THE STORY OF US

The World of My Dreams

Book One

S.L. HARRIS

authorHOUSE®

AuthorHouse™
1663 Liberty Drive
Bloomington, IN 47403
www.authorhouse.com
Phone: 1 (800) 839-8640

This is a work of fiction. All of the characters, names, incidents,
organizations, and dialogue in this novel are either the products
of the author's imagination or are used fictitiously.

Published by AuthorHouse 06/05/2018

ISBN: 978-1-5462-4498-1 (sc)
ISBN: 978-1-5462-4497-4 (e)

Library of Congress Control Number: 2018906633

Print information available on the last page.

CONTENTS

ACKNOWLEDGMENTS

I would like to send out a very special thank-you to my longtime friend James Howard; my bestie, Victoria Dooley; and my loving, supportive, and beautiful mother, Ruth Cooper, for helping me on this creative endeavor. Thank you all for giving me the confidence to see this project through to the end and for believing in me. It means a lot. Your edits, insights, and suggestions did not go unnoticed or unappreciated. Thank you for your encouragement and love.

Jeffery Calvert, you inspire me to write. I dedicate this book to you. You show me what love feels like, and I am forever grateful.

Justus Barnes, my intelligent, sweet and loving son, words cannot express how much I love you. The title selection was perfect. I think you are very insightful and smart beyond your years.

Shantell Harris, you are the best cheerleader of all. Your interest in my story encouraged me to keep writing. I am forever indebted.

Gloria Harris, you are the best big sister a girl could ever have. You have been there for me unconditionally through every challenge and celebration in my life. I love you and appreciate you so much.

Grethel Ruth, I love you dearly. Thank you for being there for me emotionally and spiritually throughout the years. You have coached me through so many milestones in life, this being one of them. I would not be who I am today, if it were not for you and your support, enthusiasm, and concern for me. Thank you, Fairy Godmother.

To all my family and friends, I love you all. I just want to give a special shout-out to my loving brothers, Patrick Harris, Sam Harris, and Al Harris, much love.

CHAPTER 1—THE BUSINESS

November 29

It is three in the morning, and I am baking in my kitchen. Partly to calm my nerves about the news that came about inadvertently yesterday afternoon, but mostly to be prepared for the grand opening of S & S Cafe and Lounge. My sister, Samantha, and I have been working on this for years. It has spun from a simple idea to a business proposal to drafting the floor plan to accommodate how we could incorporate food, relaxation, and spiritual absolution into a profitable business. Things are working out nicely. I have clientele who has been waiting for this place to open since there has been talk of it over a year ago. I've been running a catering business for ten years now in conjunction with other various pursuits. I sell foods and desserts to the local police stations, fire departments and construction sites in the area.

My menu consists of foods ranging from baked chicken to simply burgers and fries all made with a touch of love and from scratch. My dessert menu consists of red velvet, carrot, to simple vanilla cakes. The list goes on, combining both gourmet and old-fashioned recipes. Some of these recipes were passed down from my great-aunt, and others I learned along the way at cooking classes and online tutorials. I spruced up most of the recipes a bit and added my own flair. I like being creative in the kitchen; it is truly calming to my soul.

Samantha, also known by me as Sammie, is a licensed massage therapist going on three years now. She has grown exhausted working for other people. She is tired of massage studios overcharging the clients and only providing half of the services she could offer. She feels restricted to say the least. She strongly believes she can make her sessions more affordable and offer a package that goes beyond just the physical. Sammie is also a practicing Reiki healer.

Reiki is a Japanese technique for stress reduction and relaxation that promotes healing and is administered by laying of hands. *Rei* means God's wisdom or higher power. *Ki* means life- force energy. The effects of a session are bliss. I know because I was her first client after her Reiki master, Adu, passed on his life-force energy to her during the attunement, which was a ceremony I was blessed to be a part of. The only reason I was able to attend is because we are twins. Sammie was so excited and nervous that Adu felt my presence would help her calm down to receive more freely the life-force energy he was passing on to her for her future clients. Not to mention Sammie and I are like the Chinese yin and yang symbol. She and I are so opposite on so many levels, but when we work together, we are in perfect harmony spiritually, emotionally, and mentally. The past three years have been a series of spiritual attacks that affected our family and threatened our closest relationships, even our relationship with each other at one point. We had to work together to pull through successfully.

My abilities expand past my cooking skills. I'm what they call an empath. I'm able to pick up on people's intentions, feelings, and emotions before they can even figure out why they are feeling that way. Sammie has a way in which she can help me filter through impressions to get to the root of the problem with people. The third part of our business consists of spiritual absolution. We had a small loft space above the café/lounge added to the floor plan, where Sammie will do her massages and Reiki healings and I will practice spiritual counseling to those who are lost emotionally, mentally, and/or spiritually.

As I continue to bake, my thoughts take me back to one year ago today, when Sammie and I applied for the vendor license through the county office in Tampa, Florida. Everything took off from that point. Developing the business plan was easy. Eleven years of undergrad and graduate school prepared us for that. All the endless papers and reports actually had some use in helping us organize and structure our thoughts and ideas. My undergraduate degree is in psychology with a minor in sociology. Sammie's bachelor's degree is in physics and mathematics. I have a master's degree and certification in mental health counseling. Sammie's master's degree is in biology. See, we are completely opposite, hence the yin and yang.

I worked for a mental health agency for twelve years. I felt like I was barely scratching the surface with helping people. I had strict guidelines to follow on the treatment plans, which left no room for my nontraditional approach to helping people. I could feel what they needed, yet I was so bent on not losing my license by approaching things from a spiritual standpoint that I stuck to the plan. This left me feeling stuck in a career I wasn't happy with. That is, until I started to explore alternative avenues to counseling. I signed up for classes through Spiritual Health Care Professionals. I received a certification in spiritual counseling.

Let me tell you, life has not been the same since my augmented career adjustment. I mean, I still counsel people, but instead of looking at their issues as mental ones, I approach things from a spiritual perspective and I have made worlds of difference in my clients' lives. I feel like I am actually doing what God has called me to do.

Back to the business: The more challenging part of starting our business was getting investors to help in the funding of our little café and lounge idea. Sammie and I both had a little savings from over the years, and combined with the inheritance we received from our parents' auto insurance settlement, we were able to successfully launch our idea from dream to reality. We knew we would need more than cash to make this business a success. We needed people to buy into the idea. We conducted surveys in the area where we were going to purchase the storefront. We offered free slices of pie or cake for the people who would take the time to fill out a survey, which consisted of four simple questions:

1. *Do you like baked goods?*
2. *Do you like massages?*
3. *Is this a convenient location to receive both?*
4. *Would you tell a friend or family member about this survey?*

Okay, so maybe it was not an actual survey with quality questions for statistical computation and data gathering purposes, but it was an excellent marketing ploy. We were able to network with people and get contact information to send out flyers about the cafe. We even advertised that if they brought the flyer back once the café opened, they would receive a free dessert. We did this every few months for a couple of hours in the mornings outside of the café. We set up a booth where I brought in different desserts for people to try for free, and met all types of people. In fact, this was exactly where I first met him, the where-have-you-been-all-of-my-life guy, Kelvin.

CHAPTER 2—OUR FIRST ENCOUNTER BACK DOWN MEMORY LANE

Two months ago

"Ladies, good morning. So, if I fill out this little slip of paper, I get a choice of a free slice of cake or pie?" Kelvin asks.

"Yes, but you have to give your honest opinion on the survey," I reply.

"And your honest opinion of the baked good that you try today," Sammie chimes in. "My sister is the best baker in all of Florida."

Kelvin grabs the survey and a pencil, circling yes to every question. "So, when will this place open?"

"Forty- nine days from now. On November 29," I say, halfway in a trance, not fully understanding why when this man flashes those pearly whites, it sends shivers down my spine. Is it me, or is he checking me out? It's very breezy outside, so why am I so hot? I grab a stack of the surveys and begin fanning myself frantically.

Sammie turns and looks at me. "You okay, girl?" she asks then smiles, looking back at Mr. Tall, Slender, and Handsome then at me again.

"I'm good—a little hot. Are you hot?" I ask Samantha.

"No," she responds calmly, however Sammie starts to smirk a little. "So, Mister, what will it be? Cake or pie?" she asks holding one in each hand.

"I'll have the cake, please," Kelvin replied.

"Okay." Sammie hands him the slice of cake with a plastic fork.

"Thanks." He slowly unwraps the pink plastic wrap from the cake and takes a bite. Moments later, he nods a sign of approval.

"So, do you like it?" I ask, waiting as patiently as I can.

"No. I don't like it," he replies, his eyes still on the cake. When he looks up, my heart drops. "I love it. Is it pound cake?"

"Yes. It's 7-Up pound cake," I respond, relieved.

"It's delicious. So in forty-nine days from today, I'll be able to drop by this beautiful storefront to get a slice of 7-Up pound cake every day?"

"Yes," I reply. "If that's what you desire, Mister...?" I hinted in a questioning tone, trying to signal if I know his name, I can address him more personally.

"Oh, I'm sorry. My name is Kelvin—Kelvin Jerome Frey," he says as he sets the cake down. I can't help but notice as he reaches for his wallet, he seems a bit scattered. Not by anyone else's standard, but from what I can pick up on him emotionally through my sixed sense, so to speak. He is maintaining a cool and collected outer shell, but there is something else I can't quite put my finger on.

He hands a card to Samantha first.

"Thanks. My name is Samantha, but everyone calls me Sammie." She hands him some brochures with a coupon to get a free dessert on his first visit to S & S Café and Lounge.

He turns to look at me, then clears his throat. As he is eyeing me, it feels as if he is looking right through me. "Are you twins?" he asks.

"Yes," both Sammie and I respond in unison.

"I can see the difference in you two. You are both very beautiful. And your name?" he turns and gazes at me. His light brown eyes are like liquid pools inviting me to take a dive inside them.

"Sabine, but most people call me Seme." I reach out to grab the business card he extends to me and slip it into my back pocket, then I shake his hand, and he smiles at me.

"Seme, huh?" he questions as he stands there pulling me in to him emotionally with the way he's looking at me, which is focused.

His smile is friendly, in combination with the soothing sound of his voice, which hums like music to my ears. It's all so captivating.

I nod, still caught in the trance Kelvin seems to have put me in. When our hands touch...oh my. The sweetest, warmest feeling covers my entire body. When I look at him, I feel like it's just us standing there in our own little world—a world where time stands still and all of my senses are finely tuned.

I notice his smell. It's a very mild scent, yet so invigorating. Polo Sport...that's the cologne he is wearing. It smells so good on him, like it's his own personal brand of Polo. I am very aware of my heart and how hard it's beating. My palms are sweaty, and I feel a little out of breath. Damn. Is this a good sign or bad? He holds my right hand in his, then places his left one on top of mine. It instantly calms my soul. We both just stand there looking at each other, taking each other in—mind, body, and soul.

He towers over me by at least six inches. He is caramel complected, and his skin is smooth. He has an angular jawline, a perfectly sculpted nose, nice thick lips, and a goatee, which is neatly shaven. He has a nice hair texture, with threads of gray scattered throughout and those brown eyes...they seem to be taking me somewhere.

"I have to go," he says quietly, as if he's trying to convince himself of his own words. Then he bends, lowering himself closer to my face. "I hope to see you around. I'm new to town—I just moved here from Michigan. I'm expanding on my logistics business. This seems like a lucrative business you two are starting. I know a place where you can get good deals on some kitchen supplies and maybe a few investors if you're interested." He pulls his cell phone out. "How about this, tonight dinner on me? You pick the place, and we can talk. What's your number?"

CHAPTER 3—THE DATE

Kelvin made reservations for us at The Sweet Spot, but there is still a little wait before we are seated, so we order drinks at the bar. As luck would have it, he orders a Yin and Yang martini for me, which is right up my alley. It consists of Godiva white chocolate liqueur and vodka blended with ice cream then topped with chocolate shavings. This drink is like a liquid candy bar, and I absolutely love chocolate. He is definitely winning my heart already. Kelvin warns me on the car ride to the restaurant there was a strong possibility I might fall in love with him during dinner. He says the whole scene at the restaurant is like an aphrodisiac—the low lights, the private seating, and how the food is served all add to the excitement.

"So, Seme, where did you grow up?" Kelvin ask before taking a sip of beer.

"I was born and raised in Pensacola, Florida," I reply stirring my drink with my straw.

"Do you have any other siblings, excluding Sammie?"

"No, it's just me and Sammie. What about you, any brothers or sisters?

"I have an older brother who lives in Michigan with my father."

"Were you born in Michigan?" I ask.

"Yes, born and raised in Detroit," he replied.

"Tell me about your last relationship. . ."

"Wow, that's a loaded conversation. Let's just say, I wasn't her only love. We had been on and off for over seven years. It was like one minute we were made for each other, the next we were like poison to one another. I don't know, call it passion gone wrong,"

Kelvin shakes his head, then he continues to speak. "She wanted it all: marriage, children, and the nice house. I guess I wasn't able to give her everything in the time frame that she desired, if that makes sense."

He looks at me as if to make sure I'm still following. I nod my head sipping more of my drink, but remain silent wanting him to continue his story.

"She felt with my degree and background knowledge that I should've been making a six figure salary—and I wasn't at that point at that time. She pushed me to leave one job and to take another. I think the problem was that I hadn't completely discover who I was, and what my place was in this world. It wasn't until my mom's passing that the meaning of my life became clear."

"Oh," I respond shocked, then with all sincerity I say, "I'm sorry to hear about your mother passing."

"Thank you," Kelvin says, "I appreciate that. It's been a few years, I've come to terms with it. I look at death as a passing from one state of existence to another; from the physical back to the spiritual. I don't want to get too deep but, I've always looked at life as having a human experience as a spiritual being. For me, being human is the hardest of all the things we could be in a life time," Kelvin pauses and smiles at me as if he is trying to gauge how receptive I am to what he is saying.

"Interesting," I voice weakly.

"Does it make you uncomfortable, me talking about death, and my spiritual beliefs?"

"No. Actually, it doesn't," I reply, thinking on how much his views about death mirror's my own ideas and spiritual concepts, yet I'm unsure of how deep I want to go on this subject. I ask, "Where did you attend school?" Changing the subject to give myself time to reflect a little on this experience as it is unfolding very fast.

"Eastern Michigan University. I majored in construction management. I worked in that field for ten years before switching over to logistics."

"Impressive," I respond.

"You think?" He asks smiling at me looking into my eyes.

"Yes," I reply. This time when I look at him, a familiar feeling comes over me, as if I've known him before. A connection takes hold of my soul and sparks something within me and leads me to ask him, "What did you mean by your meaning of life becoming clear after your mother passed away? If you don't mind me asking?"

He looks at me, and grins briefly before taking on a more solemn look. This time when he stares at me, it looks as though he is looking past me into some other world. "My mom was wise beyond her years. She was a great woman. She kept everything together in our family. She was one of those people who never met a stranger. She knew that I wasn't happy with the woman I was dating or happy with how my life was at that time. Things just didn't seem satisfying to me. I needed a change, and she could sense it. She said, 'Kelvin, don't waste time on people who don't really care about who you are and what you have to offer. Sometimes people chase ghosts: ideas of what they want, most times it's not realistic or healthy. Don't get caught in their web of lies, son.' She said that people can get so caught up into what society says they should have or want in a spouse that they ignore what the soul needs." Kelvin's eyes refocuses on mine and he continues, "My mom had cancer, she had been fighting it for years. I guess when she finally left me . . . left this earth, something clicked in me that said, 'Follow your heart. Don't let life pass you by. Being content in life is not enough, you have to aim high and not settle for less," Kelvin finishes his beer off, then excuses himself to the restroom.

I sit there thinking about what he just expressed to me. I find it refreshing that he is so open and honest. I spend half of my working life trying to get people to admit their true feelings, so it feels good to relax and have someone open up so freely to me. It also makes me feel special that he trust me with the information he revealed. I know firsthand that it's not easy talking about a parent who passed away. When Kelvin returns to the bar, I change topics to something not as deep.

"So, how long have you been in Florida?" I ask.

"About three weeks now. I am living out of a hotel. Most of my stuff is in storage. I'm looking for a house to rent."

"Your table is ready," the sweet blond hostess announces as we gather our things and follow her to our booth. By the time we're seated, I'm already feeling the effects of the alcohol. When I turn to look at Kelvin, our eyes meet in the way that seems to occur often since meeting him that morning. It's as if I'm being drawn toward him on some other level. To add to matters, my defenses are down now that the alcohol has weakened my resolve. My nerves are calm, and I am ready for anything. Here we are, sitting in an intimate booth right next to each other, and the lights are dim. The backs of the booths are so high it blocks out the people who are sitting in front of us and the traffic from behind us. We're at the corner of an entranceway, so it's very private. It really feels like we're the only ones here. Those eyes...he's pulling me in, those lips, I can't resist. Our faces are moving closer and closer together. Just as I buy into the illusion that it's only us there and I'm about to feel those soft-looking lips on mine, our waiter interrupts us.

"I'm Vaugh, I will be your waiter for tonight. Can I start you off with some appetizers?" Kelvin and I scan our menus quickly and decide on Buffalo wings. The waiter scribbles our order down and walk away. I move over closer to Kelvin hoping to continue where we left off —ending with my lips touching his, but instead Kelvin pulls away and start to speak again. I sit back to listen, hoping that my disappointment doesn't show too much on my face.

"Were you able to get in contact with Sam over at Kitchen Supply Plus?" Kelvin ask.

"Yes, I was. Thank you for that. Sam was very helpful and I'm meeting with him next week to see if he has any supplies that I could use at the café."

"No problem. I know how it is starting up a new business. Any way that I can help, I will," Kelvin says sincerely.

The food is delicious and Kelvin is a gentlemen. We spend the rest of the night flirting with one another. In addition to Kelvin being insightful and soulful, he also has a great sense of humor.

I could spend weeks on end with this guy and never get bored of his stories.

Minutes after we get into his car, I can feel my eye lids getting heavy. The food is settling on my belly and this was a long day. What feels like moments later, I open my eyes to find that we are in the driveway of my home. "I can't believe I fell asleep on you. You had to drive the fifty minutes by yourself? I'm so sorry, Kelvin," I say as I open my door to exit his jeep.

He rushes over to the passenger side to hold my door open and grabs my hand to help me out of the jeep. "Seme, it's okay. We had a good time, you had a busy day, and you were tired. Let other people take care of you sometimes. The ride wasn't that bad; besides, I stopped by the gas station and bought an energy drink."

I smile.

We walk to my doorstep and he sweeps a piece of hair behind my ear, then bends and plants the sweetest kiss on my forehead, then cheek, then lips. But it's too brief. "I'm sorry, sweetie, but I have to go. I got a call that one of my truckers got into a mini crash, and I need to go handle some business. I'll call you tomorrow."

"Okay," I say, disappointment in my voice as I watch him walk back over to his jeep.

Before he pulls off, I let myself into my house. As soon as I step in, I have an eerie feeling.

"Is someone here?" I ask. Taking all of my spiritual precautions, not limiting myself to my current spiritual practices nor my previous religious rituals. Even though in recent times I have come to accept the idea of God as a Universal Force of Nature, I still acknowledge and practice, at times, my Baptist upbringing. I instantly called on the name of Jesus, I ask for the help and protection of Archangel Michael, then I say a silent prayer for protection and courage, envisioning my angels and spirit guides circling me. I offer a chant from mythical teacher Hermes Trismegistus: "God is a circle whose center is everywhere and whose circumference is nowhere."

As I walk past the foyer, I send light and love before me, as a form of protection in the same way that a person ask that Holy Spirit surround them. I flick on a light in the kitchen. I look around assessing things. Everything look in place. I reach into my purse to grab my cell phone, reserving the right to call for help if I need to. I also grab a dry dishcloth from the stove handle and instinctively place it over my mouth, as I'm feeling a little nauseous. I set my purse and cell phone down on the counter.

I yell out, "Sammie, is that you, girl?" as she's the only other person who has a key to my house.

No answer.

The farther I walk into the house, the fuzzier my head gets. There's a penetrating pain in the center of my belly. I walk toward the patio area to close the blinds and check the lock, as this is the only other entrance to my house. I notice the automatic patio light that comes on after dusk is flickering nonstop. I open the patio door, step out, and lift myself onto one of the outdoor chairs so I can reach the light fixture. I unscrew the dome then use the dishcloth to protect my hand as I unscrew the lightbulb. I shake it a little, to get the circuits connecting again. Then, I screw it back in place.

The flickering stops and the light comes back on. I put the dome back in place, step down, and look around. The pain in my belly has subsided a little. I take three deep, calming breaths, as a way of releasing the nervous energy that I just experienced. When I look at the clock in the kitchen through the patio glass, it reads 11:11 P.M. I quietly tell myself, *focus upon your desires not your fears.* As this number sequence is a signal to take note of your thoughts as they are manifesting at rapid speed. This is something that I remember through my spiritual numerology studies. Eleven is also a master number which signifies spiritual ascension or at times 1 1 1 1 provide a code or message about a spiritual situation occurring multi-dimensional. My phone rings. I quickly run inside, lock the patio door and answer the phone.

CHAPTER 4 – THE DREAM

It's Sammie.

"Are you okay, girl?" Sammie asks over the phone, "I had a weird dream."

"I'm okay. What did you dream?" I ask, relieved she called me, dismissing the fear that was just gripping me.

Sammie is whispering and I can tell that she is walking out of her bedroom, trying not to disturb Malik by the way she pauses and the ruffling sounds I hear. "Is Kelvin there?"

"No. He dropped me off. He had some type of emergency from work after dinner," I say as I walk into my bedroom after checking the guest room and office windows, making sure they're locked.

"Oh. So, what are you doing now?" Sammie asks.

"I'm walking into the bathroom to take off my clothes and makeup," I say as I put the phone on speaker and set it on the bathroom counter.

Sammie goes on to say, "When I woke up, girl, my stomach was killing me. It hurt so bad I couldn't even stand. I slid out of the bed. I was sitting on the floor for a little bit before I decided to call you. I had to wait until the pain subsided. I'm going downstairs to get some ice water."

"Wow. My stomach was hurting too. When I walked in my house, I felt something—a presence," I say as I take my eye makeup off. It isn't abnormal for Sammie and me to feel each other's pain psychically and physically. At least now, I know why my belly was hurting.

"Oh my God, Seme. So in the dream we were at the grand

opening of our café. You remember that woman who came to me and Malik's wedding uninvited?"

"Yeah. Casey? That was her name, right?" I ask, recalling her… the uninvited wedding guest, who made an inappropriate speech during the reception.

"Yes. She was in the dream. You know Malik and I ran into her at the theater today and before that last week at the mall. She's so strange, girl. If I didn't know any better, I would think she was following us. We keep running into her."

Sammie says in the dream, Casey comes to our café for the grand opening. Instead of staying downstairs with all of the other guests, she goes upstairs to our sacred space meant for my spiritual counseling and Sammie's Reiki healings. Sammie says I follow Casey up there to find out what she's doing. When I get up there, Casey is sitting in the middle of the floor in a deep trance, unaware I'm there. As I gaze at her, she seems to transform into another person. Casey's facial features start to resemble Samantha's. I walk over to touch her, to try to understand what's happening, according to Sammie. The instant I touch Casey's shoulder, I fall to my knees in agonizing pain. Sammie, because it's her dream, can see everything that's happening, but is unable to control any of it. Sammie says she kept yelling, "Seme, don't touch her. It isn't me. Stop." In seconds, I am on the floor in so much pain I am balled up in the fetal position. Suddenly, Casey's eyes open and she comes out of her trance and her face transforms back to her own physical features. The sight of Casey up close frightened Samantha so much she woke up from the dream.

"Geez, girl," I say. "That was a horrible dream. Maybe it's just your nerves about us starting a new venture of opening up our own business. You've been doing most of the planning, maybe it is taking a toll on you. The same way when you feel sleepy you sometimes think you are depressed. You are just tired girl. Plus, you keep running into that psychopath. She would freak anyone out." I laugh a little, thinking back on the wedding.

"Yeah, I guess you're right," Sammie says very solemn-like, which leads me to believe she's still very uneasy. "Well, I'm going to try to get some sleep. I'll call you in the morning so you can tell me about your date." Sammie yawns. "Let me go back upstairs before Malik notices I'm not in bed."

"I know, right? We can't have Malik all like, 'Sammie, nights are reserved for us. Doesn't your sister have any boundaries?'" I say in the deep voice I use when I mimic Malik, successful in my attempt to make Sammie laugh.

"Okay, girl. Talk to you later. Bye."

"Bye."

As I walk out of the bathroom, I hear three hard, rapid knocks on the door. It startles me. Who could be coming to visit me so late? Maybe it's Kelvin. I slowly creep over to the front of my house and look out of the peek hole. No one is there. I then go over to the window and pull the curtains slightly, and I still don't see anybody. I wait for a little while, then grab one of my dining room chairs and wedge it under the door knob.

Walking back to my room, I think to myself, *Great . . . now I'm going to have a paranoid night.* I lay in bed feeling as if something or someone is in the room with me. Yet I see no one. I turn on the lamp next to my bed, and the volume to the television up to drown out the excessive thoughts that are running through my mind.

CHAPTER 5—THE UNEXPECTED MEETING

I wake up refreshed with Kelvin on my mind and happy that I got through the night without any more bizarre events. The thought of Kelvin automatically brings a smile to my face. I pick up my phone before getting out of bed and I text: *Thanks for last night. I had a wonderful time. I hope your truck driver is okay and that the truck didn't endure too much damage. Thinking of you. —Seme*

I roll out of bed to start my day. What should I plan to do? It's Saturday morning, and Sammie and I don't need to worry about going to the storefront until the walk-through, which is in eight weeks or so, November 28 at eleven in the morning to be exact, the day before the opening and incidentally, the day before our thirty-ninth birthday. Everything is ahead of schedule in regards to the cafe; we are just waiting on the inspector to tell us everything checks out. The one client I planned to see today canceled on me. I should be thinking of the menu for the café or be worried about the turnout to our grand opening or the meditative technique I'm going to use to guide my resistant client through on Monday, but I'm not at all worried about any of that. My mind is so clear, and I feel like a new person today.

I take a refreshing shower, throw on some shorts and a tank top and head toward the mall. Before exiting my car, I shoot Sammie a quick text, asking how she's feeling. She replies instantly: *I'm good, a little sleepy. Out at breakfast with Malik. Call you later.*

Four stores and six bags later, I realize I'm starving. I totally skipped breakfast. My phone rings for the first time all day. I answer without even looking due to all the bags in my hands and the length of time it has taken me to get the phone out of my junky purse.

"Hello?" I speak into the phone after a five-second delay because I accidentally drop the phone trying to swipe right to answer. It is as if the phone flew out of my hand.

"Ummm, hello. Is everything okay over there?" asks the sexy, calm voice that seems to be finding comedy in my unorganization.

"Kelvin? Hold on a second. Let me have a seat so I can get organized." Just as I am about to put the phone down, he walks over to me and grabs some of my bags to help me.

"Oh my, how did you...when did you... how are you here?" I question, very pleasantly surprised and a bit embarrassed.

He laughs and slowly explains. "Sweetie, I was already at the mall, and I was going to call you to see if you wanted to grab a bite to eat. Then, when I looked over here, I couldn't believe it was you—all beautiful and disorganized. So, I called you, and I watched you frantically search for your phone in your purse, then when I saw the phone fly out of your hand, I decided I would be less observant and more helpful, so here I am," he finishes with a smile.

We both laugh. He sets the bags down and embraces me in a long, close, sweet bear hug. After a little while, I pull away.

I shyly ask, "So, you want to do lunch?"

"If you have time, yes," he responds.

Kelvin helps me take the bags to my car, and he gives me an update on the trucking accident last night. It was nothing major—the driver fell asleep at the wheel, and the truck hit the curb. A superficial dent was all the damage that the truck endured. He did have to make the driver check into a hotel room to get some sleep before he could get on the road again. Kelvin had to get another driver to take over the load, as there was a time schedule to abide by.

Kelvin rode with me in my car to the Burger Stop, not far from the mall. We ate and talked for hours. He gave me more details about the woman he almost married, which from what I gather was his last serious relationship. This is the woman that he made the comment about "not being her only love" last night at the restaurant.

I spoke of my breakup with a person I had been dating seriously for about a year, yet had known for six years. How I felt I was in the relationship by myself—how he was preoccupied with his own life and career that he didn't have time to focus on what I needed or wanted from him. I expressed how I got tired of pulling all of the weight and asking for things—simple things, like going out to a movie or for a bite to eat—that I would never receive from him.

Kelvin listened. He took it all in with a sense of compassion and concern. It was as if, when I spoke it, Kelvin felt it with me—my pain, my hurt, my heartache. The truth is, in my heart, I am done with relationships. Done with opening myself up time after time to be hurt all over again. Searching for something I am never able to find.

As I tell Kelvin of my latest heartbreak, it is as if my mind goes back to the last three years of pain and hurt in my life. The depression I had endured after my parents passed away, which I never want to talk about, yet it seems to keep showing its ugly face about every six months. How I felt displaced in this life. How I often wondered if God had forsaken me. But, I couldn't tell him all of this. What would he think of me? Here I am, the counselor needing counseling.

"It shouldn't be this hard," I whisper to myself, caught up in my own head sorting through my thoughts about life and love. I am thinking that maybe I shouldn't be discussing my latest breakup because to say it starts a chain reaction and makes it real again. I don't think I'm strong enough to experience the pain again. Not just from my last relationship, but also from the pain I endured when the accident happened—when both of my parents left this earth together in a horrible head-on collision with a drunk driver. How Richard, my ex, had been there for the funeral, but absent through my sleepless nights and tear-filled days. My thoughts took me to how Sammie and I felt lost for a few months, not registering that our parents were gone permanently. Of course, she had Malik to support her during that time, which grew their love to what it is today.

"What shouldn't be hard, sweetie?" Kelvin asks looking at me confused and concerned.

"What?" I question not realizing I said that out loud. "Love," I reply, looking baffled.

Before I can even finish my last thought, Kelvin asks, "Where did you go earlier?" As if he could feel me drift away for a minute into my thoughts and memories of the past.

"I'm here. I was here," I reply. "But...I need to go home, Kelvin. Let me drive you to your car," I say as I feel my mood spiraling down into that dark place, and I just want to be alone to collect my feelings and process the emotions that have come up unexpected in this beautiful moment with this very beautiful man.

"Okay. Did I say something wrong?" Kelvin asks.

"No, I just don't feel well. I want to go home and lay down for a bit," I reply.

"Okay. Let me pay for this food and we can go." His eyes are searching for answers as he pays the tab. The car ride is silent. He grabs my hand, holding it until we pull up to his jeep.

"I hope you feel better, Sabine," he says as he reaches over and kisses me on the cheek.

"Thank you for lunch. I will talk to you soon." I say, as I force a smile.

I lay in my bed at 5:30 in the afternoon, reminiscing on the dialogue Kelvin and I had, trying to figure out how such an innocent conversation can trigger so much pain for me. Pain that I thought I had recovered from months ago. I loved Richard, and at one point, I think that I was in love with him. It was hard for me to get over the fact that he seemed to take on more hours at the police station and have less time to spend with me after my parents' funeral. We weren't exactly a couple, more so friends with benefits, but we tried to make it work. He had always been there for me in the past whenever I needed him for small things that really mattered. I was there for him too, through the loss of a job, family disputes, and I practically completed a course for him when he was working on his undergraduate degree. Why was it, when I needed him the most, he backed away? These are the questions that still haunt me.

It is times like these when I need my mom or dad's guidance the most, yet this time, they are the cause of most of my heartache. I miss them so much. It has been three years since I heard their voices, enjoyed their company on a Sunday afternoon at the beach, or just enjoyed dinner with them at the house. I fall off to sleep thinking about life without them.

I awake a couple of hours later feeling better than I did before falling asleep. I text Kelvin: *Sorry I was a little off today. Let me make it up to you. Meet me for ice cream in a half an hour at Joe's Ice Cream Parlor, my treat, if you're available.*

As soon as I pull up to Joe's, Kelvin is outside waiting on me. He opens my car door and pulls me into his arms. His lips are pressing hard against mine in an instant, parted slightly waiting on my response. I return his gesture, kissing him with as much desire as he is giving to me. He's holding me so tight. I needed this. His touch, this passion, and his desire for me awakens something inside of me, making me forget about my failed relationship with Richard. I feel a glimmer of hope inside of my heart.

"I'm sorry, baby. Am I hurting you?" he asks as he loosens his grip a little.

"No. It feels good. You feel good," I reply, pressing my cheek against his as I stand on my tippy toes to maintain facial contact with him.

"I know this may be strange to say so early on," Kelvin whispers, "but I missed you. I'm happy you wanted to see me again today." He pulls away and looks at me. "You are okay, right?" He asks with an etch of concern in his voice.

"Yes. I am now," I respond and smile.

Kelvin follows me to my house after eating what feels like pounds of ice cream. As I am searching for my keys in my purse to open the door, he says, "You were right."

"I was right about what?" I ask, still searching my purse for my keys- wishing I combined both my house and car keys on the same key chain.

"Joe's does have the best ice cream in town. Thank you for taking me there."

Just as I am putting the key in the door to unlock it, Kelvin stands so close behind me that I can feel the heat radiating from his body, his breath on my neck, and his desire to be inside of me. I turn around. My back is leaning against the door because I don't think my knees can sustain the weight of my own body right now. He extends his left arm on the outer side of my body as he places his hand on the door. His eyes are gazing straight into mine. It seems as if the longer he stares, the deeper our connection gets. He moves in even closer to me and kisses my neck gently. With his right hand, he rubs my upper back and pulls me into him as his soft kisses become gentle sucks on my neck, collarbone, then shoulder.

My purse falls to the ground. He lifts both of my legs up, and I wrap them around his waist as he pulls me in forcefully to his body. His breathing has changed from calm—normal—to out of breath and heady.

As I begin to speak, I realize the words are harder to get out than I thought. "Can we go inside before my neighbors get an eye full?"

Without saying a word, he swiftly bends down with my legs still wrapped around him to grab my purse, then deliberately slow, he comes back up with a thrust as he twists the doorknob and then pulls the key out of the lock and hands it to me. He pushes the door open with my booty. Once we're inside, he closes the door with my booty and continues the same sweet seduction he started outside.

He places my purse on the hook by the door. I hand my key chains to him to hang up. He does it. Then, he thrust several times, standing up, maintaining a great balance. My arms are wrapping around his neck. My head is tilting back, my lips are parting and moans are escaping me. His lips have moved down to my breasts, and he is pulling down my bra with his teeth, still thrusting his manhood in between my legs, infrequently yet systematically, if that is even possible. My nipples are very sensitive to the feel of his tongue flicking them. It sends signals down to my womanhood. Now, his lips are around my nipples, sucking, teasing, and nibbling.

"If you continue doing that, I might cum right here," I whisper to him.

"Ummmmm, I would love that very much, Seme." He moans and continues to seduce me.

As if on command, I cum hard. My body is shaking. I am moaning so loud I think my next-door neighbor hears me. I wish I could feel him inside of me as the walls of my vagina squeeze together uncontrollably, spasming over and over. Then I hear Kelvin whisper to me, "Soon, baby."

"Soon what?" I ask between catching my breath.

"Soon, I will be inside of you," he says, which has me questioning if I said anything out loud during my orgasm.

My body becomes so limp that Kelvin has to carry me over to the sofa and lay me down. As he gently positions me on the sofa, he rubs my hair out of my face and plants the sultriest kiss on my lips. With my eyelids still closed, I relish in what just happened by the door. It's as if every move he made was custom designed for my enjoyment and pleasure. Did he know this was going to happen today—he and I being intimate in this way?

Minutes have gone by, and I am curious as to what Kelvin is up to. When I open my eyes, I find him completely naked and ripping a condom open. After placing it over his elongated penis, his hands are all over my body...on my breasts, squeezing and rubbing them, my butt, pulling me in close to him as he grinds his manhood on my fully clothed womanhood. He lifts himself briefly, and removes my shorts and panties in one swoop, then my t-shirt and bra in another swoop.

Wow, he is good, and his penis is...enormous... is my last thought before he flips me around and proceeds to take me from behind. This feels much different than what I experienced by the front door. He is much more aggressive sexually, yet, still gentle in his technique. He slowly glides inside of me, expanding to what feels like the end of my vagina.

"Oh, you feel so good, Sabine," is what I think I hear him whisper. He is barely audible—more grunts and moans.

He pulls back slowly then pounds himself inside of me, holding himself there, taking up all the moisture. The walls of my vagina seem to be closing in around his thick, long man part. His dick is rubbing on my sweet spot as I nuzzle my butt comfortably back toward him, making him fall a little deeper inside of me. Just like when I do yoga...I relax into the position, and I find that I open up a little more. I can already feel myself building up again. He is taking me closer to my release already. It has been a long time since I felt this connected, this satisfied, this much desire for a person as I am linked with them in the act.

I begin pulling in the opposite direction, my booty away from his penis, straightening my core using the sofa arm to help steady myself, then I lift my booty up toward him, and as if on cue, he pounds his dick hard back inside of me. I pull away several times to get the same response from him repeatedly until I am spiraling out of control, lost in the pleasure just inflicted on me by this beautiful man. Not too shortly after, he follows suit and is pumping faster and cumming loudly. I can actually feel the ejaculation leaving his body in slow, consecutive squirts. Kelvin is yelling out, calling my name.

"Awwwwww, Sabine!"

"I'm going to get us some ice water," I say after finally managing to get up from underneath Kelvin.

"Okay, sweetie," he mumbles, still exhausted from our escapade.

"Why don't you meet me in my bedroom?" I yell from the kitchen. As I am pouring our drinks, I peek around the corner to see how he responds.

He is slowly sitting up on the sofa, and at that moment pauses as if he is thinking about whether he really wants to get up. He looks a little confused and a lot exhausted.

"It's this way, sweetie." He follows me to my bedroom with his clothes and mine in his arms. It looks as though he is in deep thought as we walk through the kitchen. I hand him his water as we enter the bedroom. He neatly places my shorts, tank top, panties and bra on the bed along with his pants, shirt, underwear and t-shirt. He drinks the whole glass of water down in seconds.

"Thirsty, huh?" I ask sarcastically, feeling feisty and playful.

"Very. If you only knew," he responds as he sets the glass on the nightstand next to my glass. "May I use your bathroom?" he asks.

"Yes. It's right through there." I point in the general direction. "There are towels in the closet if you want one."

"Thank you, babe." He grabs his t-shirt and underwear and a towel from the closet, and as he gets closer to the bathroom, he disappears out of sight.

This gives me the opportunity to sexy myself up a bit. I change into a short erotic laced nightgown, all black, fluff my hair up and put on some lip gloss, which I retrieved from the nightstand drawer by my bed. As he walks out of the bathroom, I pull the covers down on his side of the bed, inviting him to come join me. He has on his T-shirt and boxers. As he gets closer to the bed, I say, "You are only allowed in if you take off the rest of your clothes."

He smiles and does it. Completely naked, he slides in the bed beside me. I turn to face him, kiss his chest and lick his nipples. I move my hand down to his penis. I grip it, then say, "Very nice equipment, Mr. Frey. I'm glad to know you operate it very well."

He smiles, looking down at me, but is so distracted by what my hands and tongue are doing to his wanting body that it seems he can't really stay focused on what I'm saying to him. I kiss my way down his stomach, and when I reach his pubic hairs, I look up at him again. His breathing has become heavy.

"May I?" I ask.

"Seme, at this point, you can have anything you want," he says, looking somewhat stunned and nervous at the same time.

When Kelvin finally awakes at 10:30 A.M., he walks into a kitchen decked out with a spread of omelet, bacon, toast with grape jelly, fresh fruit, and a nice cold glass of orange juice waiting for him.

25

He is only wearing his pants, which are hanging off his hips, making me notice he doesn't have underwear on. "What smells so good out here?" he asks, looking around the kitchen.

I motion toward the table.

"Wow, sweetie!" He walks over to me, plants the sweetest kiss on my lips, then holds me in his arms for a little while, staring down into my eyes. "Good morning, beautiful," he says.

"Good morning, sexy man," I respond.

He shakes his head. "What am I going to do with you?"

"Sit down and eat breakfast with me," I demand.

"Your wish is my command." He sits down, says a silent grace and begins eating.

We spend much of Sunday lounging around and watching Netflix movies. I make a light lunch—turkey, bacon, and avocado sandwiches with some decaf sweet iced tea and fried plantains. For dessert, I prepare some chocolate-filled croissants. We eat strawberries, drink Baileys over ice as a late after-lunch snack, then lay around on the sofa together. Throughout the day, Kelvin takes several business calls in regards to coordinating pickups and drop-offs of numerous loads from Michigan to Ohio, Ohio to Illinois, and Illinois back to Florida. I pause the Netflix movie as he goes in and out on the patio to talk business.

Kelvin walks back into the house and informs me, "I'm going to be leaving for a few days on business, sweetie. I have to make a long-distance trip, so most likely I'll be gone the whole week." He walks over and sits next to me on the sofa.

I sit up to face him. "Well, I'll be waiting here for you until you come back."

"Yeah?" he questions as he rubs my hair. "Sweetie, what do you want from me?" He pauses and goes into thought. "I ask because I feel something here between us, and I don't want to dismiss what I'm feeling. Maybe we should talk about what this is." His gaze look genuine.

"Okay. Well, you don't have a wife in Michigan, do you?" I ask.

"No. I don't," he responds.

"Are you married, sweetie? Is your husband on vacation?" he asks me.

I smile. "No. I'm not married."

"Well, whoever let you go was a dumb ass," he says with the most serious expression.

"Well, whoever let you go, can you please thank them for me? I want you all to myself," I reply.

He reaches over and hugs me. We stay this way for a while, then he says, "Well, it's official..."

"What's official?" I ask, confused.

"I'm your man, if you'll have me?" he ask in the smoothest tone.

"Yes," is the only thing I can muster after such a direct question.

"Just so you know, I knew you would be my woman when I first saw you."

"Really?" I inquire.

"Yes. Really. And you know what?" he asks.

"What's that?"

"There will never be another. One heart, one mind, one love." He grabs my hand and intertwines his fingers through mine.

I stare at him. "And how do you know this?"

"It is a feeling. Trust me. You'll see, Seme."

CHAPTER 6 —THE MELTDOWN

Samantha is a hot mess.

"Girl, slow down and start from the top," I say, confused, trying to understand what she's talking about.

"Sabine, this woman is a lunatic," she yells as she paces. "I just can't believe it. I mean, if it had not have happened to me and I hadn't experienced it with my own two eyes, I wouldn't believe it!"

I pour us both a tall glass of wine and hand her glass to her. "Okay, so tell me, calmly." I stress the word *calmly*.

After taking a big swallow of wine, Samantha proceeds to tell me how Casey is causing all kinds of havoc in her and Malik's life. What started as an innocent "friendship" per Casey's confession turned into a world of chaos in a matter of days. Turns out that Casey is madly in love with Malik, well according to Samantha anyways. Not only is she in love with Malik, but she felt it was necessary to communicate this in so many words and actions to my sister. Big mistake. Like our dad always said, never mess with a Stallworth woman.

Sammie communicates how when she came home from work last night, after a ten-hour shift, Casey was in her and Malik's house and had made dinner. The table was only set up for two. Initially, Sammie thought that Malik was surprising her with a romantic candlelight dinner—until Casey came out of the kitchen dressed in three-inch heels, a short red fitted dress and Sammie's apron on that read "Kiss the Cook."

"For a minute, I thought that I walked into the wrong house," Sammie says with comicalness for the first time throughout our whole conversation. I smile. As she goes into the storyline of how

28

the conversation went between them, I envision it as if it is happing before my eyes, as a movie playing at the sound of Sammie's voice. I'm in Malik and Sammie's house on that day, looking in on the incident as if it is happening right now.

"I'm sorry. Did I walk into the twilight zone?" Samantha asks Casey.

"Oh, Samantha, I didn't know you would be home so early." Casey smiles as she places salmon and yellow rice down on the center of the table.

"Where's Malik?" Sammie asks, looking around the house but not letting this woman out of her sight.

"He's not home yet. He gave me the code to the door, and I let myself in." Casey states casually.

I interrupt Sammie's detailed account of what happened. "Oh my God. Samantha, she had the code to the house?"

"Seme!" Samantha shakes her head, remembering the whole evening in disgust.

"Okay, so then what happened?" I question, equally disgusted.

She explains that Malik walks in the house moments later. All calm, like nothing was wrong. Malik thought that Sammie had invited Casey over for dinner. After a semiprivate conversation with Malik, she found out he had given her the code over a year ago when she had stopped into town and needed a place to crash before they were married. When Sammie and Malik went back into the dining room area, Casey had sat up a third plate for dinner.

"Will you be joining us for dinner, Samantha?" Casey asks.

"What? Will I be joining you for dinner? This is my house! What do you mean?" Sammie shouts.

"I mean, Malik told me you don't like fish. I wasn't sure if maybe you just wanted the rice?" was Casey's response.

At that point, Sammie begin to call Casey every derogatory name in the book and forced her out of the house. Sammie threw all of the food away, and she had a long and unpleasant conversation with Malik about the nature of Casey and his relationship after changing the code to the house door.

"Wow," I say, speechless. Finally adding, "What did Malik say?"

"Malik thinks I overreacted." Sammie turns and looks at me as she comes out of the recent memory of events pulling us both back into this reality.

"Really?" I question sarcastically.

"I mean, he agreed it was kind of weird that she was in the house cooking and hadn't been invited over. But..." She trails off.

"But what?" I question, aware Samantha isn't telling me the entire story.

"I don't know. Maybe she told him she would make him dinner," Sammie says in thought. "I have a bad feeling about this woman. Not just the typical, oh, she's-trying-to-steal-my-man feeling. But something else."

"Like what something else?" I question.

"Like maybe it's something I don't know or that I'm missing. I mean, Malik seems too nonchalant about the whole thing," she says in a daze, very slowly. "So, how's it going with Kelvin?" Sammie effectively changes the subject.

"It is going. I like him," I say, feeling that pull in my heart as I think of him and totally downplaying how I am really feeling. "He has some business to attend to in Michigan, Ohio, and Illinois, so he'll be gone until the end of the week."

"Oh. How's work?" Sammie asks.

"Work is good. I can't wait until we have our own space to do my counseling sessions in. I have two college students interested in the cashier position at the café, and one interested in waiting the tables. Let me grab their résumés for you to look at. I think it would be idea for them part-time." I walk toward my office to grab the résumés.

As I walk into the room, a strange sensation hits me. The same sensation I had a few days ago, but not as extreme. Sick to the stomach, I feel as if someone is in the office with me. But when I look around, there isn't a soul around that I can see.

When I come back out of the office, Sammie looks exhausted. "Here, girl, maybe look them over tomorrow? Go home and get some rest. Malik loves you. Just let things calm down, and you'll get to the bottom of whatever is going on," I say to her as I hand her the résumés.

"Okay, girl. Thanks for listening. See you tomorrow. We can set up some interviews soon. We still need a dishwasher and an aide in the kitchen. I'll post the positions online tonight," Sammie says as she walks toward the door. "Can you do me a favor?" Sammie asks.

"Yeah. Sure," I respond.

"Can you tune into Casey and see what you pick up on her psychically?

"Okay. I will."

I make a nice warm bubble bath after Samantha leaves. I soak for an hour, clearing myself of all toxins that I have absorbed throughout the day. I send love and light energy to all of the clients I met with over the weeks, then to my sister and her husband. This helps me to psychically cleanse them on a spiritual level of any and all negative energies they are experiencing, almost like a prayer of release but a step higher. I relax more, feeling my body's release of tension and stress. I then go to that mental space in my mind's eye, the third eye, where only love exists. I am surrounded by loving beings of light, what we call angels.

I feel one with all life and all creation in this space. I am at my usual spot, by a tree, which I have named Hawthorne. I am dressed in all white in my mind's eye. Everything seems to flow here, like there is a continual nice breeze on a warm summer day. Except that it's not daytime, and it looks the way I envisioned outer space might look— lots of stars surrounding me in this sacred space. There is no sky or ground, just imagine a dark backdrop illuminated by the stars. This is where I am.

I call in Archangel Michael for protection. He shows up ten times my size and calmly walks around the space with his golden sword in his hand. I send loving light to all of the angels who now surround me. As I do this, I can feel my soul rejuvenate, as if warm beams of light are streaming throughout my body, connecting me to my angels. At this moment, it feels like I have everything

I've ever wanted, a sense of peace and satisfaction beyond what I currently know in this lifetime covers me (covers my soul). It is more like an understanding. At this point, I know I am ready to do my spiritual work.

I start my prayer aloud, "Jesus Christ, Ascended Master, please surround this space with your blood for protection. Only things that are of the highest good are to come through. Please make me aware of anything you want me to know pertaining to my sister, Samantha, and her husband, Malik. Amen." I instantly see them both in my mind's eye, wearing white flowing clothing. They are facing each other, holding hands, gazing lovingly into each other's eyes. Then they turn to look at me. "What do you want me to know in regards to their relationship? Is it in danger?"

What I experience next completely throws me off guard, even in my current peaceful state. I can feel the love between the two of them, however there is a waning occurring, the same way a telephone loses reception. I'm feeling a disconnect or a block in my abilities. Then all of a sudden, it is just me in a circle surrounded by three angels. The angels say, "It is okay, Sabine. Say the prayer of protection once more." As I say it, my angels continue to circle me and communicate they want me to stay in the water to maintain the connection. I take several deep breaths to reestablish the connection, which comes back in focus over the course of minutes. The angels tell me to always, when asking about the relationship of Samantha and Malik, be around, in, or near water for my own protection. They inform me that there is some interference from lower energies, that I need to do some clearing of both Samantha's house and mine and to not be afraid.

The angels communicate, "Just as you know love, there are times when there is an absence of love."

I ask, "What do you mean? Is there a problem with Samantha and Malik's relationship?"

"Yes. Malik needs to be aware of the company that he keeps."

"Does Casey have anything to do with this absence of love?" I ask, confused.

"Yes, very much so. Casey is dabbling in some things she

should not be in. If you want to help your sister, get to know Casey, Sabine. We need to warn you, this woman is operating from a different space—a space that is not of your highest good nor your sister's. Pray for protection before each encounter."

I send light and love to my angels and spirit guides. I take several deep breaths, and I come up out of this meditative state of mind, back up into this consciousness. I unplug my tub to drain the water, get up, grab a towel, and walk over to the mirror.

I grab my phone and call Sammie. "Hey, girl. Invite Casey over to my house for lunch tomorrow. Tell her you want me to meet her and we can have a girls' afternoon."

"Okay. Why?" Sammie asks.

"So that I can get a feel for her," I answer.

CHAPTER 7—THE GIRLS' AFTERNOON OUT

I had a couple of afternoon counseling appointments that I rescheduled for tomorrow, to accommodate for our girls' afternoon. My mornings are typically dedicated to baking and delivering lunches and desserts to the fire station, police station, and local businesses in the area. Today, I woke up at four o'clock in the morning and worked on the lunch orders I had taken yesterday for today's deliveries.

Samantha has requested the afternoon off. She told me over the phone she would meet me at my place after she leaves work at noon. I just completed my last delivery twenty minutes ago. It is 11:40 AM. I have enough time to stop by the bank to deposit my earnings into the business account. The first thing I do when I walk into the house, besides wash my hands, is throw together a salad which consists of spinach spring mixed lettuce, candied pecans, cranberries, strawberries, ham, and a vinaigrette dressing. I boil six eggs and slice and season some red tomatoes to add beside our salads. I bake a batch of sweet potato fries and whip together a quick lemon cream pie. I text Sammie to let her know I'm about to get in the shower and that she should let herself in, if I'm not out before she gets to the house.

As I shower under the warm cascading water, I remember what my angels suggested last night, that I put a protection around Sammie and myself. I envision a protective white light surrounding Sammie and my energy fields from intrusion of lower energies. As I put the protection around my sister and myself, I imagine us standing together completely shielded in the white light, which covers our entire aura, preventing any foreign energy from getting into our space.

I ask that both our angels come in for protection and support, then I say a simple prayer: "May the love of God enfold us. Please help me to see, feel, hear, or understand anything that you want me to know in regards to this woman, Casey. Protect us from anything that is not of our highest good. Amen." I let the warm water run down my body to wash away all doubts and fears that I temporarily picked up on at the mention of this woman's name. I then end my shower and spiritual cleansing session with a prayer—"Thank you, God, for blessing me. I am grateful for all that I am receiving in regards to the business, love, and family. Amen."

I throw on some white fitted jeans and a purple cutoff top that reads *Diva*. Then slip on silver sandals that match the silver letters on my shirt. After checking myself out in the mirror, I decide to pull my hair into a high ponytail. I put on some big silver hoop earrings and a little blush, mascara, and finally I lightly spray perfume over my clothes. The woman looking at me in the mirror looks decent. I am actually looking forward to a girls' afternoon.

Just as I am walking out into my bedroom, I hear Sammie's voice. "Hey, girl. Where are you?"

I answer, "I'm in my bedroom." Shortly after, Sammie walks in to meet me.

Sammie looks very nice. She has her hair hanging down. It looks very fluffy and silky, as if she has just washed it. She also has on large hoop gold earrings, tight black fitted jeans, silver sandals, and a skintight pink top, which is showing a lot of cleavage.

"Wow," I say. "You look hot. Malik let you out of the house like that?"

She laughs. "Malik's at work. Besides, I'm a grown woman. I can wear whatever I want." We both laugh. Sammie whispers to me that Casey is waiting on us in the kitchen. She informs me they pulled up at the same time.

As we walk out into the kitchen, Casey greets me. "Hi, Sabine. I'm Casey. It's nice to meet you." She extends her hand to shake mine, and I reach out to hug her. "Oh my God, you guys do look a lot alike," she says as she pulls away from the hug looking between Sammie and me. "Even down to the earrings! Good thing your hair is up, Sabine. I wouldn't be able to tell you two apart."

I laugh. "Yeah we get that a lot, but there are some differences. You will become more aware of them more as you get to know us better." I walk over to the kitchen table. "I made lunch for us."

Sammie chimes in. "You know that cooking is her specialty."

"Yes, you told me," Casey says. "I can't wait to dig in."

Sammie and Casey sit down, and I fill all three of our plates up with salad, fries, two boiled eggs and slices of tomatoes. "I kept it light today. I did make a yummy dessert." As I sit down, I smile and take a good look at Casey. She is wearing blue jeans and open-toe sandals with a black cut off shirt that hangs off her shoulders. She is very curvy—big hips, legs and thighs. "Casey, are you a runner?" I ask.

"Yes. I run every morning for one hour," she replies.

"I can tell. Your body is cut, girl."

She blushes and laughs. "Thanks. I try."

I walk into the dining room to turn some music on. I find R. Kelly on the iPod and let that play in the background as we eat and discuss life. As I pour us all a glass of Verdi, I think, surprisingly, I like Casey. We all seem to make a good trio, too. She seems down to earth. She is a little blunt but funny. She tells Sammie and me that she owns her own hair salon where she employs seven people. In the past, she worked as an attorney for a law firm in Jacksonville, Florida, but she wanted a change of venue. Now, she takes cases now and then, but her primary focus is on her salon.

"I can understand wanting to leave the professional world to enter a more creative occupation," I comment.

"Yes, girl. Sometimes I get tired of enforcing the law." She smiles flashing her perfectly straight pearly white teeth. "Sometimes it's more fun to break the rules a little." Casey turns toward Samantha.

As I grab the empty plates to place them in the dishwasher, I turn to Casey. "So, Casey, Samantha told me you two got into some kind of disagreement the other day. What happened?" I question.

"It was just a misunderstanding. We both apologized to each other yesterday before she invited me over here for this girls' afternoon, which I totally needed by the way. "What's for dessert?" Casey asks.

"I made a pie. It is in the refrigerator, you can help yourself. Can you slice me a piece also?" I ask, thinking this would be the perfect opportunity to do a little prying on Samantha's behalf.

"Sure. Samantha, do you want a slice?" Casey asks as she takes the pie out of the refrigerator.

Sammie responds, "No, I'm good for now."

"This has been a great afternoon, and Sammie and I needed this time to relax. We've been working hard trying to open up our dream business. It's a lot of work." I say as Casey hands me a slice of pie. "Thanks. Plus with Sammie being married for only a year, I can only imagine how difficult it can be trying to balance a husband and his needs and just adjusting to married life," I add on, looking at Sammie, thinking she would chime in, but she doesn't.

I can't help notice that Sammie seems a bit uneasy now. She excuses herself from the table. When I look back at Casey, I notice a smirk. "What happened that started the disagreement between you two?" I ask, concerned by Sammie's despondent mood.

"Well, I've known Malik since childhood. We went to elementary, middle, and high school together. We are just really good friends, and I think that makes Sammie feel threatened," she says proudly, with a hint of arrogance. Casey comes across as very nonchalant as if she does not have to explain herself any more than she already has. It appears that Casey feels that her words are justified by the fact that she and Malik have a history.

"Oh, I see. What makes you think that Samantha feels threatened?" I ask, curious as to how she will respond. Her personality is taking a completely different turn than how things were during the first hour of this visit.

Sammie steps back in to the room and informs us she's going to the store to get some more Verdi and that she'll be back shortly. Casey continues after Sammie closes the front door, "Well, it is not so much her as it is the things that Malik says about how she feels about our interaction."

"Please, elaborate," I state, taking a bite of my pie. She goes on to tell me how Malik reached out to her after years of no contact and how she would not have known about the wedding if Malik had not mentioned it to her the week before.

"He invited me to the wedding, unofficially. I mean, I never got an invitation, but...he was cool with me coming. I think he was a little stressed about marrying your sister. He needed some moral support, so when he asked me to come up, I was there for him," Casey states.

"So, you came up before the wedding?" I ask, trying to put this all together.

"Yes. Three days before the wedding. I stayed in the house with Malik."

I couldn't help the thoughts that were entering my brain—that during the three days that Sammie and I stayed at the resort, busting our butts off in preparation for their wedding, Malik was home chillin' with Casey, his longtime friend. Who knows what else they were doing? *I can't believe this. Wait a minute: Does Casey want me to know this? Is this why she's confessing?* Either she wants me to know what went on, which could mean that Malik did cheat with Casey, or she wants me to believe he cheated to cause drama in my sister's marriage. *This woman is playing games.*

"Malik has repeatedly told Sammie how he wants to have kids right away, but she wants to wait until the business is up and running smoothly," Casey stressed how this bothers Malik because he has always wanted a big family and once he got married, he wanted to start right away. "Honestly, Sabine, I think it's selfish that Samantha married Malik and is not willing to consider his needs. I mean, why get married if you are not going to start a family right away. They could've just continued dating." Casey pauses and looks at me, "I know that she's your sister, but I feel that's wrong. "Casey states looking at me for a response.

"So, the issue has to do with having children? I don't understand how that would make Sammie feel insecure. They've been married a little over a year. Besides, the period of time that you are speaking of; they were not even married yet. Decisions like that take time. Kids are a big decision, and it's life changing," I say, somewhat annoyed by Casey at this point.

"The issue has to do with her not giving him what he wants right now. This is a current issue with Malik. He wants children." She sorts of yells this to me, then calms herself down. "Malik is a good man. There are other women out there who would be willing to meet his needs."

"And, you are one of them?" I voice coolly, meeting her gaze.

She smiles as Sammie walks back in the door. "Hey, I got two bottles, and I got us some chips and a RedBox movie," Sammie says as she sets the bag down on the table and takes the wines out.

I get up and grab a bottle of the Verdi to put it in the freezer, momentarily thinking about hitting Casey over the head with it, but then I regain my composure. "So Casey, are you dating anyone right now?" I ask, trying to figure out if she is really after Malik or just wants to cause mayhem between my sister and her husband.

"Yes. I'm dating a guy I knew back in college, his name is Billy," she says as she takes the chips out of the bag and throws the empty grocery bag away.

"How is that going?" I ask, genuinely interested in her response.

"It's okay. He needs to loosen up a bit," she says.

The rest of the afternoon goes by with no problems. We have more drinks and watch the movie Samantha picked out. They leave around four. Overall, it was a good afternoon. Minus Casey's smart out-of-line comments every now and then.

Hi, baby. I know I said I would be back by Thursday night, but I picked up another job in Chicago," Kelvin relays sadly over the phone.

"So, will I see you by the weekend?" I ask.

"Ummmm, no. I have some things to attend to back in Michigan. Something has come up with my brother, and I need to help him with a few things."

"I understand. Well, you know where I am, and you have my number. Don't be a stranger," I reply.

"Sweetie, I am so sorry. I'll make it up to you." Kelvin's voice is soft and sweet, but I feel unforgiving at the moment.

I get into my feelings for a little bit after the conversation with Kelvin, then I tell myself this is what happens when you jump in full power with someone you barely even know. I force that thought to the back of my head, and something or someone says to me, "He's just busy trying to build an empire for you and him. It would be worth it to keep him around, my dear."

Okay, so my morning wasn't starting out so great. I was up doing my usual routine of cooking and replying to emails, then Sammie calls me.

"Hey, girl. So, what did you think of Casey?" she asks.

"She is something else. On the one end, I want to like her. And on the other end, she's shady," I reply, and then we both start laughing.

"I know, right? It's like one minute you want to hang out and go shopping with her, and the next minute you want to slap her," Sammie replies.

"Exactly. She definitely has some issues. How are you and Malik doing?"

"He's grumpy and distant. I think he's cheating," Sammie replies casually.

"With Casey?"

"Among others," she replies dryly.

"Why do you think that?" I ask, kind of shocked.

"I just know. I'm not going to make accusations until I have proof."

"Well, give me some time to process things, and I'll let you know what I think."

After hanging up from Samantha, I think back to some of the things Casey said the previous night. Of course I won't tell Sammie of the conversation. She'd probably murder that woman, or even worse murder Malik, and I would hate to see my sister's story on that television crime show, *Snapped.*

Just as I am closing up shop for the day, blowing out candles and clearing a deck of angel cards I had used with my last client, I hear a knock at my door. I walk over to open it, and there is a bleak looking man dressed in a blue suit standing outside. He has nice creamy brown skin; he is short and has a stocky built. If it weren't for the fact that he looks so sad, he would come across as very attractive.

"Can I help you?" I ask.

"Yes. So I've passed by this place several times and said I would stop by one day to see what this place was about. I told myself, today before I grabbed some food from around the way—" he motions toward the Chinese restaurant within the plaza— "that I would stop by, and here I am," he says melancholy, as if he's searching for something or waiting on an explanation of what I am selling.

"There's not much to see here but a waiting room. I'm a counselor," I reply.

"What kind of counselor?" he asks and beams a very charming smile, which seems to lighten up his dreary demeanor.

"My background is in mental health, but I have branched out into different things," I reply. "It really just depends on the issue that the client presents. That determines which method I will use."

"I see," the man replies. "Can I set up an appointment?"

"Ummm, yes. Come in. Let me grab the intake package. Have a seat." He walks in and sits on the sofa I have in the waiting room. I step to the back room and grab the paperwork and a clipboard. "What's your name?" I ask, handing him the clipboard.

"William Witford. I work for the law firm right up the street," he says as he fills out the short form that I use to gather information on new clients.

"You mean Witford Associates?" I ask, remembering the signs advertising the law firm, as I see them every day when I drive in to work.

"Yes. Exactly." He glances up at me and smile.

"So you own the firm?" I ask.

41

"My father actually owns the firm, but he's prepping me to take over for him one day."

"I see. That seems challenging and rewarding," I respond.

He smiles. "It is." This time when his eyes meet mine, it is brief as they dart to specific areas of my body such as my legs and hips. As he hands me the clipboard, his attention has been refocused to my face. "If you don't mind me asking, what's your name?"

I briefly check over the paperwork, ensuring that he has filled in everything.

"Sabine Stallworth, mental health therapist and licensed spiritual counselor at your service."

"Ahhh, I knew there was something different about you. You don't seem like the typical clinical therapist."

"Okay. I don't know how to take that," I respond.

"Take it as a compliment," he says.

"So, do you have any specific issues you would like to address during our sessions?"

"Relationships," he answers. "I've been having a lot of issues in my current relationship."

I write this down on the notes section of my paperwork. "Are you married?"

"No," he says.

"Let's set a date and a time for us to meet." I look at my calendar. "How does tomorrow at 5:30 P.M. sound?"

"Sounds great."

"The charge will be sixty-five dollars for an hour, unless you have one of these insurances." I hand him a laminated list to review the insurances. "Then you would only pay what your co-pay requires. I always let my clients know upfront that I also do hypnotherapy, which is a form of spiritual counseling. The insurance companies do not cover this, so if you ever wanted to engage in an alternative therapy or counseling session, you would pay the full price, which ranges from forty to sixty-five dollars per session. The sessions last one hour."

"Well, I'd rather not get my insurance company involved, so I'll pay cash." He hands me the list back. "Besides, my co-pay is about forty dollars anyway. That's only twenty-five dollars more if I don't go through the insurance."

"Okay. It's your choice," I state. As I take the list from him, our hands touch briefly.

"Why would someone need hypnotherapy?" William Witford inquire.

"Most times, I only suggest hypnotherapy if I feel there's a block in your progress, something that extends beyond the current situation we're focused on. For example, you may be talking about your relationship with your girlfriend, and I notice you've linked it to a situation in your past with your mom. In order for us to truly deal with the situation with the girlfriend, we would have to go back in time and address the situation with your mom. I would use hypnotherapy to take us there. Make sense?"

Yeah. It does… Makes perfect sense," he says as he gazes into space as if he is thinking on that concept.

"Do you have any more questions?"

"No," he responds.

"You can look me up on the Florida Board of Clinical Social Work, Marriage and Family Therapy, and Mental Health Counseling." I hand him a card with the website. "Also, I'm certified as a spiritual counselor through the Spiritual Health Care Professionals. If you flip the card over, you can see that information there." It briefly describes how sometimes science and psychology cannot answer existential problems. By helping people understand their own spirituality, it helps to promote peace, healing and a union with God. The methods to reach this healing consist of meditation, stress management, hypnotherapy and anger management.

"I will see you tomorrow at 5:30 P.M., Ms. Stallworth," he says as he gets up from the sofa and moves toward the door. He reaches out to shake my hand. I oblige. "I'm glad I stopped by," he says as he walks out of the door.

"Me too."

When I arrive home, I notice a beautiful bouquet of flowers

sitting outside of my door. I bend to read the card: *Even though distance sets us apart right now, you are always close to my heart. Kelvin.*

I set the flowers on my dining room table, and it brings life to the room. I pull out my phone and text Kelvin: *The flowers are beautiful. Thank you so much,* then I snap a picture and send it to him. He sends back a heart emoji. This is all I need to spark my heart and eliminate any doubt I was feeling this morning about him and us rushing in so quickly.

After taking a long, hot shower and getting settled into bed, I open up my photo gallery on my phone and look through pictures Kelvin and I took together this past weekend. He snapped a few of us kissing, us lying in bed and me covering my face, and one with us looking at each other making funny faces. As I scroll through some more, I find one of him standing out on the patio, talking on his phone. His jeans hanging off his waist, boxerless. This man is mesmerizing. Just as I am staring at the picture, my phone rings.

I pick up., "Hello?"

"Hi, baby. I miss you," Kelvin says all heartfelt and lovely.

"I miss you too," I say, all giddy and shylike, smiling ear to ear.

"I'm sorry I'm not with you right now," he says, then pauses.

"Me too." Then I realize I feel like I'm in a daze pining over this man, as if I'm a high school girl. "I was looking at our pictures from this past weekend."

"Yeah? Any good ones?" Kelvin asks.

"Hold on. Let me send you a few, and you be the judge."

I can hear Kelvin tapping on his phone to view the photos that I just sent, and he laughs as he scrolls through them. The last one I send is of me in sexy lingerie, more half-naked and posing the sexiest pose I could come up with after my shower this afternoon.

"Wow. You're beautiful, baby. Thank you for the pictures, especially the last one. You're going to have me leave my brother stranded tonight. If I leave right now, I'll be there by nine A.M. I can do it, baby. Just say the word."

I laugh. "Don't leave your brother stranded. I am tempted to say the word."

"I'll try to leave by Sunday night and make it to you by Monday morning," Kelvin says.

"Sounds like a plan," I reply.

CHAPTER 8—THE SESSION

It is fifteen minutes after five, and I am preparing for William Witford's session on this Friday afternoon. It's a bit windy outside, and the rain has just started to come down—hard. It's like buckets of water falling from the sky. Within seconds, it went from a warm, sunny day to hurricane weather. The lights are flickering a little from the high winds.

I light two white unscented candles that sit on a high table behind the turquoise sofa in my office, then I pour some primrose essential oil mixed with water into a burner. Aromatherapy has a high therapeutic value. It is very important for me that the setting is welcoming and calm for my clients. I like them to feel comfortable, especially new clients who may feel uncomfortable initially about opening up. In addition, the aroma of primrose calms my soul, and I have to admit the loud thunder has me a bit high strung.

The scent of the oil is mild and sweet, mixed with the dainty smell of roses. It kind of reminds me of a summer day, inside of a cozy beach home when the winds are high, sort of like today. Whenever I burn it, I picture myself sitting in a window overlooking the ocean as waves crash to the shoreline. It makes me feel protected and safe. Overall, the sent is calm and invigorating at the same time. Old mystics say primrose oil is believed to draw the truth from any liar, so it never hurts to burn this on my first session with someone so I can understand their truth.

I only purchase thirty-watt lightbulbs for the three lamps in this room. The subtle glow creates an ambiance that sets a warm mood for my clients. There are lots of colors scattered around the room, mostly pastels—pink, mauve, and baby blue—as they are soothing and soft, which relaxes the mind. The sofa is a turquoise color with silver and mauve pillows, which look almost tan with a touch of pink.

I have a picture posted above the sofa that reads *Reflect-Renew*. On the opposite wall, there is a picture of a tropical beach paradise sunset. The sky is filled with many colors. Two palm trees are in view, the trunk of the trees in the shape of a V. The palms on the tree seem to be swaying in the wind. As the sun sets on the ocean, the light reflects the hue of blue, purple, red and orange blending like a rainbow onto the water. To me, a rainbow or variety of bright colors symbolize healing. This is exactly how I use this picture, as a focal point to help in the healing process. This is the picture I direct my clients to look at when they're feeling out of sorts or feeling stress and anxiety. I ask them to pretend they're in that picture, walking along the shoreline, looking at the beautiful colors and to try to see where one color ends and the other begins. The more they stare at the photo, the more they are less in this reality and more in that fantasy of calm. This helps me bring them back to a calm emotional and mental state.

I hear the bell ding as William has arrived. I walk out to greet him. When I get to him, he is soaked as he closes his umbrella and takes off his suit jacket and shoes.

"Oh my. Let me get you some towels." I grab some out of a closet.

"Thanks, love," he says as he pats his wet face with the soft, dry towel that smells of fabric softener.

"Should we reschedule? You're soaked, and I don't want you to get sick staying in those wet clothes. You probably should go home and change into something warm and dry. I don't have any men's clothes here for you," I say, concerned.

He points to a gym bag he has sitting beside him at the door. "I have my gym clothes in here. If you have a restroom, I could change, and we could still have the session."

"Sure. The restroom is right through there." I point to the left of the door. "When you come out, meet me in the room to the right."

When William walks into the counseling room, he looks like a completely different person. He appears refreshed, comfortable, more relaxed and down to earth. Yesterday he was all professional and stuffy. He has on gray jogging pants, a white t-shirt, and some white-and-gray gym shoes.

"It smells good in here. What is that?" he asks.

"Essential oils for relaxation," I reply.

"Nice. I hung my clothes on the towel rack in the restroom. I hope that's okay."

"That is fine. Have a seat, William. Is it okay if I call you that?"

He smiles, "Sure. I'm accustom to people addressing me as Counsel, but I'll let it slide with you." He chuckles.

I smirk at him sarcastically. "I like to start my sessions out with a few relaxation techniques. Close your eyes. We're going to start with a few deep and cleansing breaths."

We spend the first ten minutes breathing deep. I guide William through what he tells me is his first meditation ever in life. Once he gets past the giggles and sexual innuendos he makes in reference to the deep breathing, he does pretty well. Clairvoyantly, I pick up that he is very focused, has a pure heart, is sincere in his thoughts and actions. He has a problem with alcohol—it appears that he likes to drink, but not because of some childhood situation that he couldn't cope with—but because he really enjoys the effects of the alcohol in his system. Because of this, he is caught in situations he shouldn't be in, which could jeopardize his practice. I also pick up that his father is sick—very sick.

"You did a good job, William. I'm proud of you. How do you feel now?" I ask, keeping my voice as calm as possible as I am prone to be very hyperactive, but I want to keep him in this calm space.

"Actually, I feel really good. Thank you for that," he says sincerely.

"Guiding you through that meditation was calming for me also. It helps me to get centered within myself and be able to focus on you and your needs," I say. Then I think, *it also helps me tune into you psychically, but that isn't for you to know.*

"My needs, huh?" William asks with a grin.

"Yes, your needs," I reiterate. "Now, I need to bring you back up to this consciousness. Blink your eyes, wiggle your toes, and stretch your arms and legs," I say as I demonstrate. He follows my demonstration as if we are warming up for an aerobics class.

"So William, what's on your mind today?" I ask as I grab my note pad.

William shuffles around a little. He looks at me, then looks down. He fiddles with the drawstring on his jogging pants, then he looks up and stares me straight into the eyes.

"Well, Ms. Stallworth—" he says, but I interrupt.

"Call me Sabine."

"Well, Sabine, relationship issues brings me here today. I'm dating this fine-ass woman who is as smart as a whip, but that's the problem, I think she has me whipped!"

"How so?" I ask.

"I don't take orders well, but she gives orders pretty damn well."

"Okay."

"The problem is I'm doing things I normally wouldn't do."

"Like what?"

"Like I got rid of some friends because she felt they weren't up to my level. She said some shit like they were holding me back. These were friends I talked to and hung out with regularly."

"How long has it been since you last hung out with your friends?" I ask.

"At least three months."

"Wow, that's a long time."

"Yes. She takes up most of my time. It's like she practically lives at my place now. Sometimes I need a break from my house to get peace of mind away from her."

"Let's back this conversation up. How do you feel about this woman who has you whipped?"

"Like I said, she's good-looking and smart, and I admire those qualities, but she isn't totally my type."

"How did she get to the point of living with you?"

"Good question." He pauses. "I'm still trying to figure that one out."

"Before she came into the picture, were you serious with someone else?"

"Yes." He goes into deep thought and appears a little sad.

"If you don't want to talk about it, that's perfectly okay."

"No, I can talk about it. I need to talk about it. Her name was Sara. We met in law school. We dated on and off for ten years. About two months ago, we got into this huge argument over the woman who is living in my house now."

"Why the argument? What happened?"

"She felt I was spending way too much time with her. They knew each other back in college, and Sara didn't have a lot of nice things to say about this woman."

"I noticed that you mentioned Sara's name but you haven't mentioned your new friend's name. Is that on purpose?"

"Yes, that's on purpose. She likes a low profile."

"Okay. Can we call your new friend Kelly for all intents and purposes?"

"Sure."

"So, you were spending way too much time with Kelly..." I say to get him back on track.

"Yes. Kelly really knows how to party, but that's the thing; I like hanging out with her in certain scenes like parties and clubs because she socializes well and she's fun. As far as Kelly hanging out in my house seven days a week, not a good scene for her. In my opinion, she isn't the wifey type. She's a fun girl. Sara was the wifey type. I miss her," he confesses.

"Where is Sara now?"

"Sara is in her skin, I guess," he says sarcastically, then adds more seriously, "I don't know. She doesn't return my calls, and she has moved from her old condo downtown. I can't locate her."

"Well you two share friends, right? Have any of them seen her?"

"I don't know because I haven't talked to them. Those are the same friends Kelly feels I'm too good for."

"William, you're an attorney. If you want to find her, I'm sure you have resources. Use them."

"I know, but I don't want to put Sara through more hurt. Plus, Kelly is living with me now, by her own invitation."

"Do you want Kelly in your house?"

"It has its perks." He smirks.

"I see. Let's do this…on a scale from one to ten, how do you rate your relationship with Sara? Ten is the best relationship you've ever experienced."

"Eight and a half or a nine."

"Rate your relationship with Kelly," I challenge.

"If you want to call it a relationship. A five," he says matter-of-factly.

"What would you call it?" I ask.

"Great sex from a houseguest who's overdue to leave. I would rate the sex a nine. The situation is shitty. I would rate that a two."

"Okay, this is what I want you to do tonight. Make a list of the qualities that you like in Kelly. Make the same list of Sara. Bring it back to our next session so you can make some decisions, not necessarily about going back to Sara, but about deciding on a relationship that's best for you. We're going to use Sara as the one to measure others by."

William and I engaged in conversation about his family over the course of the counseling session. He has a younger brother who is currently in law school and due to graduate in a few months. He spoke of his mother and how supportive she is and how his father is the rock in their family. He reports a happy childhood growing up. He lived alone before Kelly. Whenever he spoke of Sara, I could feel the sadness and dread in his heart. As we got to the end of the session, I reminded William about making the list comparing Sara and Kelly. I informed him that it's a technique to help him in distinguishing what qualities he looks for in a mate.

"Okay, Sabine. Will do. When can you see me again?"

"I usually don't work on Saturdays unless I have an emergency with one of my clients or had to re-schedule an appointment from earlier in the week."

"What would classify as an emergency?" William asks.

"Mental breakdown." I direct William to the card I gave him earlier that has numbers to call if you are feeling suicidal. "At the bottom of the card is my work cell phone number. You use this in emergencies only. If I don't answer right away, I will check my voicemail and call you back." I grab my planner. "I like to give you at least three days to process your feelings about what we discuss here. If you want to meet on Monday at 5:30 P.M., we can. Or we can wait until next Friday," I say as I flip through the pages of my planner.

William interrupts, "Friday is too long. Monday is great. I will have the lists for you. He hands me a fifty and a twenty-dollar bill.

"Hold on. Let me get your change." I walk over to my safe and pull out a five-dollar bill.

"Thanks," he replies as he puts the five in his wallet and throws the wallet into his gym bag.

"Thank you. I don't know where my mind was. I normally take the cash before the session. You almost got a freebie."

"I would pay seventy dollars for the meditation alone. That was very relaxing," he says.

"I'm glad you enjoyed it."

"I'm going to grab my clothes from the restroom." William picks up his bag and walks out.

"I'll meet you at the door," I call after him as I finish my notes.

When I see him at the door, I hand him the card with his next appointment listed, and he reaches for a hug. "Thank you Sabine. I'm glad I have someone to talk to. I've been feeling lost these days." When he pulls back from the hug, it looks as if there is a storm in his eyes. Chaos surrounds him. I can tell this is the most relaxed he's felt in months.

"I'm so happy to help. See you on Monday. Don't forget the lists."

"I won't." William walks to his car. The rain has stopped. There's a nice breeze outside, but there is an overcast; the sky is grey. It kind of puts me in a solemn mood, unless I'm picking up on William's mood. Yeah, that's more likely. I need to get out and do something fun. I decide to call Sammie to see if she wants to eat out at a place where we can get good steak and an entertaining fine dining experience.

CHAPTER 9—KELVIN'S GIFTS AKA "SUPERPOWERS"

I call Sammie once I'm in my car. She doesn't answer her phone. I wonder what's going on with her. She's so distant lately. I leave a voicemail message: *Hey, girl, I was leaving work and wanted to see if you're interested in going to the Asian Steak House for dinner. Call me. I'll be in your area in thirty minutes. I could scoop you up.* My phone rings, and I answer it thinking it's Samantha.

"Hey, girl. Want to go to the steak house? They have this new appetizer I want to try. Plus, I need to get out and do something fun. You know how entertaining it is watching the chef make that onion choo choo, and my taste buds are set on Asian cuisine… " There is a long pause on the other end.

"Hello?"

I look at the screen to see who I'm actually talking to. It says unknown caller. All I hear is heavy breathing on the other end. I hang up the phone. *That felt creepy,* I think. *Mental note to self: next time look at the caller ID before beginning a long, drawn-out conversation with a creepy unknown stranger on the other end.*

The phone rings again. I look at the screen, and it shows Sammie's picture.

"Hey," I answer.

"Hey, girl. Yes, I want to go to the steak house. Come pick me up."

"On my way. Did you just call me one minute ago?" I ask, confused.

"Nope. I just returned your phone call. Why?"

"Someone called me from an unknown number and just held the line. It was weird," I respond, "then you called."

"Wasn't me."

I think to myself, *a lot of strange things are happening lately, from odd creepy feelings in my gut to malfunctions with electronics. The other day, it was the flickering light outside on my patio, then there was the knocks on the door, now I got a phone call with a heavy breather on the other end. It feels as if this is meant to scare me.*

"Where's Malik?" I ask, taking my mind away from the eerie situation.

"Out, I guess."

"You guess?" I question, curious as to why she's so nonchalant.

"Yup."

"Okay. Well, I'll see you in a few minutes. Kelvin is calling me." I click over.

"Hello, lady."

I love the sound of Kelvin's voice. It's just so mellow and sexy. It's as if he's standing right next to me whispering into my ear.

"Hello, Kelvin."

"Did I catch you at a bad time?" he asks.

"No. I'm driving to my sister's house."

"Samantha's?" he asks.

"Yes. We're going out to dinner. I needed a break, and want to catch up with her about some things going on in her marriage. She thinks her husband is cheating on her," I blurt out, opening up to him as if I've known him for years, *it feels like I've known him for years.*

"Really? That's not good," he responds.

"Yeah, well, they dated for three years, and all throughout their dating, they argue like cats and dogs for about a week, then they make up. It seems like every time they argue and make up, the love is stronger between them, so I'm not worried about the relationship. I just hope they don't drive each other insane during the process of challenging each other."

"Interesting," Kelvin states. "This conversation is perking me up on my long drive. It's like a real-life soap opera."

"Actually, that's exactly what it's like." I laugh. "I try not to get too involved because I know they'll work it out between them sooner or later. Love always wins, right?"

"Awww. You're a romantic," Kelvin states, and I can tell he's smiling.

"I think you are too, Mr. Surprise, here are some flowers and a nice sweet note to brighten your day."

Kelvin laughs. "So, I brightened your day yesterday?"

"For sure. It was a very nice gesture, and I really appreciate it. I just wish you were here with me now."

"I know, baby. I'm working on it. I do have a surprise for you. I think you'll like it."

"Kelvin, you're going to spoil me."

"That's the intent."

I pull up to Sammie's house and honk the horn lightly. "Where are you now?" I ask Kelvin.

"I actually finished the job in Chicago and got my brother squared away sooner than I thought. I'm on my way to see you. Surprise. I'll be there around eleven, if that's okay with you."

"What?" I exclaim with a smile.

"Is that too late, baby?"

"Are you kidding? No, it isn't too late! Kelvin, I can't wait to see you."

"The feeling is so mutual, baby. I'll let you go enjoy dinner with your sister. Leave room for dessert. I'll contact you when I'm thirty minutes out. I have to park my truck and pick up my car."

"Okay. Be careful. I'm so happy I'll see you tonight," I say.

"Bye, sweetie."

"Bye." After I hang up from Kelvin, I feel like I'm floating on air. How does he do that to me?

Sammie gets into the car. "Hey, girl!" She beams a wide smile at me as if she has something to tell me that she's excited about, but she doesn't say anything more. There seems to be pure joy radiating from her aura.

"What's up girl? You seem extremely happy," I say looking suspiciously at her wanting her to tell me what is going on with her.

"Nothing, just happy to be having dinner with my sister, is all."

During the car ride, we discuss some ideas for S & S Café and Lounge. She informs me she's interviewed a few people and wants me to do a second interview with them. We agree to set this up for tomorrow morning. She sends emails out to the four people she is interested in hiring for Saturday morning interviews. She does all of this on her smart phone in the car.

"So, we're working Saturday morning, huh?" I question, giving her a hard time.

"Yeah, why? Did you make plans?" She asks, looking as though she has made a mistake sending those emails.

"No, I'm good. Kelvin will be here tonight, though," I reply.

"Wow, you guys are kind of serious to just have met. Is he your lobster?" Samantha asks.

We both laugh, but in all honesty, I really do hope he's my lobster. *Lobster* is the term Sammie and I picked up from watching *Friends*, that funny television series when Phoebe asked Ross if Rachel was his lobster. Meaning, his mate for life.

Dinner was great, and we are stuffed. To my surprise, Sammie didn't talk much about her relationship issues, and I didn't talk much about Kelvin. We both shared in our excitement about the business, picking up ideas on how we would want our business to run in comparison to the steak house. We decided we needed to eat out at least three times per week, for research purposes for S & S Café' and Lounge, and not necessarily just restaurants, but bakeries, delis, and any place that sells food, desserts, and coffee. We want to stand out from the rest; have that extra special touch that maybe some of the commercial businesses don't have. We aren't total critics. We'll be looking at the things we like about these places also, and we'll do the things we like about a restaurant or eatery better at our cafe. We both agreed that sounded like a solid plan.

As we are walking out, we see this couple in front of us giggling with each other. When we walk to the parking lot, we notice that they are about three cars down and a row in front of us. For some reason, my focus is on them. When the woman turns around, Sammie and I recognize her immediately. It's Casey.

Casey is all over him, flirting like a goddess. He is leaning on the car, and she's standing very close to him, whispering to him, then stepping back and laughing piercingly. She stumbles a few times almost falling, and he grabs her by the arm. It's obvious that they are both drunk. By far, she appears more intoxicated than he is. Then he turns his face towards us. I recognize him too...

"Oh my God, Samantha."

"What? Do you know that guy?" She asks.

"Yes. That's William."

"Who's William?" Samantha asks.

"My new client."

"Well, I'm just happy it's not Malik Marks." She laughs.

"Let's get in the car before they see us," I whisper.

Sammie starts singing "I Spy with My Little Eye." I shush her and roll my window down a little to see if I can make out what is being said. Casey jumps into the passenger side of the car. William is still standing outside, looking down at his watch. I can't help but wonder if they are sober enough to drive.

"Sammie, maybe we should see if they need a ride."

"Really, Sabine?"

"Yes. They're drunk," I state, looking at her dumbfounded, as if she's forgotten that's how we lost our parents, to a drunk driver.

"We could call them a cab," she says calmly.

"Sammie," I exclaim, as I turn my head to look at her.

"Okay, girl," she says, more so to appease me.

We both get out of the car and walk toward them. William recognizes me immediately. "Sabine, how are you love?" He reaches for a hug.

"I'm good. How are you?" I ask, assessing him as I pull away from the hug.

"I'm great. Who's this beautiful woman who looks just like you?" he asks.

58

"This is Samantha, my twin sister."

Sammie shakes his hand. "Nice to meet you. Looks like you guys are having a good time tonight." Sammie looks inside of the car and see Casey passed out.

"We are. We're thinking of going to a club. You guys want to come?" William asks, excited.

"I don't know. It looks as if your date is done for the night. Plus, you seem pretty intoxicated yourself. Is it safe for you to drive?" I ask, concerned.

"It's all good. I just called Uber," William says with a smile.

"Okay, but is she going to be okay? She looks pretty wasted," Sammie states.

He looks in the car. "You're right. I'll have the Uber driver drop her off at home first," he smiles, then adds, "Just kidding. She'll sober up by the time we get to the club. I really appreciate your concern, ladies. It's heartwarming," he is convincingly displaying an appreciative facial expression, even though I can tell that he is being sarcastic.

I look at my watch; it reads 9:30 P.M. *I really need to go home and prepare for Kelvin,* I think. "We're not dressed for the club," I blurt out, then Uber pulls up. "Maybe next time, William. Have fun and be safe," I say as Sammie and I head back to the car. We watch William help Casey out of his car and into the Uber, then he gets in.

Then as if we're on the same wavelength, Sammie says, "Let's follow them."

"Sammie, you read my mind," I say excitedly.

We stay at least two car spaces behind them. We take a few back roads and then come to a building that has several cars in the parking lot and what looks like a private entryway. There's no name on the building. Women are dressed in mini-skirts or tight pants with revealing tops. We see all types of couples: women and men; men and men; women and women; woman, man and man; and man, woman, and woman.

"Interesting," I say. "Sammie, do you think this is a swingers club?" I ask.

"I know this is a swingers club." Sammie is looking out the window checking out the scene. William and Casey get out of the car and walk to the door. His arm is around her neck. They are smiling, and William is shaking hands with people, then they disappear into the building. Sammie saves this location in the navigation on her phone. "Sabine, we are totally coming here tomorrow night."

"What?" I question, somewhat shocked.

"Aren't you curious a little?" she asks.

"Maybe," I say. "Are you going to invite Malik?"

"Of course. This might be exactly what our relationship needs," she says as her thoughts seems to go wild. I drive off from the club and drop Sammie at her house by 10:45. As I'm about to pull out of her driveway, I get a text from Kelvin saying he'll be at my place in thirty minutes. I text him back and tell him I'll leave the key under the mat and for him to let himself in.

Sammie turns around from her doorstep and yells, "Don't forget the interviews in the morning. All four confirmed. We're meeting at the coffee shop. See you there at eight A.M." I watch Samantha walk in the house, then I head home.

What an interesting night. I'm very curious about that club, and I'm looking forward to hanging out tomorrow, but what I'm really looking forward to right at this moment is seeing Kelvin.

When I get home, I put my spare key under the mat, then I lock up, run some bathwater, and light some candles. I pour some lavender bubble bath into the tub. I grab the Verdi Sammie brought over here the other day and two wineglasses. I set them on the ledge of the bathtub. I grab two fluffy towels and set them on the chair next to the tub. I use the toilet, brush my teeth, and take a quick shower. I dim the lights in my room and turn the lights off completely in the bathroom. The only thing that's keeping the bathroom lit are the four candles posted around the tub. I hear the front door open. I slide into the warm, soothing water. Kelvin walks in seconds later.

"Wow, Sabine. Aren't you the romantic?" he says as he bends

down to kiss me ever so softly. His lips and his indulgent touch have me craving for more.

"Please. Take your clothes off and join me," I say, feeling desire racing through me, yearning for more of his kisses, more of his touches. He turns around and walks toward the sink. He removes all of his clothes, leaving them at a puddle by his feet before slowly striding back toward me. His gaze is intense as he stares at me slowly, seductively moving the tip of his tongue across his lips. I find myself instinctually rising so he can sit behind me. The water slowly runs down the curves of my body, creating an enticing sight for him as I placate to his natural male tendencies for erotic visuals. He steps in to the tub. I watch his physique as he grips both sides and as the muscles in his arms tense and flex as he slides down underneath me. I use his body for leverage as I rotate in the water to face him. I've made the water purposely hotter than normal to add glisten and a hint of perspiration to give my face a sultry look. I face him. Our eyes lock. I have him; his smooth lips to mine are imminent. I smile then break the tension by looking away and grabbing the sponge. He releases a breath as I rub the sponge lightly from his neck to his shoulders, then firmly grip them, squeezing the water from the sponge, I notice that his arms are strong and hard. My mind naturally gravitates to the image of him manhandling me sexually.

His skin is soft and smooth. He smells like the embodiment of man and cologne. The steam rising from the water makes him glisten. I dip the sponge in the water once more and squeeze it over his chest. His body is so warm—hell, hotter than the water we're in. I wipe the sponge over his chest and press my lips against his collarbone, leaving a soft kiss. He moans. I can feel his erection as I continue to play with his body. I position myself so that our faces meet. He grabs my head and pulls me in for a very passionate kiss. No longer imminent, it has initiated the kiss I've been longing for.

He lifts my body and positions me so my legs straddle each side of him. My knees are bent, and I lift up to grab the condom I placed between the towels. I quickly open it and roll it down on his throbbing penis as I look him in the eyes. I position his erection on my clitoris and rub it up and down. I can instantly feel my body wanting to explode. We are kissing and grinding, then I feel his penis slide slowly inside of me, stretching me out and filling me up. He pauses for several seconds, holding my waist, keeping me still on him.

"Don't move, baby. I don't want to cum. You feel so good," he says. I continue to place soft, brief kisses on his lips, teasing and enticing him. He kisses me back with so much thirst and urgency that I've already started cycling toward my looming orgasm. He then takes control of my hips, slamming me into him at least ten times. That does it for me. I am cumming, hard, moaning and crying out.

"That's it, baby. Just like that. I love to hear you cum," he says as he slows it down, letting me get myself together. He kisses my neck softly, kisses all over my breasts, then he begins to pumps his body into mine again, building up his speed. Every stroke hits my spot and sends aftershocks through my body. It's almost as if I'm having a continuous orgasm. "Baby, this may not be the best time for me to tell you this, but..." He pauses for several seconds.

"But what, Kelvin?" I whisper, barely able to get my words out.

"I'm falling for you... I mean..." He kisses my neck, then pulls my face to his. "Look at me, Sabine."

I open my eyes and stare into his beautiful brown ones. "Yes?" I continue to meet his grinds, both of our bodies crashing into each other...the water splashing.

"I'm falling in love with you," he says, then his head tilts back, and he yells, "Shit, baby, I'm cumming." Then, "Awwwww!" as his body jerks. I continue grinding faster until I'm cumming with him.

Seconds later, he lifts my body up and pulls off the condom. He ties it up and reaches out of the tub to place it on the floor. I turn around so my back is to his stomach. I interlace my fingers through his. I can feel his body still jerking from his orgasm. His head is resting back on the tub. I'm thinking about what he's just said to me—*I am falling in love with you*. Then instantly, like a dream flashing before my eyes, I see myself standing in a laced off-white gown with long sleeves. I see him standing next to me with a light gray suit on. It looks like we're taking pictures on our wedding day. Our fingers are intertwined the way they are right now. I snatch my fingers away.

He sits up. "Are you okay, baby?" he asks, concerned.

"Yes. Let's get out of the tub," I suggest and hand him a towel.

Kelvin drifts off to sleep almost instantly when we are in bed. I look at his face, rubbing the facial hair that is growing out on his cheeks. Then I whisper, "I am in love with you too, Mr. Kelvin Jerome Frey." I kiss his lips. When I pull away, I hear him groan lightly as if he's heard me. Kelvin pulls me in close to him and hugs me tightly before I drift off to sleep.

I awake in a panic at 4:44 A.M. I glance over at Kelvin. He is sound asleep. I hurry out of the bed and into the bathroom to splash water on my face, as if I am trying to wash away the horrid memories of the dream. Tears fill my eyes. Looking in the mirror makes it hard for me to determine my reality right now, versus what I just experienced in my dream. My head is spinning, and I feel woozy. What bothers me is that it seemed less like a dream and more like a replay of events for my eyes to see. The question is, whose events?

In the dream, I am in this house that has three floors—a basement, a middle floor, and an upstairs. Between the middle floor and the basement is a side door. There are men outside—at least seven. They're drunk and belligerent. It seems as if they're trying to get into the house. All of the window blinds and curtains are open; I feel so exposed. I am hiding on the stairwell near the side door. My boyfriend is on the opposite side of the door, outside trying to block these men from entering. I can sense they are over powering him. I run upstairs to the bedroom, run into the bathroom, and lock the door. By this time, I am sobbing out of control, and I am out of breath. I already know I'm doomed. No one can do anything to save me. I can hear the men in the house. My boyfriend is saying, "Baby, I'm so sorry." He is crying. The other man is saying, "Open the door or I'm going to tear it off the hinges," which is exactly what he does ten seconds later. One man proceeds to have his way with me, then the other, and so on. My boyfriend's hands are tied in front of him. Two men are holding him down by the shoulders. He is on his knees, and they are forcing him to watch as each man takes his turn on me.

As I come out of the memory of this dream, I feel sick to the stomach. I run to the toilet, heaving my guts out several times until it feels like there is nothing left to throw up. I grab some tissue and wipe my mouth, then flush what I just emptied into the toilet. I walk out to the sink, rinse my mouth then grab my electric toothbrush. Either the sound of my vomit or the buzzing from the toothbrush wake Kelvin up. He walks in. "Are you okay baby? Are you sick?"

I finish brushing and rinse my mouth once more. "Kelvin, I'm sorry you heard that," I say, embarrassed.

He turns me around. "Sabine, are you okay?" he asks with concern etched on his face.

"Yes. I just had a bad dream."

He hugs me, then he leans his forehead into mine. "Let me see," he says. A couple of minutes pass by and he says, "It wasn't a dream, Sabine. It was insight into someone's life."

"Kelvin, how do you know that?" I ask, shocked.

"I have gifts, baby, just like you." He kisses my forehead. "Come on. Let's go to bed."

CHAPTER 10—THE INTERVIEWS

I wake up again at 6:40 A.M. I hear Kelvin in the kitchen moving around, and I smell bacon and eggs cooking. It has my stomach growling. I am so hungry. When I walk into the kitchen, Kelvin is fully dressed and is looking like a culinary master.

"Good morning," I say to him.

"Good morning, sweetheart. I made you some breakfast." He sets the plate in front of me.

"Thank you." I grab my fork.

"So, how are you feeling this morning?" Kelvin asks as he grabs his plate and sits across from me.

"Okay. Are you leaving?" I ask, kind of hoping he's not getting on the road again so soon.

"No. I'm just going to handle some business in town. You know I have an office here, right?"

"No, I didn't know that."

"Yeah, it is right near the mall—Frey Transportation Services, Inc. They're putting the sign up today on the building."

"Oh. Nice," I say with a full mouth.

"And I think I've found a house I want to rent. I'm going to look at it today," he says as he eats his eggs. "How's the food?" he asks.

"It's great. Thank you for cooking me breakfast. Later tonight, Sammie and I want to check out this club. I want to know if you would be my date."

"Of course, Sabine. Do you want me to meet you here?"

"Yes. Let's meet back at my place tonight at 9:30."

"Okay. I'll be here. Here's your key." He slides the key across the table.

I slide it back to him. "Keep it. I was wondering if you would stay with me for the weekend and maybe longer...or, at least until you find a place, if you want to."

"I would love to. Thank you, Sabine." He smiles and puts the key in his pocket.

"I've gotta shower. I'm suppose to meet Sammie at the coffee shop at eight. We have some interviews lined up for the café." I rush to the bathroom to get ready.

Once I am dressed and walking out of the bedroom, Kelvin gets up from the kitchen counter and walks with me to the door. He turns me around to face him.

"I really meant what I said last night. I love you, Sabine." He kisses my lips slowly.

I swear his kisses take me to a different world. "I believe you." I blush, then I say, "I love you too, Kelvin." We smile at each other for a few seconds. He hugs me, pulls away, looks me deep in the eyes, then opens the front door for me. He walks me to my car.

"So, I'll see you tonight then," he says as he opens my car door.

"Yes." We kiss once more before I get into my car.

On my drive over to the coffee shop, I keep thinking about what Kelvin said: *I have gifts, like you.* How does he know about my abilities? And how was he able to channel my dream by just touching his forehead against mine? And how did he know it wasn't just a dream. Whose life was I experiencing?

I walk into the coffee shop and check my phone. The time reads 7:45. I have fifteen minutes to spare. I order two tall decaf iced cafe mochas, then I grab a table and take my laptop out.

I pull up the email Sammie sent to me with the four potential employees whom she has screened for this second interview. She has written a little synopsis next to their names: The waiter, Lamar, is a sophomore at the University of South Florida. He is studying interdisciplinary social sciences with a concentration in religious studies. He has three years of experience waiting tables. The kitchen aid, Julissa, is working on her degree at Florida Technical College in baking and pastry making. She has no job experience, but she has three letters of recommendations from her teachers at the Florida Technical College. It appears as if she is the best in her class. The second kitchen aid, Wendy is a retired schoolteacher who likes to bake as a hobby and has been doing so for over twenty years now. She has several reviews by clients who have purchased her baked goods. Lastly is the cashier and manager, Lydia, who has over twenty years of experience managing other employees. She has worked for a department store as a department head for fifteen years, and she has spent the last five years managing a coffee shop. Samantha walks in at eight on the dot.

"Wow, Samantha. You did a good job screening." I comment. "I like all of them and I haven't even met them yet."

"I know, right? Is this my drink?" Sammie asks.

"Yes." I slide her drink over to her.

"Lamar, Julissa, Wendy, and Lydia sound great. I can't wait to meet them," I reply, looking over their résumés.

The interviews go extremely well. Their personalities are so different, their age and experience varies, and this is exactly the climate we are looking for. Lamar is very warm and friendly, perfect for a waiter. Julissa is on top of her game—she definitely knows what she is doing. Wendy is so graceful and has so much experience and great ideas. I think Julissa and Wendy will make a great team in the kitchen, they will learn a lot from each other. Lydia has spunk and seems like she can settle any dispute.

"Well, I guess we need to get the offer letters together," I say to Sammie.

"I'll work on those on Sunday," Sammie replies.

We finish up around noon, then we finalize our plans to meet at my place tonight. I head home, not realizing how sleepy I am until I get in the car. I did have a busy night last night. Plus, I didn't sleep very well. When I get into the house, I immediately take off my clothes and lay out across the unmade bed. I can smell Kelvin's scent on the sheets and just like that, my thoughts turn to him. I pull out my phone and text him: *Send me a picture of the sign they put up today on your building.* Seconds later Kelvin sends the photo, then he calls me.

"Sabine, what do you think of it?" he asks.

"I think it looks great. I think all of it is great. It's wonderful that you own Frey Transportation Services. How long have you been doing this?" I ask.

"The main branch is in Michigan. My brother, father, and I have been running it for three years. We have three drivers right now. The company is doing so well, that's why I decided to expand. That's why I am here in Florida. I'm putting some ads out on Craig's List advertising for drivers as we speak."

"That's great, Kelvin. So you won't always be on the road once you find drivers?"

"No. I'll be doing more of the logistics. But now, I'm building new accounts, and as jobs come in, I have to take them."

"Makes sense, businessman," I say with a smile.

"So, how is your day so far, sweetie?" he asks.

"So far, so good. We're going to hire all four of the people we interviewed today. Sammie's preparing the offer letters."

"Seems like everything is coming along," Kelvin says.

"It is. You know Sammie and I like to do things differently; we tend to take a nontraditional approach. We would like to open the café up at night for the grand opening. We're going to make it like a party. We'll have samples of our food out at the tables and music. We'll raffle off gift cards, and we'll have an area to take pictures so we can advertise on Facebook, Instagram and Twitter. We figure the party should be from seven to ten. We're trying to target an older crowd. What do you think?" I ask.

"I think that the party—I mean opening—will be amazing, Sabine."

"Thanks, Kelvin."

"So, tonight, what should I wear?" Kelvin asks.

"I'm so happy you asked that. If you don't mind, I'd like to dress you for the evening. Can you meet me at the mall in a few hours?"

Kelvin laughs. "Okay. Should I be scared?"

"No, don't be scared. You have such a perfect frame—tall, slender, and just a nice build to your body. I want to dress you up tonight, like my own personal Ken doll. If you want, you can dress me. It will be fun," I say with excitement.

"Okay. I guess it will be fun," Kelvin says, sort of feeling the spirit of fun.

"I could come by your office first then we can walk over to the mall," I suggest.

"Okay, baby. See you around two?" he says.

"Yes, see you at two."

"I'll text you the address in case you want to put it in the navigation," Kelvin says before he hangs up the phone.

I'm walking out of the door around 1:30. On my drive to Frey Transportation Services, Inc., I decide to stop by the frozen yogurt shop to pick up some strawberry frozen yogurt for Kelvin and me to enjoy before we begin our shopping expedition. I pull up in the parking lot. The sign really does look great. It makes the building stand out. The ground is freshly paved, and I see two semi-trucks parked over to the left. One is royal blue and the other is midnight black. I get out of the car, carefully holding both large cups of yogurt and walk up to the door. Kelvin opens it.

"The sign looks even better in person," I comment excitedly. I am unorganized because my hands are full and I am wondering where I can set these cups as there are papers all over the desk and on the table in front of me.

"Yeah?" he questions and smiles. He takes both cups and sets them on the desk after shuffling some papers around, then reaches for me and gives me the most loving hug. I relax in his arms. That song by Method Man and Mary J Blige comes to my mind, *You're all I need...*

"I'm sorry, sweetie. Am I holding us up?" he asks.

"No. This is good," I say feeling beyond relaxed and more like I'm melting in his arms.

"Oh, wait, I got us a treat. We should eat it before it melts," I say, coming back to reality.

As we walk over to the mall with our yogurts in hand, I explain to Kelvin this is not an ordinary club.

"What do you mean?" he asks, looking inquisitive.

"I mean, Sammie and I think it's a swingers club."

"What?" he questions, shocked initially, then he smiles.

"For the record, I'm not a swinger. I have never been to one of these clubs, but Sammie and I ran across it yesterday, and we're curious and want to check it out. It'll be fun. We don't have to do anything; we can just...watch."

"Is Sammie bringing her husband?"

"Yes."

"I find it interesting that the first time I meet Sammie's husband will be at a swingers club."

"Well...you'll actually meet him at my house at 9:30 tonight before we go to the club," I say sarcastically.

"I'm glad you told me what type of club we're going to tonight, and I'm kind of happy you're dressing me up for tonight."

I smile and take my spoon filled with frozen yogurt and put some on the tip of Kelvin's nose and run into the mall.

"Sabine!" he yells. I throw my cup in the garbage and come back out.

"I'm so sorry, baby," I say, trying to be sincere, but I can't stop the smile that has already formed on my face. I take my hand and wipe the yogurt off his nose.

I pick out athletic skinny jeans, a short-sleeve V-neck button cuffs grey cardigan shirt and tan Timberland Groveton high-top sneakers for Kelvin. As for me, he picks out a long-sleeved, tight polyester dress that is knee length and has a white-and-tan pattern. The front of the dress has a rounded neckline, which extends right below my neck and around the shoulders, and the back exposes my upper back. He purchases some neon coral Angelica Lilian stiletto sandals that go perfectly with the dress.

"I think we did a pretty good job, Kelvin," I say to him as I feed him some of my cinnamon pretzel while we wait on our pizza.

"You think?" he asks.

"Yes. This was fun. Thank you for the dress and the shoes."

"You're welcome, Seme. Thank you for being my personal shopper."

"Any time." I stare at Kelvin longer than I probably should.

"What is it, baby? Do I have some cinnamon on my lips?" He rubs his lips.

"No. Your lips are perfect. I was thinking about what you said this morning to me about my dream."

"Yeah. It wasn't a dream, sweetie, it was insight into someone's life."

"That's the thing. How do you know what I dreamt or had insight into?"

"Baby, listen, okay?" He grabs my hand. He pauses as he gathers his thoughts.

"I knew that you were disturbed beyond what a nightmare does to a person because I felt it when I came into the bathroom to check on you. Then, when I moved in closer to you, it was as if I was being ported into another world. I could feel your memory like flashes, as if I was coming in and out of another reality. Then when I pulled you close, I saw the woman who you portrayed in this vision, and I felt her pain—the pain of being raped repeatedly."

He grabs my hand a little tighter. "I felt her bleakness and her despair. I saw her boyfriend, and I felt his powerlessness in this situation. I also know he committed suicide after that incident because he couldn't live with the fact that he let that happen to her. It had something to do with his gambling debts. The woman in your vision carries that hurt with her to this day. There's a void or an absence about her that she covers up with a tough façade." Hearing Kelvin narrate my dream as if it was his, makes me uneasy as to how he is privy to this knowledge. I look down towards my lap trying to search my brain for an answer to how he knows so much.

"Look at me, Seme, "She's hurt and angry. She's also very dangerous—ruthless. Everything she had that was good in her dissipated on that day. To her, there's no God, no such thing as love. Life is a series of events that occurs by chance and then you die. She has nothing to live for."

"Kelvin, stop. I don't understand," I say, hurt and shaken, remembering the dream all too vividly.

"You don't have to understand. You just need to accept it," he says sincerely.

"Are you psychic?" I ask, looking up at him.

"I have insight into some things. My abilities are not identical to yours. I have noticed that somehow, being around you opens me up to a different world. It amplifies my awareness, if that makes sense. Excuse me, baby." Kelvin gets up to grab the pizza we're waiting on. As he walks back over, he continues his story. "My mom could see things. She had the gift of prophecy." He pauses for a while, then proceeds. "When she was alive, she told me I would meet a woman one day whose life force would give spark to mine. She said she would be what I've been searching for all of these years, and that once I met her, my life would take a turn for the better. She said I'd know she was the one instantly." He smiles at me, recalling that memory.

"I didn't believe her because it hadn't happened before she passed away." I was looking too hard, and in all of the wrong places. I was trying to find what my mom said that I would find. Then, one day, I stopped looking, and I focused all of my energies into my business." He looks at me. "The business brought me here...to you." I stare at him in awe. "I know this is a lot to take in, Seme, but the first day I met you outside advertising for the café, I knew you were the one my mom spoke of. I felt it when I looked into your eyes. I got confirmation when you shook my hand. It was like I could see little snapshots of our life together." He smiles. "I know you felt it last night in the bathtub. I felt it too. I feel at peace when I'm around you. There are no games or gimmicks, just pure, honest conversations and love with you."

There are so many emotions going through me at the moment, but most of what I feel is relief that I've found someone so insightful and honest. All my fears about Kelvin and I are relieved because now I know that he feels the same about me.

I finally speak up. "It feels good."

"What feels good, Sabine?"

"It feels good to be loved by you, Kelvin, and thank you."

"Thanks for what exactly?" he asks.

"For opening up to me about your mom." I look at him and squeeze his hand. "And for telling me how you feel about me. It means a lot to me."

"No problem, baby." He reaches over and kisses my cheek. "Well, I guess we need to go back to your place to prepare for this club." He stands and grabs all of the bags and reaches for my hand.

CHAPTER 11—THE CLUB

Once Kelvin and I are home, we eat pizza and have a drink of wine. Shortly after, I walk into the bedroom to prepare our outfits for the night. As I go into the bathroom, I turn the shower water on, reflect on what Kelvin spoke of in the mall today about the message his mother left for him. I also keep contemplating on how Kelvin said that he feels that I'm the one for him, and his ability to tune into my thoughts- I never experienced anything like this with anyone before, not even Sammie. I feel content that I've finally met someone who understands my ability and that I don't have to hide that part of myself with him.

Sammie and Malik arrive at 8:30, which is perfect. It leaves just enough time for a few drinks and introductions. Malik and Kelvin shake hands, and Kelvin hugs Samantha as we greet them at the door. "Nice to see you again, Samantha," Kelvin says.

"Same here," Samantha states, as she looks Kelvin up and down. "Nice outfit."

"Thanks. Sabine picked it out."

"She did good." Samantha looks at me, giving me the seal of approval on Kelvin.

As we walk into the living room, Malik turns toward Kelvin's direction and asks, "Kelvin, so what kind of work do you do?" before having a seat on the sofa.

"I'm in transportation and logistics. I started my own company three years ago," Kelvin answers as he sits across from Malik.

"That's great. I've been thinking about starting my own business. I want to open a care facility for people with disabilities,"

Malik says. "I'm an occupational therapist. I work with people who are recovering from injuries."

"So, is that how you and Samantha met, at work?" Kelvin asks. "Sabine told me Samantha does massage therapy."

"No. We had a friend set us up on a blind date," Malik says as he reflects on that time, revealing less than what his thoughts seem to be uncovering.

When I hand Malik his drink, I realize that I haven't seen him in weeks. "Malik, I haven't seen you in ages. Where have you been?" I ask.

"Samantha has been holding me hostage," he replies, cutting his eyes at me insinuating she isn't letting him out of her sight. He might be right about that. After that situation with Casey, I wouldn't put it past her.

"Well, brother-in-law, tonight you have a free pass," I say, looking in Sammie's direction for a reaction.

Sammie has that expression that says, *Please do not try me.* "You know, I am glad y'all brought that up, this 'free pass' business. Let's establish some ground rules," Sammie replies.

"We don't know what to expect. How can we establish rules without knowing what to expect?" Kelvin questions.

"Easy. I think since this is our first time going to a club like this, we should just observe—maybe do a little dancing and have a few drinks, but nothing too out of the ordinary," Sammie says, and everybody seems to be in agreeance with this rule, or should I say, general guideline. Sammie goes on to tell us how she's done some research on this club and that there are two parts to it. One side is actually just dancing, food, and drinks and the other has playrooms, which consist of several private rooms with different themes and some open rooms where you have the opportunity to observe.

We all jump into Kelvin's jeep, excited to see what awaits us at Club Enticement. Sammie exits the jeep first. Malik steps out and walks over to her side and puts his hands around her waist as they start there stroll up to the entrance. Samantha looks stunning. She has on a black-and-tan dress, which stops right above her knees and contours to her body. The material is a lacy black with a light shade of a tan in the background with one strap across her shoulder. The tall black stilettos she's wearing enhances her calf muscles just right. Her hair accentuates her soft facial features. It's pinned up in a bun with pieces of stray hair curling toward her face. She looks very natural and sexy. Malik has on black dress slacks and a tan shirt, which matches well with Sammy's dress.

They walk up to the door, looking back just as Kelvin and I are about to exit the jeep. Once we are out, he and I walk toward the front of his ride. I grab Kelvin's hand, gaze into his eyes, and grin. For a split second, I wonder if this is a bad date idea, being that it's so early in our relationship. He grabs my face and says, "I'm so happy I met you, Sabine," then he plants a very adoring kiss on my lips before we walk up to the door where Samantha and Malik are standing.

At the desk, upon entering, we are required to sign a waiver about confidentiality and a no cell phone policy in certain parts of the club, and present identification. The charge is $65 per couple. Once we've paid, we go through a metal detector. It reminds me of going through airport security. When we enter the actual club, at first sight, it looks like a normal club. There's a bar in the far end and people dancing. We all have a seat at the bar to scope the place out.

As the night continues and our confidence increases, we decide to explore a little. As we are walking through the halls, we see couples making out against the walls and others peeking into windows watching people perform. I have to admit, I thought that this place would be somewhat sleazy before actually being here, but in all actuality it's all very sexy, exotic, and exciting.

Kelvin and I go off on our own path, and before long, we find ourselves in one of the themed rooms, kissing and bumping against the walls, trying to take each other's clothes off. He is grabbing my butt and lifting my dress up, pulling me in to him. I am trying to push him away to unzip his pants and take his belt off. Finally, I shove him into a chair, and I begin to do a strip tease for him, removing the top part of my dress one shoulder at a time. He's looking up at me taking one pant leg off at a time. When he's done removing his pants, he says, "Come here, Seme."

I bend close to his face. He kisses me briefly before pulling me down into his lap—my back to his front— then he maneuvers me so that I'm laid out across his lap in the same way a man scoops a woman off her feet before he walks her over the threshold to start their honeymoon. My nipples are in his mouth within seconds, and his lips are all over my neck and shoulders. There is so much passion and vigor in his touch that it feels like I'm undergoing a deep-tissue massage. He slides my panties off and throws them on the floor, then he looks up and pauses. "Sabine, we have an audience."

When I look up, there are at least four people peeking into the window beside the door. "Oh, let me close the curtains," I say as I attempt to scoot up out of his lap.

He pulls me down. "You don't have to, unless you want to." He looks at me in a very stimulating way, as if he is trying to figure out how I feel about people watching us. I turn to face him and move in closer to his face, kiss his lips once, and slowly slide down his body, grabbing his penis and teasingly circle my tongue around the tip. His hands are in my hair, massaging my scalp, and before long, all of him is in my mouth. I'm sucking up and down the shaft of his penis as he lets out moans expressing his gratitude with each lick, suck, and stroke that I apply to his man part. He uses the palm of his hand to cup my head as I continue to pleasure him, stopping me just as I feel his penis jerk involuntarily.

"Sabine, I don't want to cum," he says, then lifts me up and rolls the condom down on his penis right before positioning me right on top of him. I commence to ride him, up and down in a slow deliberate motion, feeling every stroke in every part of my body from my head down to my toes. My head slants back. Kelvin is gripping my booty, sucking on my breasts, thrusting into me, meeting all of my strokes. All of my senses are heightened, and I feel myself reaching that high.

Kelvin says, "Baby, that's right. Let it go." As I do, and my body is crumbling around him, Kelvin slows his motion, and each stroke from that point seems to set me off again, triggering multiple orgasms. When he finally stops moving, I lay my head on his shoulder, feeling washed out. I dare ask him, "Aren't you going to finish?" Knowing if he continues, I may not be able to walk for a while. He rubs my hair softly.

"Not right now, baby," he responds. After a few minutes have passed, I lift up off him, pull my dress down over my hips, and pull the top portion up over my shoulders. When I turn around to look for my panties, the eyes that are staring at me through the window take me completely off guard. I kneel to the floor still searching for my panties and in a feeble attempt to hide.

"Baby, what are you doing?" Kelvin asks, looking at me on my hands and knees.

"I'm looking for my panties," I reply as I continue to search.

"These panties right here?" I look up at Kelvin who is now standing and tucking the panties in his pocket. "You don't need these tonight." He reaches for my hand and helps me up.

"That was great Kelvin, thank you," I say as I steady myself in his arms, regaining my composure and poise. He responds by kissing my forehead. As we turn to exit the room, I notice William is no longer standing at the window. I'm relieved and somewhat embarrassed. Somehow I feel I'm violating some unspoken rule between counselor and patient. Plus, the whole reason Sammie and I even found out about this club was because we followed him and Casey here. Who comes back to a club like this two days in a row? I ask myself. I wonder if Casey is here. Should I tell Kelvin about William being here and him being a client?

Midway into my thoughts, Kelvin interrupts, "Sabine, are you okay?"

"Yes. Why?" I answer and ask way too quickly.

"You seem distracted. Do you want to grab a drink?" Kelvin asks.

"Yes, that would be great."

Kelvin leads me through a few hallways and back to the bar area where we started our night a few hours ago. He orders a platinum margarita for both of us. It tastes great, and it's exactly what I need to clear my head of my excessive thought process of "Should I tell him or not?" in regards to William. As Kelvin and I are taking in the scene, we spot this gorgeous woman holding a conversation with who we assume is her boyfriend or husband. They look our way a few times, and we are tempted to walk over to start a conversation, however, we don't have enough alcohol in our system. In addition, we are nowhere near ready for that type of excitement, swapping partners seems too farfetched; we're still trying to learn each other.

Besides, we need to stick to the ground rules we've established— or more like the ground rules Samantha established, which we've already modified— at least the part about observing. Instead of engaging in conversation that may lead to who knows where, we head to the dance floor because dancing feels safe.

When Kelvin is not twirling me around and dipping me backwards, I'm standing close to him, and we sway to the sound of music, but to a beat all of our own. Never mind that a fast-paced party song is on, we are moving to a very different tempo at a much slower speed. We dance like this for a while, then as if an alarm clock is going off, jolting me out of a restful night's sleep, someone bumps into us.

"I'm sorry love. Did we bump you?" I hear a man's voice in my haze.

"It's okay," I say before looking up.

"Sabine, is that you?" I hear a familiar female voice.

When I finally look up, we are dancing next to none other than William Witford and Casey—whatever her last name is.

"Hi, Casey," I say, trying to sound excited but it comes off as stunned.

"Hey, girl. You having fun?" she asks very animated.

"I'm having a great time. I see you are too." I smile at her and motion my eyes toward William.

"Yeah, this is Billy—the guy that I told you about the other day." I nod at William, pretending to just meet him. He nods and smiles back at me as they continue to dance at a fast pace on the floor.

79

"This is Kelvin, my—" Just as I'm about to say the word, Kelvin jumps into the conversation.

"Boyfriend. Nice to meet you, Casey and Billy." I am so relieved that Kelvin took over the conversation. I feel if I continue to speak, I will say too much and reveal to both Casey and Kelvin about already knowing William. Not to mention, William just saw me and Kelvin doing the do. Could this situation be any more awkward? "Do you guys want to grab a seat and talk?" Kelvin asks.

"Yeah!" Casey says. "Let's do that." We all walk off the dance floor to sit at a booth. I feel so exposed. I look over in Williams' direction and he grins and winks an eye at me, walks over to the counter, orders some wings for us, and brings back a round of beers. As I sit down, I tug at my dress making sure that my bra strap is in place. Then I pull at the hem of my dress to make sure that it's not rising too far up my thighs.

"Sabine, I thought that was you. I saw Samantha and Malik in the other room," Casey says as she grabs a beer, interrupting my awkward state.

"Kelvin, Casey is Malik's friend from childhood," I explain, attempting to break the ice.

"I see. Nice to meet you, Casey." He shakes her hand. "Is it Billy?" Kelvin reaches out to shake hands with William.

"Yes, I'm Casey's date," William replies as he shakes hands with Kelvin. I cut my eyes away from William, feeling awkward as if maybe I should let Kelvin know how I know William. Yet, I don't. I just let him think that he's Casey's date, which he is.

"So do you two come here often?" I ask, not sure how or what we should be discussing.

"At least four times a month," William says. "This place is awesome." Just then, Kelvin and William toast beer mugs smiling ear to ear, then their conversation segue into LeBron James and the NBA finals.

"Casey, have you guys ever swapped partners?" I ask, curious.

"Yes, girl, several times. It's not all about switching partners as it is the experience. Is this your first time being at a place like this?" Casey asks.

"Yes," I reply.

"It's invigorating, right?" she asks.

"I have to say that it is. Who knew?" I question with a smile. "Did you get to talk to Malik and Samantha?"

"No, they didn't see me. They were occupied." She smiles.

"Wow. I guess they jumped right in." I say as I assess the situation. Kelvin and William are totally engaged in their own conversation about sports. Here I am holding a conversation with Casey about the nature of this club. Our wings are ready, and I know this because the beautiful woman who was looking me and Kelvin's way earlier brings them to our table along with her partner.

"Hi, I'm Amanda, and this is Steven," she says as she hands us the chicken wing basket. "We were wondering if maybe later tonight, we could buy you and your husband a drink." She stares directly into my eyes. I glance over at Kelvin, and he takes the basket.

Kelvin answers. "That would be great. I'm Kelvin, and she's Sabine. And this is Billy and Casey."

"Okay. Nice to meet everyone. We will be around." Amanda smiles at me, and they walk away.

"Awww, look at you Sabine, getting hit on by Amanda," William jokes. I roll my eyes at him, and we all start laughing. I turn to Kelvin, feeling a little awkward.

"Looks like you guys will be diving right in tonight. See, this is better than Vegas," William boasts and laughs very vociferously.

We eat a few wings and converse about the rules to the club. One of the rules being that of the couple, the woman has to be the one to approach the couple that she is interested in, it is strictly prohibited for a man to walk up to a woman who has come in alone or as a couple. My guess is that this is to keep the harassment down to a minimum. Kelvin and I find this so fascinating.

"It's like a secret society," I say. "Who knew there was a whole other world like this?" I question.

Kelvin slides out of his seat, stands, and reaches for my hand. I join him. He pulls two twenty-dollar bills out of his wallet and places them on the table. William hands them back to him. "My treat! Have a good time tonight." He smiles, and Kelvin and I walk off.

"How do you know Billy?" Kelvin asks.

I look at Kelvin dumbfounded. "How do you know I know him?"

"He seems comfortable with you, like you two have made contact before," Kelvin responds.

I nod. Kelvin is so observant. "He's actually a client and I know him as William. We've only had one session together," I respond, waiting on Kelvin's rebuttal, except there is none.

Kelvin and I walk over to the restroom area. "I'll be right back, sweetie." He disappears into the men's room.

Amanda walks up to me as I am standing outside of the men's room. She has on a white long flowing dress that has slits up the leg, which reveals her thigh every time she takes a step. It's sort of mesmerizing and sexy at the same time. "Hi, baby girl," she whispers to me. "What do you think of the club?"

I turn to look at her because there is something familiar about her, like she is a longtime friend, but why does she have a motherly feel? "The club is nice. It's different, and that's nice within itself."

She smiles and walks with me as I head towards the ladies' room. Once we're inside, she grabs my hand and places it over her chest. My eyes close automatically, and I feel warm tingling vibrations move through my body from hers. There's a familiarity, an esoteric message here for me; this is the same way I feel when I go into a deep meditation. I take several deep breaths then open my eyes.

Telepathically, she communicates to me. I can hear her; it's more of a knowing of what she is trying to tell me, she's saying: *I'm coming to you as a friend, as your guides have led me to you to deliver this message. Be wary of the woman you were eating dinner with this evening. She means you and your friend no good. She has an agenda, which is not in your best interest, and it is tied to your family affairs. It is something that isn't known at this time, which will be revealed. Be careful and watch your man.* Just as the message is complete, three women walk into the restroom, and

Amanda takes my hand off her chest and nods at me. "Be careful, baby girl," she says before exiting the restroom.

I look in the mirror, feeling a little buzzed from the beer and margarita and a little confused by what just happened. I tease my hair with my fingers, wash my hands, and exit the restroom to find Kelvin waiting on me. "We have to go, Sabine!" Kelvin states, taking my hand and pulling me through the club.

"Why? What's wrong?" I ask.

"Samantha and Malik had an incident."

"What kind of incident?" I ask, becoming nervous.

"The kind that requires us to leave, now," he demands.

We exit the club, jump into the jeep, and he tells me to call Sammie on my cell phone. My heart feels as if it's about to jump out of my chest, but I dial her number. Sammie answers, and I hear people in the background yelling out stats on blood pressure and pulse rate. "Where are you, girl?" I question with fear.

"I'm in the ambulance with Malik." She sounds nervous and a bit high strung.

"What happened?" I question in fear of the worst.

"That witch put something in his drink, and now he's out of it," she blurts.

"What hospital are you going to?"

"Tampa Receiving."

We arrive to the hospital around 3:15 in the morning. Kelvin and I are asked to sit in the waiting room by the grumpy woman at the front desk. I try several times to reach Samantha on her cell phone, but since we've arrived at the hospital, I'm not able to reach her. Two hours pass before we hear any news on Malik's condition. Samantha comes out to us looking exhausted and we can tell she's been crying. Immediately, I think the worse. I hug her. "Is Malik okay?"

"Yes, he is stable now."

"Thank God," I say, relieved.

"They had to pump his stomach. They're still trying to find out what was mixed in his drink. Whatever it was, it was a lethal dosage. His blood level shows high toxicity. I spoke with the police and filed a report," Samantha says.

"Do you want to come back to my house to rest?" I ask Sammie.

"No. I'm going to stay here in the hospital with Malik. I won't feel better until I see him awake."

"Okay, well, we'll call you later today to check in. Is there anything you need right now?"

"No, but the police will probably contact you soon to ask a few questions," Sammie says, "I explained to them that we drove with you guys, but you probably don't know much because we were split up for most of the night."

"Okay," I say looking at Sammie with concern, wanting to know more of what happened, but not wanting to put her through having to tell the story over again to Kelvin and me right now. I know she had a long morning. Kelvin gives Sammie a hug, and she turns and disappears through the emergency doors.

Once Kelvin and I reach the house at six in the morning, I realize we've barely said a word to each other during the car ride home or at the hospital. I finally ask, "How did you know there was an emergency with Malik?"

Kelvin looks exhausted. "I saw the emergency medical personnel enter the club. Then a few minutes later, I saw a man on a stretcher and your sister following behind as they rolled him out."

I grab two glasses and fill them with ice then pour cold water into each. I hand one to Kelvin. "Thanks, baby," he replies.

"Do you know anything more?" I ask.

"No. No more than you know at this time," Kelvin says, then gulps down his water. "I'm going to take a shower and lay down." Kelvin walks over to me, kisses my forehead, and walks into the bedroom.

As I remain seated at the kitchen table, I feel somewhat baffled. I sip on my water and think about what Amanda said to me and I wonder if Casey is the cause of all of this. Minutes later, my doorbell rings. As I am walking to the door, Kelvin comes to my side, smelling freshly showered.

"It's the police," I say, looking out of the peephole before opening the door.

"Good morning. I'm Officer Mack. I'm looking for Sabine Stallworth and Kelvin Frey," the officer says.

"I'm Sabine and this is Kelvin," I answer.

"Great. I'd like to ask you a few questions. Do you mind if I come in?" We extend the door so the officer can come in.

Kelvin and Officer Mack sit at the kitchen nook. I brew some coffee, put some biscuits in the oven and some bacon in the microwave. Officer Mack seems friendly enough. He begins a series of questions: "How long have you known Malik Marcs? How was he acting prior to going out? Does Malik have a drug history? How was he acting in the club? Did you see anybody suspicious around him at the club? Does his wife have a drug or alcohol history? Isn't his wife your sister? When was the last time you saw him in a normal state? How is the relationship between him and his wife? Have they been in a disagreement in the past forty-eight hours? Do you know of anyone who would want to hurt Malik?"

I answer most of the questions, seeing as to how Kelvin just met Malik last night. As I am answering, I remember I really hadn't seen Malik in weeks. That sits awkwardly with me. In addition, Sammie has been behaving strangely lately toward Malik. She is distant and vague in regards to him.

"They did have a disagreement in regards to Casey, a friend of Malik's who was at the club last night." I communicate this to the officer; but, I'm sure Sammie has already provided the officer with Casey's information. "Is foul play involved?" I ask. "I mean, do you guys suspect someone poisoned Malik?"

"This is what we know at this point, ma'am: He got sent to the hospital due to a possible drug overdose, and we're conducting an investigation to find out more information." I pour three cups of coffee and sit the cream and sugar on the table.

"Officer, do you know what drug they found in Malik's system?" I ask.

Officer Mack takes a sip of his coffee. "They treated Mr.

Marcs based off his symptoms—hallucinations, blacking out, and nausea—and how his wife described his behavior after he ingested the drinks. It's unknown what was in the drinks, but he did display symptoms of being poisoned." I slide over a small plate of bacon, biscuits, and strawberries to Officer Mack and a plate to Kelvin.

The officer grabs a piece of bacon. "Thank you. I didn't get a chance to eat breakfast."

We all finish our breakfast, and Kelvin and I walk Officer Mack to the front door. He hands us his card. "Look, if you think of something that would be beneficial to the case, call me."

"Okay, we will. Thank you," Kelvin responds.

As he walks toward his car, he turns to us and says, "By the way, thanks for the coffee and breakfast. It hit the spot."

"No problem," I respond, as I stand at the door trying to process this situation with Malik and our night. I look over at Kelvin who seems so calm, cool, and collected. I feel bad that on our third date, by the end of the night we are being questioned by the police.

CHAPTER 12—DINNER GUESTS

I stretch my arms and turn around to look at the alarm clock. It reads seven P.M. I slept twelve hours. When I turn to face Kelvin, he wraps his arms around me, holding me close.

"Hey, sweetie. Are you hungry?" he asks with his eyes still closed.

"I'm starving," I reply. "I'll get up to make us some dinner." When I attempt to get out of the bed, he holds me tighter.

"No. I'll do it. You made breakfast," he replies. He sits up, taking one leg at a time out of the bed at turtle speed, then stands and walks wobbly to the bathroom.

I grab my cell phone and text Samantha: *Hey, girl. How's Malik? How are you holding up? Call me when you can. Love you, Sabine.*

Kelvin walks out of the bathroom. He looks as though he is deep in thought. "Dinner will be ready in thirty minutes, baby," he says mechanically then exits the bedroom. I lay in bed thinking about the previous night. It was a great night for Kelvin and me, and a mysterious night in regards to Samantha and Malik. What happened with them at the club that night? I walk into the bathroom, brush my teeth, and wash my face, and just as I'm grabbing my robe, Kelvin walks in looking frustrated, suspicious, and annoyed.

"What's wrong baby?" I ask, concerned.

"William is here," he states calmly.

"What? What do you mean?" I'm confused because I never gave William my home address.

"I mean he's outside this room and in your living room. Is there anything you want to tell me about you and him?" Kelvin asks.

"No, I told you before. He's a client—a very new client. I don't know how he got my address." I look at Kelvin, and he seems doubtful and in thought. "Kelvin, he has never been here before, I promise you." I say this to him as I look directly at him, rubbing his shoulder, trying to loosen his stiff posture. Kelvin doesn't say a word. His body remains rigid, and he barely looks at me. "Let him know I'll be right out. I need to put on some clothes." Kelvin walks away, and I can tell his mood has changed from loving to something else, but I don't focus on it too much.

I throw on some jogging pants and a t-shirt. As I am walking through the kitchen, I can smell whatever Kelvin is cooking, and it has my stomach growling even more. I walk cautiously into the living room to find Kelvin and William sitting across from each other talking. They both pause as I walk in and they stand up.

William walks toward me. "Sabine. Hi, love. So sorry to drop by like this." He reaches for a hug and kisses me on the cheek. "You look good, girl, even in sweats." He smiles at me, and we all sit down.

"Thanks, William. Ummm, how did you get my home address?" I ask, taking a seat, looking somewhat concerned.

"Yeah, about that." William smiles. "I don't want you to think I am a stalker or anything, but I looked you up. Google led me to you. You aren't that hard to track, especially seeing as to how you are opening a café soon. You and your sister's faces are plastered on several websites, and I have my resources."

"Okay. Well, is anything wrong?" I ask.

"Yes, I needed to talk to you. It's sort of urgent."

"Why didn't you call the cell phone number I gave you?" I ask William.

"I did. It went straight to voicemail. You have that twenty-four- or forty-eight-hour call back time, and I needed to speak to you right away. Like I said, it's important."

Kelvin shifts in his chair and takes a deep breath that seems to express his frustration. He has his index finger beneath his nose and the rest of his hand covering his mouth, as if to prevent himself from talking. William and I both look at Kelvin then back at each other to continue the conversation we started, when we realize Kelvin isn't going to leave the room to give us privacy.

William pulls out a picture and hands it to me. "I found this picture of you inside of Casey's purse the day before yesterday. Some alarms went off when I saw it. Then last night, when I realized you guys know each other, I didn't think too much of it. Casey is Kelly, the woman that I spoke of in our counseling session, if you haven't figured it out."

"I did...figure it out," I reply as I grab the photo from him. When I look at the picture, I realize it's a picture of Samantha, not me. "William, this isn't me. This is my sister in this photo."

"There's more," William says and hands me more photos. There are current shots of Kelvin and me at the mall and standing outside of his business. I hand the photos to Kelvin. He flips through them without saying a word. There are also photos of Samantha and Malik in the line at the theater and eating dinner somewhere.

"I don't understand. Who took these photos?" I ask William.

"I don't know. I assume Casey. I found the ones of you and Kelvin in her bag after we left the club last night. She was so intoxicated she passed out." William goes into thought. "When she walked in the house, she dropped her bag on the floor and passed out on my sofa. I picked up her bag and these pictures fell out, along with this. He hands me what looks like a book.

"It's a journal," I say.

"Yeah, open it," William demands. I flip through the pages and read over what looks like little chants, but most of the words are nonsense. Most of the letters on the page doesn't form an actual word, but the repeat of the same word or should I say letter pattern on each line which leads me to believe that maybe it says something in a different language; I do see Samantha's and Malik's names etched in dark print scattered in different places throughout the book. William goes on to explain how the police came to his house this morning looking for Casey to ask a few questions about the incident last night. My interest sparks even more so now...

"William, do you know what happened last night at the club?" I ask with a sense of urgency.

"Yes. Apparently, a man got rushed to the hospital due to a drug overdose. At least that was my understanding." I look at Kelvin who stares at me for a while.

"Did the police actually talk to Casey?" I ask.

"No. I told them she was inebriated and she couldn't talk." William stops and looks at me then at Kelvin. "Which was true. She would have been of no help to them at the time. The cops did try to wake her, but she was knocked out."

"Okay. Have the police been back to your house?" Kelvin asks. "I think these pictures and that book would be important to the investigation, don't you think?" Kelvin pauses. "Unless, you have something to hide."

"I don't know if the police officer came back to the house because I grabbed Casey's bag and went to my office for some privacy. That's when I called Sabine and left a voicemail message then I took a nap, did some research on how to find you, Sabine, and now I am here. I don't have anything to hide. In my humble opinion, I thought it would be better if I met with Sabine first on the matter," Williams says arrogantly and impatiently looking in Kelvin's direction, only turning to look at me when he says my name.

"Why are you here, William?" Kelvin asks. "You could have presented this information to the officer if you were concerned about these pictures and that book," Kelvin says with an aggravated expression as he throws the pictures down on the coffee table.

William takes a deep breath. "It is not just the pictures or the book." He pauses. "It's Casey's behavior in general lately. I'm concerned and maybe a little nervous," William confesses, his mood changing into a more solemn one. "When I came home from work the other day, I noticed her car was in the garage, but I had a hard time locating her in the house."

"What do you mean?" Kelvin asks with irritation.

"I couldn't locate her," William repeats.

"That isn't suspicious. Someone could have picked her up, or she could have called Uber," I suggest with my eyebrow raised.

"No, Sabine. She was in the house." He pauses and looks back and forth between Kelvin and me. "She was in a closet in one of my guest rooms. She was so engaged in what she was doing that she didn't hear me walk in or call her name." Kelvin and I listen intently waiting on William to continue. "When I pushed the door open, she was sitting on the floor with candles lit around her. Her eyes were closed, and she was chanting something that wasn't in English. I stood there for at least ten minutes before she opened her eyes." William pauses again, longer than the time before.

"William, what happened when she opened her eyes?" I ask, trying to bring him back to that moment in his memory because it reminds me so much of Samantha's dream about Casey the other day—the same night that Kelvin and I went out on our first date. Maybe it wasn't a dream—maybe Samantha had tuned in to what Casey was doing that night in the closet.

"I am sorry, love. Can I have a glass of water?" William asks.

"Sure," I reply, but as I'm about to get up, Kelvin replies, "I'll get it," and he leaves the room.

William looks nervous. I stand up and reposition myself beside him. "What is it, William?" When he looks up, there is fear in his eyes. "Sabine, I feel like I'm losing my mind. Am I talking to you as a counselor or a friend?"

"Both. You can trust me," I affirm to him softly.

"I don't want you reporting me and having me shipped off to the looney bin."

"I don't think you're crazy. Plus, I would never do that. That isn't my role. I'm a counselor, not a psychiatrist." Kelvin walks back in the room, pauses shortly as he notices that I've moved from one end of the sofa to the other end, closer to William. Kelvin clears his throat and hands William the ice water.

"Thanks, man," William says as he takes a sip. "I should probably go and let you two enjoy your dinner and prepare for your day tomorrow." William stands.

"Are you sure?" I ask and look at Kelvin, tilting my head

91

sideways and opening my eyes wider hoping he catches the hint and extends an invitation for William to join us for dinner.

Kelvin rolls his eyes a little at me, then he says, "William, I've cooked dinner. I have some chicken wings in the oven baking, steamed veggies and rice if you're hungry. You can join us if you like." Kelvin says this in the most monotone voice I've ever heard him speak in.

Dinner is delicious. Kelvin has really outdone himself. He has made homemade barbecue sauce for the chicken, the rice is light and fluffy, and the veggies are seasoned and steamed just right.

"Oh my, Kelvin. Were you a chef in your past life?" I ask.

He laughs. "No, babe. My mom taught me a few things," Kelvin replies.

"Wow. Your mom did an excellent job on you. Who knew?" I ask in awe of him.

Kelvin smiles at me from across the table.

William is very quiet, which is totally unlike what I know of his personality so far. He's usually the life of the party; at least he was last night at the club and during our counseling session a few days ago. "William, are you enjoying dinner?" I ask.

"Yes, it is great. Thank you. I haven't had a home-cooked meal in ages. Kelvin, you're the man." William nods toward Kelvin, except his eyes are blank when he goes on to say, "You definitely know your way around the kitchen."

Kelvin smile is unsure then he glances my way. When William talks, it sounds like something he would say, but not with the robustness and emotions he normally uses to convey his words. Kelvin and I look at each other and continue to eat. After we complete dinner, William helps us clean up and load the dishwasher. He fiddles with his phone for a little while as Kelvin and I grab a glass of wine.

"William, would you like a glass?" I ask.

"No. Thank you, Sabine. I'm going to check into a hotel room for the night. I'll see you tomorrow at 5:30 for our appointment, right?"

"Yes," I say and nod at the same time.

"Kelvin, thanks again for dinner. It was great, and I am sorry for dropping in like this, I just needed to talk. Sabine is a great counselor, and I've come to think of her as a friend, just so you know. I don't mean any disrespect."

"It's all good," Kelvin says. "Be safe out there."

"I will," William responds.

"William, how's your father?" I ask.

"Not so well. He's on life support at Tampa Receiving Hospital. We're getting his affairs in order now," he says sadly. "Wait. Did I tell you that he was sick?"

"No, I did a little research on my own when you told me he was prepping you to take over the firm," I say, trying to compensate for my slip-up of asking about his father's well-being, before actually hearing from him that his father was sick.

"I am sorry to hear that," Kelvin says sincerely.

"Me too," I relay sadly.

William shrugs and walks out to his car. "Such is life, I guess." He waves as he gets into his black BMW. Kelvin and I go back inside, sit at the kitchen counter, pick up our wineglasses, and toast to each other. We are somewhat melancholy and just drink our wine as we both go within ourselves for a little while.

A couple of hours later, Samantha shows up to the house. She seems very hyperactive—as if she is on a mission.

"Hey, girl. Hi, Kelvin. I called an Uber to pick me up from the hospital to drop me off over here. I needed to come pick up my car," she says as she walks into the house. "Malik is still out of it. I set his phone up on the IMO app and propped it up on the table beside him so I can see what's going on while I've stepped away for a while." She displays her phone to us, which shows Malik in view sleeping.

"Okay," I reply, wondering how much caffeine she has ingested.

"I'm hungry and wanted to take a quick shower if that's okay," she says.

"Yes. Do you want to eat first or shower?" I ask.

"Shower," she replies.

"Okay. We'll watch Malik." I grab her phone. She walks into my room, grabs a towel out of the closet, then walks back across the kitchen to the opposite side of the house past the living room and into the guest bathroom. She seems like a supercharged robot. I grab a pair of jogging pants and a t-shirt and lay them across the guest room bed for her to put on after she showers. Kelvin makes her a plate of food and pours her a tall glass of water.

By the time Samantha comes out into the kitchen, Kelvin and I are on our second slice of red velvet cake and our second glass of wine.

"Yum. Is this my plate?" Samantha asks as she takes a seat at the kitchen table. Kelvin pushes her phone up to her and her plate closer. She takes a bite of the veggies then the rice and the chicken. "This is so good."

"Kelvin made it," I comment.

"Kelvin!" Sammie exclaims as she pushes his arm in a friendly yet forceful way. "You did good. Will you cook at the café every now and then?" Sammie asks more calmly.

"I'd love to." Kelvin smiles, kind of bashful-like as he rubs his arm and looks at me mouthing, "Ouch."

"I know y'all want to know what happened last night at the club," Sammie says between bites of food.

"Yes," Kelvin and I reply in unison.

"Okay, so Malik and I went to the open room where couples are making out openly in front of each other. We watched couples perform for a little while, sipping on our strawberry daiquiris. It was like watching live porn, so intense."

Kelvin and I listen intently as Sammie continues with the story.

"We set our drinks on the table beside us as we sat down to observe the different couples." Samantha pauses for a second as she puts more food in her mouth and chews. "Then Malik and I started to kiss a little and do our thing." She smiles at that memory, then she turns to look at me. "Sabine, I could have sworn that from the side of my eye, I saw Casey walk past us. When I told Malik, he was like, 'No, Casey wouldn't be here. It isn't her style.' How does he know her style? That's a whole other conversation," Sammie says with irritation in her voice.

"Anyways, I was sure that I saw her walk right past us, so I got up to look for her. Malik follows me with both drinks in his hands. Why was he drinking both daiquiris as he follows me around the club in my feeble attempt to find Casey? After a while, I gave up, thinking I was being paranoid. Malik and I ended up going to a private room. This is where things got crazy," Samantha says.

"By this time, Malik had drank both of our daiquiris completely. You know how Malik isn't really a drinker, right?" She pauses to eat more food. I nod.

"I noticed he was acting a little strange and was complaining that his stomach hurt, but I just thought he was feeling a little tipsy. I took off my clothes while Malik laid across the bed. When I got on top of him, he kept saying, 'No. Stop, Casey. Get off me.' I tried to calm him down and reassure him that it was me, but he got violent and grabbed my arms, flipped me over, and said, 'Stop it. Now.' Then he got up and went to the corner of the room and placed his hands over his face and started crying or wailing or yelling...I don't know."

"Yelling?" Kelvin asks.

"I don't know. He was acting strange to say the least. He asked 'How did this happen?' then he said, 'Samantha is never going to forgive me!' When I walked over to him and pulled his hands off his face to show him it was me and not Casey, he looked at me like I was a stranger and said, 'Where is Samantha?' Whenever I spoke, he would cover his ears and he was looking around the room, fearful. Seconds later he passed out."

"Shit," Kelvin exclaims and drinks the rest of his wine. "That's some crazy shit."

"Sammie, I don't get it. Was he hallucinating?" I ask.

"Obviously."

"Okay, so then what happened?" Kelvin asks.

"I ran to the front and had them call 9 1 1. Minutes later the emergency personnel showed up and took him out of the club. He woke up a few times in the emergency truck and threw up each time. When we got to the hospital, the nurses were asking me all of these questions about what he drank—did he ingest any drugs. I told them about the daiquiris and explained how his behavior changed drastically after drinking them. They asked all of the typical medical questions like did you leave your drinks unattended at any time? Of course, the answer was yes. They ran some type of blood tests and started prepping him to pump his stomach." She pauses. "The thing is they don't know what type of drug it was in his system. They can't identify it."

"Wow." Kelvin shakes his head.

"Do you mind if I have another plate of food?" Sammie asks. Kelvin grabs her plate and puts more food on it. "I'm so hungry. I haven't eaten since last night before the club," Sammie says.

"I called Casey's phone at least twenty times. No answer, but I know I saw her walk past us in that open room, and I think she slipped something into both of our drinks."

"Sammie, we saw Casey at the club with William," I say cautiously.

"What?"

"Yes. She mentioned that she saw you and Malik and that you were both occupied, and you didn't see her."

"I knew it! That bit—" Sammie stops herself from saying the word.

"Did you tell the police about Casey?" Kelvin asks as he places her food in front of her.

"Yes. They asked if I knew of someone who would want to hurt Malik or me. I gave them Casey's name and phone number."

"Well, that's good," Kelvin replies, and I can tell he's relieved that someone has actually reported Casey to the police, especially after the situation with William earlier tonight.

I decide not to mention the pictures or the fact that William had just left our house. I look over at Kelvin and shake my head slowly as a signal we're not going to bring up the subject of William at the moment. Kelvin appears to be on the same page. I think with Samantha's lack of sleep and anger, to tell her would be a disservice to her.

Sammie eats her food quietly, then she speaks up, saying what she has probably been brooding over for the last five minutes in silence. "If I knew where that woman lived, I would be over there right now."

Kelvin and I exchange glances. "Are you going back to the hospital tonight?" I ask Samantha, changing the subject.

"Yes. I called out of work today, and I will call out again tomorrow. I let Malik's job know what's going on."

"I'll bring some food up to the hospital tomorrow after I finish my deliveries and check on you and Malik. I think you should get some sleep when you go back to the hospital. You're a little edgy. Lay off the caffeine," I say to Sammie with concern.

"Okay. I will. Thanks, girl." Samantha gets up, puts her dish in the dishwasher, and gives both me and Kelvin a big hug, then heads back to the hospital.

CHAPTER 13—THE TALK

It's eleven o'clock at night, and I'm in the kitchen prepping for tomorrow; making chicken salad, sandwiches and meatball subs for tomorrow's lunch deliveries. My thoughts are running all over the place because so much has happened in these past two days. Samantha seems to be handling things better in regards to Malik now that he is awake. She texted me shortly after she got back to the hospital: *Malik is up, girl. He doesn't remember anything past our experience in the open room. Interesting... See you tomorrow.*

Kelvin seems moody, and I can't say I don't understand why. Our third date turned into a disaster filled with no sleep, a hospital visit, a poisoning victim, a police visit, and more importantly William dropping by- I think that pushed Kelvin over the edge. When Sammie left, he went into the room and started watching a movie he found on Netflix. He said that he needed to wind down but wants to talk. I told him that I would join him in a few minutes after I finish my culinary prep. I needed some down time also, and cooking relaxes me. Plus, preparing at night cuts down on the amount of work I have to do in the mornings and allows me time to sleep in, and after the weekend we've had, I need to sleep in.

I wrap up my last turkey sandwich and place the package of buns on the counter for the meatball subs and the chicken salad sandwiches, which I will put together in the morning. I don't want the bread to turn soggy from the mayo, mustard, and meat sauce. I flip off the lights in the kitchen and head to the bedroom, wondering what Kelvin wants to discuss.

I slide into bed and cozy up next to Kelvin as he continues to watch the movie that seems to have his full attention right now. He rubs my hair, acknowledging my presence. I can feel him turn to look at me, then he sits up in the bed and pauses the movie.

"Sabine, we've been spending a lot of time together," Kelvin says, as I sit up in the bed to face him. I nod my head yes.

"When I am in town, most of my time is spent with you, which is a good thing," he says.

"What I'm trying to say is I found a place to rent about twenty minutes from here, and I've been debating on whether to take it or not." He pauses. "I don't want to move too fast with what we have, but I enjoy being here with you."

"I enjoy you too. You make this house feel like a home," I say and grab his hand.

"I am glad you said that." He kisses me on my hand.

"I don't want you to rent the house twenty minutes away. I want you to stay here with me," I state softly.

He smiles. "Yeah?"

"Yes." I smile back.

"How much are you paying monthly?" he asks.

"A thousand," I reply.

"How much in utilities?"

"About three hundred."

"Do you think I could get my name on the lease?" Kelvin questions.

"Yeah. I'll talk to the landlord about it tomorrow."

"And I'll talk to my guy about not taking the house he's trying to rent to me. I'll pay the rent this coming month, baby, and we can discuss the details about the budget when we're both not exhausted." He grabs me, lays back down, and un-pauses the movie. Just like that, we are roommates.

When I wake up the next morning in Kelvin's arms, I find it unbelievable we've taken this step already. It feels right, I mean, I feel good about him and this move. It feels natural, as if he should have been here all along. The communication is clear, and it doesn't seem as if he's running game. As I'm about to get up to finish my meal prep, Kelvin grabs me and pulls me back down into the bed.

"Excuse me, Ms. Stallworth?"

"Yes?" I question, feeling trapped by his grip around me.

"I'm going to need some motivation to get up."

"Yeah?" I question.

"Yes, baby. Can you help me out please?" He loosens his grip and gives me free reign of his body.

"Let me see what I can do..." I begin placing soft kisses on his neck. I move down to his chest, then toward his stomach.

Before I can go any farther, he flips me over, kisses my neck, then lifts his face toward mine and says in a raspy-just-woke-up voice, "I'm so lucky to have you. Where have you been all of my life, baby?" He moves his face toward mine and presses his lips to my lips, and his hips to my hips. I can feel his erection pressing hard against my pelvis... I gasp, unable to return his kiss because of the two points of contacts he's just made with my body. The one below my waist is calling out for more attention.

He pulls away, rubs my hair out of my face and looks to be examining my facial features. "You know you're going to be my wife, right?" he says and nibbles on my earlobes, then his lips are back on mine again parting them with his tongue.

I'm guessing that was a rhetorical question because he doesn't give me the opportunity to respond. He reaches over on the nightstand, grabs a condom, tries to open it with one hand, then pulls away from our kiss to use his teeth to rip the package open. As soon as he has the condom rolled over his penis, I grab it and place it near my opening. He slowly strokes his body until he has filled me up, then pauses. He actually stays like this for more than a little while; propped between my legs, his booty clinching tightly as he pushes his penis as far up my sex as he can. He slow kisses over my breasts, flicking his tongue over my nipples—basically driving me wild. My vagina muscles are clenching with every suck, flick and touch he's giving me. He pulls back and begins stroking slowly.

"What are you doing to me?" I ask.

"I'm loving you, babe," he replies softly. He's making deliberate, slow strokes, looking at me the whole time. Before long, I can feel my body climbing up to that high. My breathing has changed, and

I'm grabbing his butt and pulling him in deeper to me. He picks up the pace as he gets closer to his climax. Before long, my back is arching up, and I'm feeling nothing but pure pleasure, then I hear him moan as he releases inside of me. We stay this way for a while, him on top of me, me hugging his body to mine.

I turn to look at the clock, and it reads six A.M. I'm so happy I did most of my food prep last night. "Thank you, baby," I whisper to Kelvin, who has already drifted back off to sleep. I slide my body from underneath his and get up to shower and brush my teeth. I slip on a sundress, walk back in the bedroom, bend over the bed and kiss his lips. "I'm sorry I failed at motivating you to get up," I say to him.

He smiles. "You did good, baby. I'm going to get up in a few minutes."

CHAPTER 14—THE HOSPITAL

After my lunch deliveries, I head to the hospital to make my last delivery, meatball sub for Malik and chicken salad sandwich for Samantha. When I enter the room, Malik and Samantha are laughing, talking, and appear to be having a great time.

"Hi, family," I say as I walk in because I instantly feel the love as I enter the room, and in all honesty, they are my family.

"Hey, girl," Samantha says.

"Hi, Sabine," Malik says.

"I got you both something." I pull out the sub and the sandwich.

"Seme, is that a meatball sub?" Malik asks.

"Yes."

"You're the best," Malik responds.

"Sammie, can he eat this?" I ask.

"I think so. We've been feeding him bland foods since last night, but let me check with the nurse. I'll be right back." Sammie exits the room.

"Malik, I also have some chocolate cake for you." I show it to him.

His eyes widen. "Thanks, Sabine," he says, reaching for the cake.

"Don't open it until you get the okay. Samantha will be mad at me." I look at Malik and he seems normal. "How do you feel? You look great."

"I feel good. I feel like I got ripped out of my club experience because I can't remember much."

"I saw Casey at the club," I mention to Malik.

"I know. Sammie told me," he responds.

The Story of Us

"Why would she do this to you?" I ask boldly. He looks at me in a daze, then shakes his head. Samantha walks back in. The nurse is with her.

"Mr. Marcs, how are you feeling?"

"Great."

The nurse checks his vitals and says, "We're going to discharge him in a few minutes. I would wait until tomorrow for the meatball sub. Just have him eat bland foods like chicken broth, crackers, and flat soda until tomorrow morning to be on the safe side." Malik looks disappointed.

I walk away from them to check my work cell phone. I hear William's voicemail from the other day: *Hi, Sabine. I'm sorry to call you on the weekend like this. I just left the club, and it was a shock that you knew Casey...also known as Kelly. Anyway, I'm not feeling myself lately, and I need someone to talk to... I have something that I want to share with you.*

My thoughts go to William, then I remember he said his father is on life support here at this hospital. I call to the front desk and ask for William Witford, Senior's room number. Coincidently, he is on the same floor as Malik, just three doors down.

"Sammie, I'll be right back. I need to make a call," I say as I walk out of the room.

As I walk up to Room 309, I can hear the beeps of the heart monitor and the ventilator making suctioning sounds. The beeps and the suctions seem to alternate between each other. I ease my way over to Mr. Witford's bedside.

"You look so peaceful," I whisper, "If it weren't for these tubes down your throat and nose and all of the tape on your face, I would think you were just sleeping."

I touch his hand, close my eyes, as I say a prayer, "May the love of God enfold you in your transition to the next place." All of a sudden, my body feels as if is spiraling down a tunnel. I can see him; I'm tuning in to Mr. Witford.

I notice his soul is already far away from his body. He turns to look at me from the road he is walking down. It's a dirt road. Wherever this place is, it resembles a foggy fall day up north.

Maybe it's an apple orchard. The trees are shaggy, and the leaves are turning brown. When I turn to look behind me, I see Mr. Witford in the hospital bed hooked up to all of the machines. I turn to the front, a completely different scenery; I can see a pond and that same dirt road that seems to go on indefinitely. Mr. Witford is standing right beside me, no tubes or tape on his face, and he's wearing regular clothes—tan slacks and a button-up plaid shirt. He has gray eyes, wavy gray hair, his shoulders meet my shoulder. He seems peaceful.

He turns to me and says, "*I'm ready to go when my family is willing to let me go. I know this is hard on them, but they'll be okay. All my affairs are in order, and William is very capable of handling the firm. He knows he can do it.*" He looks outward toward the road. "*Tell him to get that woman out of his house and get as far away from her as possible. She is sucking the life out of him, and she'll be the ruin of him and his career. She means him no good. I've been watching. Her soul is dark—very dark.*"

All of a sudden, it feels as if I'm being ripped out of a page in a book. I blink and look around, and I'm back in the hospital room.

"Excuse me, miss. Can I help you?" asks the nurse who is standing right beside me.

"I'm sorry. I was just leaving." I rub Mr. Witford's hand, then exit the room.

When I walk back into Malik's room, they are putting him in a wheelchair. We say our goodbyes, and I tell Sammie I will call her later to check in. As I am leaving the hospital, Kelvin calls me.

"Hi, baby. Do you want to grab lunch?" he asks.

"Yes," I reply.

"Can you come to Frey Transportation?" Kelvin asks.

"Yes. Be there in twenty minutes," I report.

"See you then, sweetie. Drive safely."

"I will. Bye."

I pull up into the parking area and take a few minutes to ground myself to this current reality. That was the first time I have ever channeled someone between this world and the next. I take several deep breaths before exiting the car.

When I walk into Frey Transportation, I notice Kelvin has already ordered lunch. I see steak, baked potatoes, and wedge salads from the Steakhouse laid out on his conference table. He has candles lit and nice romantic music playing in the background.

"What is this, Kelvin?" I ask, smiling as I stare at the table.

"It's lunch, baby." He takes my purse and sets it in a chair. "And it's a celebration of our move together."

"Such a romantic," I state after a few seconds have gone by. Kelvin smiles as he pulls my chair out for me.

I call my landlord during lunch, and Robert has Kelvin fax over proof of employment, which for him is the tax identification number of his business; proof of income; Kelvin's bank statements; and a copy of his driver's license and social security card for the background check. If everything checks out okay, Kelvin will be added to the lease within twenty-four hours.

"We are almost official roommates," I say to Kelvin.

"You're meeting with William today, right?" Kelvin asks.

"Yes. His appointment is at 5:30. You've never been to my office, have you?"

"No, I haven't," Kelvin replies.

I search through my purse, then hand Kelvin a card with the address on it. "For future reference. Maybe you can stop by one day. Once the café opens, I'll no longer need to lease the space." Kelvin takes the card and places it in his wallet. "Oh, Malik got released today."

"Yeah? How is he?" Kelvin asks.

"Great. He doesn't remember any of it."

"Well, that's good because it seems like it was sort of traumatic for him." Kelvin shakes his head as he clears the small conference table where we ate. "Speaking of traumatic, what do you think is happening with William?" he asks.

I look at Kelvin then reflect on William's situation. "I think William is going through a lot right now emotionally, with his father being on his deathbed, William taking over the family business, and his relationship with Casey is taking a toll on him.

He's lost," I relay sadly. I stand. "I need to get ready to go. It takes me about thirty minutes to get over to the office."

Kelvin walks over to me and hugs me, then he says, "Look, I don't want to come off as the jealous boyfriend, but be careful with William." Kelvin pauses for a minute. "I think he has a crush on you, and because he's going through this hard time, he may be taking your professional help more personally." Kelvin looks at me.

"I guess I can see that with him," I say to Kelvin. "Plus, it's kind of awkward, considering the setting we all met in the other night and him being my client."

"Yeah, and with him dropping by the house like he did," Kelvin states.

"That was kind of strange, but in his defense, he's fragile right now. I don't think he has anyone he can go to for support who he trusts."

"Just be careful, Sabine," Kelvin says with a calm urgency. "I love you."

"I love you too, Kelvin. Thanks for lunch. I'll see you after my session. It should last for about an hour. Give me thirty minutes to wrap up. I'll be home by 7:30."

"Okay, baby. See you tonight," Kelvin says then kisses my cheek.

CHAPTER 15—THE SESSION/VISION QUEST

I make it to the office by five on the dot. I light a few candles, put some oils in the aromatherapy burner, and turn on a CD with relaxing guitar and ocean sounds. I swear a lot of my techniques are used to prepare me for my sessions with my clients. I say this because the sound of ocean waves playing low in the background seems to set my mind at ease. As I walk through the office, mentally clearing out all the energies that may have been absorbed during the weeks, I take special care to call in William's angels and spirit guides to aid in the session. I would really like to clear him of all the negative energies in his life at this time, and at the advice of his father, that would start with Casey.

I take a seat at my desk and pull out the notes from our last session. I wonder if William completed his homework assignment. Before I can ponder that thought any longer, I hear the bell to my door ring, so I walk out to the front and meet William.

"Hi, William. It's good to see you again," I say as I walk over to him. He reaches for a hug, and as I put my arms around him, he seems to relax.

"Come," I say to him. "Let's start out with our meditation, which you enjoy so much." He follows me to the back, and when I turn around, he hands me the sixty-five dollars. I smile at him. "Thank you. I would have forgotten again." I go over to my desk, write him a receipt, and hand it to him.

"I like the guitar and ocean sounds that's playing. It's calming," he says, when he finally speaks.

"Yeah? Well, good, that is exactly what I was going for with this selection." My back is to him as I place my receipt book back into the desk drawer. "You know you can go to YouTube and Google guitar and ocean sounds and just let it play in the background at work, home, or your hotel room when you are feeling stressed." When I say hotel room, I turn to look at him.

William smiles and says, "Yeah. It's sort of strange that I have to leave my home for peace."

"Let's not worry about that right now. Close your eyes and lay back on the chair. Take a deep breath in, slowly, William, then breathe out slowly. Again, breathe in..." I look toward his direction to see if he is following my instructions then continue.

"As you breathe in, imagine you're near an ocean walking in the sand near a shoreline. Your shoes are off and you feel the cool water crashing up against your feet. You feel the sand beneath your toes, grounding you to this moment in time." I pause as I describe this scenery to him to give him time to visualize the scene. "Feels good, right?"

"Yes," he responds methodically.

"Breathe out, and know in your spirit that each step you take brings you closer to peace... Breathe in and continue casually strolling this beach. Think of nothing, but feel the water and the sand on your skin. Breathe out...allow the water to wash toward your feet. Notice how it seems to draw out all impurity from your heart, mind, and soul. Breathe in, as the water pulls away; notice the sand and how grounded you feel. Breathe out." I pause for a second to let William take all of this into his psyche.

"Breathe in again, this time taking in all of the fresh ocean air that surrounds you. It feels as if it's cleaning your lungs and purifying your spirit even more, right?"

He nods.

"Breathe out, slowly through parted lips. You're releasing all the toxins you have absorbed over the last few days, weeks, months or possibly years. Breathe in, through your nose. This time, hold your breath. Feel the vibrations of purity and love as it resonates through your body, mind, and spirit. Now, slowly breathe out all doubt that you feel in regards to your abilities, all the fears that you have about your future, and every feeling of doubt in your spirit is now released." I pause once more to let this resonate with him. "Because fear and doubt don't exist here, William. Continue to breathe at this rhythm. Only love is in this place...nothing else... just love. Breathe in and feel the love permeate your heart and your mind. It feels like warm tingles throughout your body. Breathe out anything that is not of love and send that energy to the ocean to be healed right now. Breathe in, 'In truth I, William Witford, am healed.' Breathe out anything that is not of love. Breathe in love and peace. Breathe out fear and scarcity thinking. Now, just stay in this space on the shoreline of this beautiful beach where the air is crisp and the water is clear. Hold the intent that you are at peace and nothing can steal your joy." I quiet myself for two minutes. "Good."

"Know that anytime your life feels chaotic, you can come to this place. This is your special place designed specifically for you. It's designed to bring you peace anytime and anywhere. You just say, 'safe place,' and you will be here, walking on the beach, with your feet in the sand grounding you to its reality. Do you understand?" I ask.

"Yes," William says with his eyes still closed.

"Good. Stay here for a few minutes and explore the beach." I walk over close to William and have a seat beside him. "Listen to the waves. Imagine that each wave represents something in your life that isn't the way you want it to be. Can you think of one thing in your life that isn't how you want it?"

"I don't want my dad to leave me. I still need him. I have so much to learn from him," William says.

"Good. Now watch the wave crash up against you. Notice how the water pulls back out toward the ocean? Your anxiety surrounding your dad has been transferred to that wave. It's gone. Bless it and let it go. Tell me about something else that isn't the way you envisioned," I say as I write this down.

"My love life is not fulfilling the way I would want it to be."

"Do the wave exercise. The wave is coming toward you. It crashes up against your feet, drawing out your doubts and insecurities. This is helping you to focus on the real issues."

"My home is not in order, I feel lonely, and I'm afraid of her," William says, and he seems restless.

"Who are you afraid of?" I ask.

"Casey."

"Look at the waves. What is happening, William?"

"There is a storm. The sky is dark. There's water spinning all around me. I'm afraid the water is going to swallow me up," William says.

"Listen to me, and repeat after me: 'In the midst of chaos, I remain calm.'" He repeats the mantra serenely.

"Good. Now, feel the words you're reciting. Focus on the word *calm*. You are calm. You are grounded in peace right now and forever." He recites the words I have just spoken, changing the pronouns.

"Take a deep breath. Breathe in love. Remember that love is the only thing that has power in this universe. What do you see now?"

"The storm is subsiding. Thank you, Sabine, for calming the storm for me."

"It isn't me. You have all the power here." William breathes in peacefully. "Listen, you will get waves of fear, frustration, anger, anguish; waves of feeling lost, unloved, and forgotten. It's okay to feel those things, but don't let them consume you. Let them just wash right through you as if you are an observer. They're just warnings or caution signs wanting you to pay attention to your surroundings. When something doesn't feel right, trust those feelings, but then put them back where they belong—in the water, away from your mind to be cleansed... But, pay attention to the message that they bring. Do you understand, William?"

"Yes."

"When you come here to your safe place, you can calm the storm. You know why?" I ask.

"No. Why?"

"Because this is your safe place, and in here you control your emotions and not the other way around."

"Yeah, I can see that now," William says calmly.

"Go back to the wave with Casey. What are you afraid of?

Look at the situation as if you're a spectator, not a part of it and tell me what do you see?"

"Sabine, I'm so afraid. I can't."

"Yes, you can, William. You can do all things through Christ Jesus who strengthens you. See Casey in your mind's eye. Look at her face to face. Ask her why she's here."

William pauses for a while, as if he is asking the question. I close my eyes and psychically and energetically place myself on William's beach by his side. I grab his hand. "I am here with you. I am standing right next to you. I see Casey. Ask her."

In this vision, Casey walks up to us. I hold my arm out to stop her from walking any closer. I then place a protective shield around both William and myself—a white light to protect us against any negative energies. I say to her, "Casey, before you begin, I have you know the Father, the Son, and the Holy Spirit protect this space. We invited you here to get information regarding your intentions with William, so that he's clear, that's all. Anything else you're bringing, it will be transmuted to the light to be healed. I am totally prepared to deal with it." Casey stops in her tracks. William's hands are sweating. "Why is William afraid of you?" I ask Casey.

Casey smiles, then she says, "It isn't William you should be concerned about." As she speaks, a storm starts to brew in the ocean again. We hear thunder and see lightning. "William is a stepping stone, a means to an end. He possesses the resources I need to complete what needs to be completed."

I send loving energy in her direction to calm the waves that seem to erupt. I watch as the scenery calms back down. I'm then led to say, "You know Jesus Christ is in this space." She frowns, and it appears she is fading in and out. "Whatever supernatural hold that you have on William, in the name of Jesus, I invoke you to take it off," I demand. Her face is cringing, and she is falling to her knees as if someone has punched her right in the stomach. "Why are you here?" I question again.

She smiles. "You will find out soon enough." Then she disappears.

I notice William's breathing is rapid. I place my free hand over his chest, sending loving energy to his heart chakra. "I'm going to count back from five, and when I get to one, you will open your eyes and take steps in your waking life to remove Casey from your home. Five, you are coming closer to this reality; four, you are aware of your physical body; three...two...one, open your eyes, bringing with you only the good experiences from this hypnotherapy session, with a renewed sense of how to manage your situation with Casey."

As William comes to, I compliment him. "You did a good job." I rub his hand.

He sits up. "I feel clearer, Sabine. What did you do?"

"We had a hypnotherapy session—well more like a spiritual/vision quest. Do you remember the ocean?"

"Yes. It was very relaxing."

"Do you remember how to get there?"

"Yes. It is my safe place," he responds.

"You only need to hold the intent of being there, and you are there. Did you do your homework?" I ask.

"I did." He hands me a paper with the comparison between Sara and Casey.

"We'll look at this next session. We ran over by thirty minutes."

"I'm sorry. I know that Kelvin's probably waiting on you."

"It is okay. Let's plan to meet on Thursday at five thirty P.M. I'll give you a few days to process from this session." I write out the card with Thursday's date and time and hand it to him. He places it in his wallet.

"I'll wait on you to walk you to your car," he says.

"Thanks." I blow out the candles and turn off the music. We both get up and walk toward the door. William waits on me as I tap the four-digit code into the alarm system, then we exit the building. Once we're at my car, he says, "Thank you so much, Sabine. I don't know what I would do without you." He opens my car door.

"You would manage," I say to him and smile. "I'll see you on Thursday." As he closes the door, he motions for me to roll down the window.

"Hey, next weekend I'm having a Halloween party. You and Kelvin are invited if you want to come. I'll email the invitation to you. What is your email address?"

I make it home closer to eight. When I enter the house, I holler out, "Honey, I'm home."

Kelvin walks out from the living room with a smile. "Baby, if one more minute had passed, I was going to send a search party out for you," he says as he walks over to me and scoops me up in a hug.

"The session took longer than I anticipated. I'm sorry Kelvin. I did pick up some burgers." I pull the bag out of my purse and place it on the kitchen counter. Kelvin walks up and grabs me from behind, as he whispers in my ear, "Seme, what took so long with the session?" He kisses my earlobe. I can sense his anger, yet he's expressing it differently.

"I did a spiritual/vision quest and hypnotherapy with William." I relay as I turn to face Kelvin, wrapping my arms around his waist. "I wanted him to face his fears and take his power back in his home. I think it worked."

"Yeah? How so?" Kelvin ask as he sits down, pulling me into his lap on the chair with him.

"Well, it started as a meditation session because he loves the relaxation techniques that I use in the meditation session."

"Is that so?" Kelvin asks suspiciously.

"Yes," I state matter of factly. "Anyway, when I took him through the visualization, I asked him to look at his fears, and one that came up was Casey who came into our vision, as if she tuned into the session and her essence was there. I wasn't expecting that, but it happened, and William was so afraid. I thought that I was going to have to bring him back out of the meditation, I mean the spiritual/vision quest."

"Yeah?" Kelvin inquires.

"Yes, but, what I did instead was join him in his vision quest. When I saw Casey, she was strong and angry. I put a shield of protection up around William and me, then I called on the higher powers to join us, and she eventually disappeared. She told me she was using William to get where she needed to be. After that, I ingrained in William's head that he needs to get her out of his house. After the session, William felt better."

"Wow that was powerful, Sabine. Have you ever done that before?"

"What exactly?"

"Tune in that way?" Kelvin asks.

"Yes. I just never felt a force that strong from someone. It felt very dark and kind of spooky. Normally, when I tune in to people, I'm helping them deal with their own inner demons, but this time I was dealing with a whole other entity—at least it felt like it."

"I see. Well, it looks like you got some good work done," Kelvin says and smiles at me.

"Oh, I almost forgot. William invited us to his Halloween party next weekend. He said he would send the invitation via email. Do you want to go?"

"Yes. I will definitely be there," Kelvin says, somewhat monotone.

I check my email through my phone and forward the Halloween invitation from William to Kelvin. "It looks like it starts at eleven P.M. on Saturday, October 28. It says there will be drinks and live music. It's a masquerade/costume party." I put my phone down and take our sandwiches out of the bag. I hand Kelvin his Barbeque Western Burger, and I open mine.

"Sounds like fun. Are you going to invite Samantha and Malik?" Kelvin asks as he takes a bite from his burger and motions for me to get up as he walks over to the refrigerator and grabs a beer for himself and pulls out a Sprite for me.

"I don't know. Last time Malik went out, he almost died. Plus, what if Casey is there? Samantha would probably murder that woman if she saw her."

"Yeah, you're right. Maybe that isn't such a good idea. Just me and you then?" He sits in the chair across from me.

"Yeah. Did you go grocery shopping?" I ask, noticing when he open the refrigerator it seems full.

"Yes, sweetie. I just replaced some of the things I saw you use for your catering business, and I got some stuff to make you dinner tomorrow night."

"You are the sweetest man, you know that? I've never had a man as sweet as you." I feel nothing but love from him. He is so considerate, so kind and thoughtful, it is soulfully invigorating.

"It's not a problem, baby. Thank you for the burger. It tastes great. I've never had one of these," he says, downplaying his act of kindness and changing the subject. I like the fact that he is humble, too.

"Seeing as to how we have about one month for the café to open, I'm thinking of phasing out the catering and delivery, just until the café opens. Oh, that reminds me, I need to hire a delivery person. I'm sorry. I'm just thinking out loud."

"Don't apologize. I can be your sounding board. I can be whatever you want me to be, actually." He walks toward me and grabs my burger wrapper to throw it away. "I can be your waiter or your busboy," he says very seductively and silly-like. "I can be your sex slave if you want, baby." He gazes at me lovingly.

CHAPTER 16—WHO ARE YOU?

I wake up to someone shaking me gently. "Baby, wake up."

I open my eyes, and I see Kelvin fully dressed. "What time is it?"

"It's three A.M. I'm sorry to wake you, but I have to go."

"Why?" I sit up, rubbing my face, feeling a little concerned.

"One of my trucks broke down about three hours from here."

"Okay. Do you need me to do anything?"

"No. I just wanted to let you know I was leaving and that I would most likely be back later this evening. I'll be in Jacksonville. I'll call you, okay?"

"Okay. Thanks for letting me know." I reach out and touch his face. "Drive safely. I don't want anything to happen to you. I love you so much," I confess to him. He kisses my forehead and lays back down beside me for a little while. Moments later, I feel him get up to leave the house. I toss and turn for a few minutes and drift back off to sleep.

I awake again, on my own around eight A.M. I check my cell phone to see that Kelvin texted me at 7:50 to let me know he made it to Jacksonville. I quickly shower to prepare for the day. Only three deliveries scheduled, and they are all at one stop, the police station. I have my coupons for S &S Café and Lounge ready to pass out; I cannot believe there's only one month left before we open. Sammie and I will have our own space to do what we both love in one location. All of this working and prepping from home and spending my afternoons thirty minutes out of the way on the other side of town counseling clients will be over.

I only had three orders come through my email last night requesting the special, which today is spaghetti with turkey meatballs. I pack ten spaghetti meals, grab the remaining cakes I have in my refrigerator and a few of the cans of Sprites and Cokes that Kelvin bought yesterday and pack it all neatly into a cooler. With my purse and cell phone in hand, I exit my home.

As I place the cooler in the trunk, I can't help but notice how sunny and beautiful it is outside. What an excellent way to start any day, I think as I thank God for such an amazing view. When I get into the car, my heart feels light and I continue my prayer of gratitude, thanking my Creator for bringing love and passion back into my life through Kelvin, for making everything run smoothly with preparing to open this café. I also thanked God for Malik's recovery, and for William's healing. Life is good.

Once I pull up to the police station, I pop the trunk to retrieve the cooler. As I'm walking toward the entrance, I see Officer Mack escorting a very loud and belligerent woman into the station. Her hair is wild, she has one shoe on, and she seems intoxicated or as if she is on some type of drug by the way she keeps yelling and cursing the officer. I wait a few minutes before heading in that direction to create enough distance between us. Her energy feels horrible.

All of a sudden, I get that feeling in the pit of my stomach, as if I am falling off the face of the earth and there's no return. I temporarily feel like I'm going to pass out. When did I feel this way before? I keep trying to remember as I walk several feet behind them. I am caught in my thoughts trying to search my brain, then it hits me, that day I walked into my house after my first date with Kelvin, and again when I grab those résumés out of the office to give to Sammie. When I look up, Casey is staring right into my eyes. Shit, this takes me by surprise. Casey is the woman being led into the police station.

"Casey?" I ask.

She goes completely quiet; she doesn't say another word. No cursing, no yelling, she just smiles as the officer opens the door to the station. Then, I hear it again . . . three loud knocks, the same way I heard them the other night after Kelvin dropped me off after our date. This startles me and I pause in my steps, watching them as they walk inside. She seems to be searching for something within herself. I think she recognizes me, but something about her seems distant or far away. The closer I walk in that direction, the more I realize she's someone else. Then I see it...

When Officer Mack stops to readjust the handcuffs, she never takes her eyes off me. Her pupils are dilated completely, expanding the whole diameter of her cornea, and even though I am staring at a person who appears to be Casey, friend to Malik Marcs, I realize something else is there invading her body.

I put the cooler down once I walk into the station, and I sit in a chair in the waiting room. Officer Mack is getting paperwork started on Casey and she continues to stare my way, not saying a word. I call Sammie.

"Sammie, you will never believe who's at the police station."
"Who?"
"Call me back on the video phone and I will show you."
"Okay, bye." Sammie says before hanging up.

Sammie calls back on the WhatsApp. I answer the phone and flip the screen around so she can see what I'm seeing.

"Oh my God, Sabine. I see her," Sammie says.

I walk toward the desk, which puts me closer to Casey. "Good afternoon. I'm here to drop off these lunch orders." I hand the deputy a piece of paper with the names of the officers who placed the orders. Sammie is still on the phone. I tilt my phone so it's facing Casey. The deputy informs me all three officers are out on duty but will be back in the station in fifteen minutes.

"Thank you. I'll wait." I walk back over to the waiting area to sit down.

Casey is behind the desk being fingerprinted. She continues to stare at me. There are no audible words coming from her, however when I tune into Casey psychically, I hear a low, deep voice with a raspy edge to it like a growl. It actually sounds like two or three voices in one, which are in harmony with each other and it (or they) say...

Knock, knock, knock, Sabine. So, we meet again. Three time's a charm. There is a pause, as if to see if I am receiving this message. *First after your date with Kelvin, a second time during your therapy session with William, and here we are yet again with Casey. Yes, Casey is in here with me. She recognizes you, or is it your sister that she envies? Aaahhh, I see. She seeks your sister's husband. She casted a love spell. She is an amateur...*

I ask psychically, "How did you get inside of Casey?"

Happy to see that you are receptive. You hear me loud and clear today. I had a hard time getting to you the past few times; in the car over the phone, and that day your sister came to visit you. To answer your question, Casey opened a portal, so to speak, through her black magic playtime, and I slid in. She isn't as good at spells as she pretends to be. She was just playing around and putting up smoke clouds—child's play. I can help her do some real damage now.

"Who are you?" I ask.

Casey or the entity inside of her starts laughing aloud in Casey's voice and psychically in the deep, unnerving and high- and low-pitch voices in my mind. Officer Mack walks Casey to the back and now she is out of sight.

I walk back up to the desk. "Deputy, can you please leave these three lunches for the officers on this paper? Have them pay me on the cash app, they have my user name, but I'll write it on this paper, just in case." I grab the paper with the names of those who placed an order and write my cash app user name on it along with the amount next to each officer's name on the list. Then I take out the spaghetti, bread, cake, and three Cokes.

"Okay, sure. They'll be here in five minutes if you want to wait."

"I have to go. I have extra here if anyone else needs lunch today," I say, feeling the need to get as far away as possible from this police station. Far away from Casey or should I say, the entity inside of Casey.

"Wow. I'll take one," The officer says and reaches into her pocket for some cash.

"Can you do me a favor and whoever takes a lunch, give them this flyer?"

She looks at the flyer and reads it, *S & S Café and Lounge opens November 29.* "Sure thing."

I leave the police station feeling sick to my stomach. What I just experienced with Casey just doesn't sit well with me and my stomach feels unsettled. I need some fresh air.

"Samantha, are you there?" I put the phone up to my face.

"Yes, girl. I'm taking the rest of the day off. I am on my way over to your house, I have to show you something."

"Okay. Bye."

I text Kelvin:

Hi, baby. How are you? What time do you think you'll be home tonight? I miss you. Sabine

I hop into my car and slow my breathing down by taking several deep breaths. What just happened in there? Is the question that is running through my mind. I mean yes, I am able to communicate with the spirit world, but I've never experienced the dark side of spirits- not like this. I am use to dealing with people and their unresolved issues, what I term "inner demons". I am able to converse clairvoyantly with spirit guides, angels, and decease loved ones. But, this is different. What was in Casey is not a part of her, it is a complete other entity residing in her body, holding the intention of causing harm to others. I can feel the negative energy deep inside of me. It feels like a haze, as if something is being blocked out or hidden. Whatever it is, it's operating on a lower frequency and it's hard to pin point- even with my skills and abilities. I know something is wrong. I saw Casey, yet I had a conversation with someone else or something else, not of this world or of this time. It made me feel suffocated, nauseated, and sad. My mind goes back to eating chicken wings and drinking beer with Casey and William at the club the other night. I can't help but remember how perky she seemed and now, she just seems like a vessel, an empty hollow shell of a person. Like her soul is trapped somewhere inside of her, while that thing takes over. My heart goes out to her. What was she taken in for anyway? I take out my work phone and call William.

CHAPTER 17—THE SITUATION

"William, hello. It's Sabine."

"Hi, love."

"Can you meet me at my house in thirty minutes? It's an emergency."

"Okay. I'll be there," he says with concern in his voice, then he hangs up.

I walk to my car and my phone rings. "Hello?" I answer.

"Hey, girl. I'm on my way to your house now. I just left work. How are you holding up?" Samantha asks on the other end of the phone.

"Everything is surreal."

"I know, right?"

"Did you hear anything when I tuned in to Casey?" I ask.

"No, but I could feel this eerie feeling and I saw it in her face. I recorded it. Sabine, when I play it back, you can see... I'll just show you when I get there."

"I called William to find out why she was being locked up. He's on his way to the house now."

"William knows where you live?" Sammie asks.

"Yeah. I'll tell you about that later. Kelvin is calling me on the other end. I'll see you in a few minutes."

"Okay. Bye."

I click over to answer Kelvin's call. "Hi, baby. I miss you too. Are you okay?" he asks.

I start to break down a little bit; tears are rolling down my cheeks because it's such a contrast in the feeling I get from Kelvin versus what I just experienced in the police station a few minutes ago. I sense such over whelming love coming from Kelvin.

I take a deep breath. "I am okay. I just want to know when you'll be home," I say with a shaky voice.

"Baby, what's wrong?" he asks coolly, but I can sense the alarm in his tone.

"Kelvin, it's too much to talk about over the phone. I'm okay though, just shaken up. Sammie is on her way to my house. I invited William over too."

"Williams' on his way over, huh?" Kelvin mutters, "Listen, I'm on my way back now. I should be home around five or five-thirty," Kelvin says.

"Okay."

"Can you give me Sammie's number?" Kelvin asks.

"I'll text it to you." Which I do right then as I am stopped at a red light.

"I got it. I am going to call Sammie. Drive safely, baby. Focus on the road."

Once I get home, I light some candles and say a prayer for protection around my home and for all of the people in my life. I light a sage stick and smudge the house, walking around calling on the name of Jesus for protection, rebuking anything that is not of my highest good. I light my essential oil burner purely as a way to calm my senses. When I look outside my bay window, it's still a beautiful day, however, unlike this morning, when I was driving to the police station, my spirit feels heavy, worried, and stressed. The doorbell rings. I set the sage in the holder as it continues to burn. I open the door, and I see William.

"Hi, love." He reaches for a hug. When I grab a hold of him, I let everything go. I am crying uncontrollably. He walks into my house, closes the door behind him, still embracing me in the hug as minutes pass by. Then he says very calmly, "Sabine, it's okay." He lifts my face and wipes my tears away. He smiles. "Whatever it is, it's going to be okay." And for a second I believe him.

"I'm sorry, William," I say.

"No need for apologies, love."

"Come in." We walk toward the living room. "Can I get you something to drink? Water, soda, wine? I am going to have wine," I say, wiping the remaining tears from my eyes.

"Wine it is then," he says, I can tell that he is somewhat shocked that we are drinking alcohol so early in the day.

"So, I went down to the police station to drop some lunches off for a few of the officers. As I was walking in, I saw a police officer escorting Casey in handcuffs," I say as I walk into the kitchen to grab the wine and glasses. William follows me.

"Wow, you saw that?" William says as he takes the wine from me and opens it.

I nod.

"Yeah, well, this morning I told Casey she's going to have to find someplace else to stay. I told her this isn't working for me. She went ape shit," William says as he goes back to that moment in his head, pouring the wine. "She started raging out, throwing shit around my house. She broke my sixty-inch television set. I tried to get her to calm down, but she was on a rampage; slapping me a few times, scratching the back of my neck. I called 911. She continued to rage out until they got there. They witnessed it. She came at me a few times trying to throw heavy objects toward me. It was really messed up, Sabine."

"That is messed up," I say taking a sip of the wine then going to the refrigerator to pull out some cooked veggies and rice. "Have you eaten?" I ask.

"No," William responds.

I assemble my ingredients as I prepare a veggie stir-fry. "I'm happy you put her out of your home. She meant you no good. You seem like a nice person, William. I could tell that about you when I first met you."

"Thanks, Sabine. I feel the same about you."

I go on to tell him how Sammie suspects Casey and Malik had some type of affair going on. Also, how she thought Casey put something in Malik's drink at the club the other night. I even confessed that Sammie and I followed him and Casey to that club, which is how we knew about it in the first place.

"It seems like Casey was upset about Malik and Samantha getting married," I relay.

"I can see that. Remember Sara? We talked about her in counseling," William says.

"Yes, I remember."

"I allowed Casey to come between us." William pauses. "I cheated with Casey. Sara found out. The thing is I had no desire to be with Casey. I was and still am in love with Sara. It's like I was under some type of spell or something. Whatever you did to me at our last session gave me the courage to break free from her. I saw some pretty unnatural things occur at my house while Casey was there, and it freaked me the hell out." He shakes his head. "The room that she slept in, I can't go into it."

The doorbell rings, then I hear Samantha come inside. "Hey, girl. It's me," she calls out.

"We're in the kitchen," I yell. Sammie has several bags in her hand. William gets up and greets her with a kiss on the cheek, and he takes the bags out of her hand.

"I stopped by the store. I got some junk food and wine to help calm your nerves, girl."

"Thanks. I'm making some stir-fry."

"Yum. I spoke to Kelvin." She pauses and looks at me. "I filled him in on what happened at the police station. He's very concerned. He seems to really care for you Sabine."

"Yeah?" I question.

"What exactly happened at the police station?" William asks.

"Seme, you didn't tell him?"

"Not yet."

"Tell me what?" William inquires again.

"Let me go use the bathroom, and I'll show you when I come out," Sammie says.

"What happened, Sabine?" William questions, concerned.

"Oh my God, William, it's so hard for me to talk about because it's hard for me to believe it and I witnessed it."

"Run it by me. I'm all ears."

"William, do you remember our session the other day?"

"Yes. Some of it."

"Do you remember Casey coming in?"

He looks reflective. "Yes, I do."

"Do you remember what she said?"

"Sabine, it makes me sick to the stomach to try to remember. I think I blocked it out, but I know that it wasn't good."

"You didn't block it out. When I pulled you out of the session, I only wanted you to remember what was important, which was to get her out of your house."

William looks at me. "Well, that I did, so mission accomplished."

"She told me in the vision quest she had another agenda, and that I would find out what it was soon enough," I relay to William. "Today, I got a glimpse of it." I get up to add the rice and veggies to the skillet of sautéed onions and minced garlic, then I pour some soy sauce and Asian garlic sauce over the rice, stir it a little, then I turn the skillet on low to let it simmer.

Sammie joins us in the kitchen. She pulls out a glass from the cabinet and pours herself some wine. She puts the wines she bought in the freezer to chill them fast. I can tell this is going to be a wine drinking afternoon. Sammie pulls out some red vine licorice and offers some pieces to me and William.

I explain to William what I saw upon entering the police station from Casey's wild behavior, to her weird eyes, to her uncanny stares, to the conversation I heard psychically from the entity within her body. Williams sits back in his chair and takes a deep breath. "Wow." He rubs his fingers through his hair.

Sammie pulls out her phone. "And then there's this." She pulls up the video on her phone of Casey sitting at the police station getting fingerprinted. In the video she's turned around facing the camera. There appears to be a glitch in the camera phone because it looks as if there are two faces on Casey. I can see her face attached to her body facing the camera and then I see another image coming sideways off her face.

"What is that?" I ask, rewinding the video then pausing it.

"It's like you can see the entity inside of her," Sammie says.

William chimes in, "It's like it's trying to come out of her body." When we all look at it again, it does look as if it is pulling from the core of her body and it seems strained like it is trying to pull away from her, but it does not have enough energy to separate itself. It's a blur, but it's definitely there.

I get up to fix our plates of food and refill our wineglasses. We're all quiet now, thinking about what we just saw on the video. As we're eating, I ask Sammie to play the video again. We all huddle around the camera trying to make sense of the image. In my mind, I'm trying to rationalize it... "Maybe it's the light."

"Sabine, this is a full image of another face," William says. The three of us sit there eating and watching the video for the fourteenth time.

Then, a voice comes out of nowhere, "What are y'all doing?" We all drop our forks and turn to look at the origin of the voice.

"Kelvin," I say as I jump up and give him a hug.

"Oh my God, Kelvin, you scared us," Sammie says.

Kelvin has a look of concern on his face. William stands and shakes Kelvin's hand. "Nice to see you again, Kelvin."

Kelvin nods. "Same here. Sabine, what's going on baby? Can we talk in the room for a second?"

"We'll be right back," I say to Sammie and William.

When we get in the room, Kelvin rubs my hair and stares at me for a while. "Samantha filled me in on what happened today at the police station. I'm sorry I wasn't here for you," Kelvin says as if he's trying to assess the situation. "Come here. Let me see." He comes in close to me and places his forehead on to mine. He places one hand behind my head. My thoughts are racing around, and he says, "Relax, baby." He places his other hand on the side of my face, then I feel a jolt as if something is locking us in to each other. Seconds go by. Kelvin slowly pulls away from me and inhales deeply. He puts his hand to his mouth as if he's in thought. I just stare at him waiting on him to say something.

"What is it, Kelvin?" I ask becoming impatient that he is not communicating to me.

"Baby," he says, then he pauses.

"Yes?" I question.

"We're under attack."

"Why do you say that?" I ask, wanting to hear his perspective on the situation.

He inhales deeply again, then exhales. "Casey wanted to destroy Malik and Samantha's relationship, but the entity inside of Casey wants to come in between our love. It locked into you, Sabine. It felt the joy in your heart, the love you feel toward me... the love that we have toward each other." Kelvin steps back and grabs my hand. "I'm sorry, baby. I've gotta think. I'm going to take a shower and come join you for dinner in a few, if that's okay?"

I nod. He turns my hand loose and walks to the bathroom.

As I walk back out to the kitchen, I find Samantha on the phone with Malik, I assume, filling him in on what happened today. William is in the living room looking at his phone. I walk up beside him. "Are you okay?" I ask.

"Yes." He looks in my eyes, searching. "How about you?"

"I don't know," I reply. "I'm shocked and kind of scared, if you want the truth."

He rubs my lower back with his hand. "So, I just got off of the phone with Officer Mack. They're going to hold Casey until the court hearing, which will be in a couple of weeks. They put up a five-thousand-dollar bond. They have probable cause to hold her for the club poisoning investigation. I turned in the journal and the pictures to Officer Mack this morning."

"I see," I state.

William shifts as if trying to bring himself back to a normal reality. "Anyhow, the food was great. Thank you, Sabine. I'm going to leave now and give you and Kelvin some time to process all of this, and I need to do the same," William says.

"Okay. Take my personal cell number." I grab his phone and type it in. "Call me if anything comes up. I mean anything. It doesn't matter the time of day or night, okay?"

William reaches to hug me. "It's going to be okay, Sabine, I promise."

"I hope so." I walk William out to his car and ask, "Are you staying at your place or a hotel?"

He smiles. "Why, do you plan on coming over?"

I shake my head.

"Just kidding Sabine. I'll be in a hotel tonight. If you need me, I'm a phone call away."

When I walk back into the house, Samantha is showing Kelvin the video. I walk over to the stove and put some stir-fry on a plate for Kelvin. As I hand him his plate he says, "I was supposed to cook you dinner tonight." He takes the plate. "Thank you, baby."

"Seme, I spoke to Malik. He said his mom's church sisters are praying for us. I guess we just trust that everything is okay." Samantha walks over to me. "Don't feed into the fear, girl. We're going to be okay. Remember what you told me once... Love is the strongest force in the universe. At least for the time being we can find comfort in the fact that she's locked away."

She and I say the next part together, "Love and fear cannot co-exist."

I give her a hug. "I love you, Sammie."

"I love you too." She grabs her purse then opens the freezer. "I'm going to take one of these home." She grabs one of the wine bottles and puts it in her purse, and places the other in the refrigerator. "Bye, Kelvin. Take care of my sister."

"I will." He stands, and we both walk her to the door. We watch as she gets in to her car.

"Text me to let me know you made it home safely," I yell right before she closes her car door. Sammie pulls out of the driveway. As soon as the door is closed and we're back in the house, Kelvin pulls me to his chest. He holds me tightly and kisses the top of my head.

CHAPTER 18—THE DREAM

"I've made a decision for us," Kelvin tells me as I lay in his arms while we're in bed. "No work tomorrow for either of us. We're going to have a day together." I listen as I drift in and out of consciousness. "No clients or no food deliveries for you. As for me, I won't go into the office or on any emergency trips. Just you and me tomorrow, Sabine. Can you clear your schedule for me?"

"Yes," I say, barely able to keep my eyes open. Moments later, the unconscious wins. My body shuts down, and I drift off to another world. My mind goes to a place of peace. I'm in a dream state in what looks like a beach house. I'm standing on the highest floor the house, which is on a balcony outside on the third floor. The winds are high, and I'm in view of the whole ocean from where I stand. I can see a lighthouse across the waters on a small island and the sun is setting. The light is blinking every fifteen seconds from the lighthouse, and it's beautiful. I look down at myself and see I have on a long flowing white gown. When I turn away from the ocean, I see a candle lit in the middle of the balcony. I walk over to the candle, kneel beside it, and close my eyes.

In the distance, I hear a woman's voice. I open my eyes and look around, searching for the source of this familiar voice. I walk down the stairwell, which is to the side of the beach house and into a room that is enclosed with windows that extend a few inches from where the ceiling meets the wall. The entire length of the wall has windows and it rounds the whole room. The entire room is wide open, and there's glass everywhere. It's beautiful, serene, and exposed.

In the middle of the floor is a bed with four wooden posts. A white plushy comforter and several round pillows are scattered on the bed. I walk over, and I get reminiscence of scenes of romantic encounters between Kelvin and me—things I don't remember happening, yet it feels so familiar. I turn to look, and I see a dog run up to us in the bed. She's jumping around wagging her tail around us. We're laughing, then we pause and smile at each other. Suddenly, that look that seems to pull me into my own little world with Kelvin comes over Kelvin's face, and seconds later, we're kissing as if our life depends on each kiss.

That vision fades. I walk down another flight of stairs, and I'm in a kitchen. I'm cooking dinner dressed in a short silk dress with high heels on. It looks as if I'm preparing for a party. I'm setting the table and arranging flowers. Kelvin walks in drunk. "Kelvin, what are you doing? You knew we had this dinner tonight. Why would you get wasted?" I mouth this as the scene plays out for me to see.

He looks at me, his eyes barely open. "I'm okay. I'm going to shower and sober up. I'll be ready for dinner, baby. I promise." Kelvin comes over to me and leans on the counter and pulls me to him, and even in his drunken stupor, I feel the love toward him. We kiss, and I push away from him, and he looks me in the eyes. "I'm sorry baby. I only had two beers, I don't know what happened." He walks to the bathroom to shower.

After I prepare dinner and complete setting up the dining room, I go into the bathroom to find the shower water running and Kelvin on the floor passed out. I run over to him and pat him on his face. "Baby, wake up." I check his pulse and it is weak. I grab my cell phone and make a phone call. Minutes later, when I go to the door, Amanda from the club, is at the door. I show her to the bathroom where Kelvin is passed out. She immediately asks me to help lift him up and get him to the toilet. We hold his head over the commode. She proceeds to stick her fingers down his throat, effectively gagging him. His body is heaving, and he's emptying himself of all the alcohol he ingested.

The next scene, he's in the bed and I'm placing a cold towel over his forehead. Amanda tells me, "This was not alcohol poisoning, and it was not accidental." She places her hand over his body and tunes into him psychically, "He went to the bar for a couple of beers, and he met someone there who put something in his drink." The problem is she couldn't positively identify the woman. She tells me he'll be fine—that he just needs to sleep it off, and when he wakes up to prepare the tea she gives to me. She says it will cleanse the toxins out of his body.

The scene changes to the dinner party in the dining room of this beach house, and Kelvin is not in attendance. Samantha is there with Malik, and there is another couple there, and it seems as if Samantha and I are trying to impress them. There's something eerie about the couple and the situation.

I awake from my sleep, looking around the room for Kelvin as he isn't lying next to me. I hear faint clanking noises coming from the kitchen. I look at the clock. It is only thirty minutes past eleven. Wow, I drifted off early.

I walk out into the kitchen to find Kelvin putting the remaining stir-fry up and loading the dishwasher. He appears deep in thought, so much that he doesn't see me until I speak up. "Hi, baby. Thanks for cleaning up the kitchen."

He smiles, walks over to me, and embraces me in a hug. "No problem, sweetie." He kisses my head. "So, I think we should get out of town for a few days."

"Yeah? What did you have in mind?" I ask, pulling back to look at him.

He walks over to his laptop, which is sitting on the kitchen table, and turns the screen around to face me, and I see a beautiful resort in Key West. "Kelvin, it's beautiful, but we would still be in Florida."

"I know, but it's hours away, plus it's an all-inclusive resort, and we need a getaway. It's kind of hard to book something last minute and just for a few days out of state."

"Let's do it," I say with enthusiasm.

"Are you up for leaving tonight?" Kelvin asks. "It's about a seven-hour drive. We would get to Key West early in the morning. If we get tired we could check into a hotel on the way there."

"I think I'm rested. Let me go pack our bags."

Kelvin pulls me in to his arms, "Pack light, baby—just the necessities. I'm going to take you shopping."

CHAPTER 19—ROAD TRIP

I quickly pack our underwear, nightclothes, a couple of sun dresses for me, and two pairs of shorts and shirts for Kelvin.

Kelvin packs a cooler filled with juices, waters, a couple of beers, grapes, apple slices, and turkey and ham sandwiches with cheese and bacon. We put the luggage and the cooler in the back of the jeep, lock the house up, and are on our way to Key West by one o'clock in the morning.

"We should make it there by eight A.M. if we don't make too many stops," Kelvin says as he gets back in the jeep from gassing up.

The road is empty, and the night sky is clear. I check my Gmail account on my smart phone. I delete some of the junk mail. I press compose so that I can generate a message to the companies that I cater for:

> I am excited to relay that the official opening for S & S Café and Lounge is approaching. The formal count down has begun. Please be patient with me as I prepare this space for the opening on November 29. The first few weeks of November will be dedicated to the preparation of the building and the organization of the party that is scheduled on the day of opening at seven P.M. We will have samples of desserts, raffles, games and drinks. We look forward to seeing you there.
>
> Note: The catering and delivery services are suspended at this time, and will resume two weeks from the grand opening.
>
> Thank you for your understanding and continued support.

Sabine Stallworth
Co-owner of S & S Café and Lounge

After sending the email out, I realize I never interviewed a driver. I am going to need someone to do the deliveries once the café opens. I need to add that to my list of things to do. I check my calendar of counseling sessions and realize William is the only one scheduled for the remainder of the week. I will give him a call tomorrow to let him know I'm out of town, but will be back in time for his party. Maybe I will suggest to him about referring him to another counselor. It might be a conflict of interest now that we seem to be getting closer as friends. Wow. My schedule was easier to clear than I thought. I guess that's the benefit of owning your own business.

I reach into the cooler in the backseat to pull out the grapes. I pop a couple in Kelvin's mouth as he catches me up on what has been going on in his business. He tells me he has purchased two more trucks for Frey Transportation. He has also hired two drivers and a logistics manager for the office in Michigan. He's put procedures in place in the event of an emergency with tow companies within a 300-mile radius of Florida and Michigan. He is still coordinating with other tow companies in different states.

"Business is going very well, and things are branching out beyond what I dreamed they would," Kelvin states.

"I'm so happy for you Kelvin," I say to him as I look at him with admiration.

"I want to make you proud of me, baby. This has been a dream of mine for years, and now I'm finally starting to see the fruits of my labor."

"You've already made a big impression on me. I love your business mind, your forthrightness with getting things done, and your ability to balance life. You know that's hard to pull off, right?" I place my hand on his leg. "It is not just about your success, but the people you help along the way. You working in partnership with other companies brings business in for them also, which increases your company's karma. You're doing excellent."

"Company karma?" Kelvin asks with a grin.

"You know what I mean. Everything you put out comes back to you threefold, and you're putting some good vibes out there. You even helped me and Sammie out with our business, and we appreciate it so much." I turn the radio on and go into a daze. I think about things coming back to people threefold and the concept of karma.

My mind focuses on Casey, and I keep thinking about how she came between William and Sara's relationship and tried to come between Sammie and Malik's union, and now I'm a little worried about me and Kelvin's relationship. And what's up with that dream I had? Was it a dream or insight? Let me see if I can remember: I start backwards. Who could the couple at the table have represented? It seemed as if Sammie and I were trying to impress them. Maybe someone lucrative to our café? Then there was Kelvin who appeared to be intoxicated. Yet, according to Amanda, in my dream, Kelvin did not have alcohol poisoning, but someone had put something in his drink. Maybe Kelvin represented Malik, and it was sort of a reenactment. But why would my subconscious reenact the part I already knew and not the part that I didn't see, like when someone slipped whatever was slipped into his drink?

Kelvin interrupts my thoughts. "Are you okay, baby?"

"What?"

"You seem deep in thought."

"I'm fine. My mind is just wondering. I had this dream, and I was trying to figure it out."

"Do you want to tell me about the dream?"

"I could, but it wouldn't make sense, and I don't want you doing your little mind reading thing. It freaks me out," I say to him, looking startled and quickly removing my hand from his leg, cutting off all contact to limit him trying to read my mind.

"Try me the normal way. Tell me your dream." Kelvin turns down the music, which has now gone to commercials anyway.

"Do you need me to drive? I did take a nap earlier, and you already drove like six hours yesterday."

"I'm fine, baby. I do this for a living. If I get tired, I won't hesitate to let you know. Now, the dream."

I tell him the dream from the beginning to the end.

"Interesting. Let me think on it for a while," he says. "Can you hand me a sandwich from the cooler?" I pull out a turkey and ham sandwich with bacon and open it for him. I take one bite first and then give him the rest.

"How is it?" Kelvin asks.

"It's delicious," I reply, savoring the bite I just took.

"I made one for you too."

"I'm going to save mine for a little later." I pull out my laptop and open up a blank page in Microsoft Word and place a "Q:" for question on the screen. I go into my mind's eye then I ask a question. What was my dream trying to reveal to me? I type this on the page and let my automatic writing take over. 'A': is the answer from my higher self.

Q: What was my dream trying to reveal to me?

A: Love is felt in the soul, experienced in the mind, and expressed through the heart. Your mind replays instances of love, what has been felt through your soul over the ages. Your mind replays the experiences to remind you and renew your love, and the expression is through the heart, although sex represents one way to express love in our physical form. Your dream showed you love in its many forms: feelings, experience, and expression. Your connection with Kelvin is true love—several lifetimes of love.

Q: What about the kitchen scene in the dream?

A: It was a warning in regards to the obstacles that are currently in place. The things that come along to try to block what is real. Everything else that comes with love is a byproduct of the situation and the person whom you are with and how they choose to honor your relationship—not all people understand this part. However, this scene is not entirely related to you and Kelvin, as much as it relates to Samantha, Malik, Sara, and William.

Q: How do you mean?

A: *It is a lesson for you to witness and grow from, about how the people who are in your life affect the success and failure of your relationship, if allowed. In Samantha and Malik's case, one person in particular is trying to pull them apart for the sheer ability to do so. What may have started as one thing mutated into another and from more than one point of view. What Casey thought she wanted disappeared out of focus when she realized what your sister and her husband experience is real. Nonetheless, that doesn't stop Casey from trying to break up the relationship; it just changes her reasons behind doing what she does. If she is not to gain Malik, she still wants your sister to lose him. Malik's purpose was not to hurt your sister. It was to fulfill a desire to feel needed and secure in himself as a man. When you're in a relationship, your desires and focus should become one in regards to your goals for the relationship. Of course, not all things are together; you have your own hobbies and interests, however, as things pertain directly to your partner and yourself—the goal should be one. If there is a gain in regards to one person and not the other, there is an imbalance in the relationship and a possible threat to the future of the relationship. These are the byproducts that Malik temporarily forgot about in his selfish actions. It's something he has been reminded of since the act and must face the consequences for his actions (karma, so to speak), and he will because he loves your sister. Some don't recover from selfish acts such as William and Sara. With these types of things, while one person must suffer the consequences, there's a possibility that some consequences aren't forgiving. Whether or not someone forgives determines if the relationship will be enhanced or demoted. Sara demoted William; however, he learned his lesson, so not all was lost here.*

Q: *Who was the couple in the dream at the dinner party?*
A: *It isn't so much the couple who was important, as it was the message the scene was trying to convey. The*

message being that you and your sister, Samantha, are very serious about getting your café up and running smoothly. This requires your focus and your attention to even the smallest details. You arranging the flowers, setting the table, and cooking the dinner represented your need to set your business up for success. You were and are crossing the t's and dotting the i's. However, there are many distractions at this time that are taking away your focus, Sabine. Therefore, it's a warning about possible disasters and how you should proceed in the midst of chaos, while at the same time taking care of home; this message is for both you and your sister. This requires grace, patience, focus, and prioritizing.

Q: Thank you. Love and Light.

I save the message and close my laptop.

"Wow, were you writing a book over there?" Kelvin asks with a smile and a ton of sarcasm.

"No, silly. Just trying to organize my thoughts."

"Oh. Well, you were organizing your thoughts for about an hour," he says.

"Yeah?" I ask.

Kelvin nods. "Anything insightful?"

"It was all very insightful actually."

"Well, seeing as to how we still have about five more hours on the road, do you care to share your insightful thoughts?"

I explain to Kelvin another one of my "gifts," my ability to write to my higher self and get a renewed perspective on a situation, and in this case, a perspective on a dream.

"Automatic writing, huh?" he asks.

"Yes. It allows a person to produce written words without consciously writing them."

"So, even though I watched you write a book for an hour, you're telling me you didn't write those things."

"Something like that. Let me take over driving. You can read what my subconscious or higher self-wrote. Q: is for question, which is what I asked, and A: is for answer, which is what was written in response." Kelvin pulls over and we switch seats.

"By the way, I know what my dream means now," I say as I cut my eyes at him.

Kelvin looks at me and smiles, "Okay, the directions are on my phone. I'll be sitting here reading, and I'll determine if I think this is a correct interpretation of your dream."

"Interesting," Kelvin says as he stares at the computer after reading what I wrote.

"What?"

"This is a pretty good interpretation of your dream," Kelvin states, still looking at the computer.

I smirk. "You think?"

"I think you have a lot of great gifts, Sabine," Kelvin says as he closes the laptop down and slides it into my bag in the backseat. He adjusts his seat so that it is lying back. "I'm going to take a quick nap. Are you okay driving, or do you need us to pull over?"

"I'm good, sweetie. Take your nap." I grab his knee reassuringly. "I'll wake you up if I need you. I have the directions here." I point to his phone.

And just like that, Kelvin drifts off to sleep.

CHAPTER 20—THE RESORT

It is a little past seven in the morning, and according to the navigation, we only have less than an hour left on our road trip. I pull off at the exit to get some gas for the jeep. Plus, I need to use the restroom.

Kelvin wakes up. "What's up, baby? What time is it?"

"It's seven thirty A.M.," I respond as I turn off the ignition.

"I've been out for four hours," he states puzzled.

"Yes, some well-deserved sleep. You had a busy day yesterday," I respond, just as I'm about to exit the car.

"I got the gas, baby." Kelvin gets out of the car, walks over to the driver side, slides his debit card into the machine, and begins pumping the gas. I get out of the car shortly after him to use the restroom and freshen up a little.

When I come back to the car, Kelvin is checking the tire pressure. "Let's go to The Breakfast Nook to get something to eat," he says looking at the next driveway. The Breakfast Nook is conveniently located next to the gas station. We park the car and walk over.

I order a waffle with hash browns and bacon and a cup of decaf coffee. Kelvin orders an omelet that has sausage stuffed inside, hash brown, and a tall glass of orange juice. The food is delicious, and it hits the spot. After we finish our meals, we head back to the car. Kelvin drives the remainder of the way to the resort. Forty-five minutes later, we arrive to a place that looks like Paradise.

What really stands out initially about this resort is that it's surrounded by so much water, both man-made and natural. It's astonishing. The palm trees look greener, and the sun seems to shine a little brighter here. I instantly feel revitalized and very hopeful about this trip.

Kelvin parks the jeep in the underground garage, and we take the elevator up to the main lobby. Once we reach the front desk, a beautiful woman named Cindy greets us. She has naturally blond hair, which is shoulder length, bright red lipstick, and is dressed in a navy blue skirt and white collared shirt that has her name tag pinned to it.

Her professionalism and enthusiasm matches very well with the quality of this hotel and resort. She tells us that our room will be ready in one hour. She takes Kelvin's phone number and informs us she'll notify us when the room is ready. The bellhop takes our bags and encourages us to explore the grounds. I order a strawberry daiquiri, and Kelvin orders a platinum margarita from the hotel bar.

"Oh my, Kelvin. This place is perfect!" I exclaim.

When I look around, I see several shops. The inside of this place resembles a mall, a restaurant, and a day spa all combined. There are clothing shops and several restaurants and bakeries scattered throughout. The skylights on the ceiling create the impression we're outside. I can hear the birds chirping, and the sun provides natural light to the space. Kelvin smiles and sips his margarita, trying to keep his cool, but I know he's feeling the magic the same way I am.

We hear live music playing outside. Kelvin hands his debit card to the bartender, and she says, "This is an all-inclusive resort. If you want to leave a tip you can, but the drinks are included in your package." I reach into my purse, pull out a ten-dollar bill, and put it in the glass that reads Tips. Kelvin takes his card back and smiles an even wider grin.

"Can we take our drinks outside?" Kelvin asks the bartender.

"Yes. Enjoy yourselves and welcome," she responds.

As we walk out, we touch our glasses together. "To a good time, baby," Kelvin says.

We walk down three steps and open a door to a view that surpasses any description I could try to give. All I see is clear blue water, palm trees, exotic flowers, cabanas, an in-pool bar, a live band playing tropical music, gorgeous people walking around, and a view of the ocean beyond the pool that looks like it could be on a post card. We stand there for at least a minute just letting the beauty sink into our minds. This place is sharp, crisp, and refreshing, kind of like this strawberry daiquiri I'm sipping on.

Kelvin grabs my free hand and walks me through the pool area. He finds a cabana with two plush beach chairs laid out like a bed with a table separating them. He motions for me to sit, then takes my drink and places it on the table along with his. He then walks over to the other chair, lays back, and exhales loudly.

I watch as a few people get in and out of the pool, retrieving drinks from the bar, which is in the deeper end. I see a family playing water volleyball. Next thing I see are the back of my eyelids as I rest them from the long drive.

What seems like moments later, Kelvin wakes me up to inform me our room is ready. We walk up to the front lobby. Cindy, who is no longer behind the desk, greets us. She is offering to give us the grand tour of the grounds. She informs us that the tour comes with the package we selected.

The first stop is to our room, which Cindy informs us before we go in, has two floors and a balcony view of the ocean. As we walk into the room, the foyer area offers a place to sit. Conveniently located near the door is a two-seater plush bench, which opens up and can be used for storage. To the right of the storage bench is a full-sized bathroom, which is equipped with a glass walk-in shower trimmed with brass, matching faucets and showerhead. It has his and her sinks with a ton of counter space and mirrors. A shelf is positioned in the corner to store personal items and towels. There is another bench with storage space inside the bathroom across from the sink. The toilet is in a separate space, which closes off from the rest of the bathroom.

As we exit the bathroom, a winding stairwell is in view, which leads to the master bedroom upstairs. To the right of the stairwell, a living room area with two sofas and end tables and sliding glass doors lead to the balcony. Out on the balcony is a beautiful view of the ocean, just as Cindy mentioned.

Around the stairwell, there is a kitchen and nook area with a full sized refrigerator and stove and a mini island. Circling back around this room leads back to the entrance and the stairs. The top of the stairs opens out into the bedroom, with the bed being in the center of the room. Because this room is lined up with the living room below, the back wall is completely made of glass and looks out to the beach. A huge walk-in closet is positioned to the left, through the closet and out the other side is a small bathroom with a toilet and a sink.

"Impressive," Kelvin says and smiles at me.

"I'll give you guys time to put your things up. When you're ready for the rest of the tour, I'll be waiting outside. Take your time." Cindy walks down the stairs and out of the room—or should I say mini house.

I walk down the stairs and grab the cooler, roll it to the kitchen, and unload the remaining juices, waters and beers into the refrigerator. When I walk back upstairs, I notice Kelvin has hung up our outfits, taken the shoes out and laid everything out nicely in the huge closet that comes equipped with a dresser and hangers. I grab the bag that Kelvin has partially unpacked, take it downstairs to the large bathroom, and place our toiletries on either side of the sink, then I head out to the balcony to enjoy the view while I wait on Kelvin to come downstairs.

He walks up behind me moments later and asks, "Are you ready, sweetie?"

We walk out of the room together to meet Cindy, who is standing outside of the door tapping away on her cell phone. She quickly puts the phone away as she shows us the vending machines, icemaker, emergency exits and stairwell. We take the elevator down several floors to what looks like an underground spa and indoor pool.

"This area is open all night. You just have to use your door key to access it from the elevator." She shows us a heated pool, a sauna, and an exercise room. There are no windows in this area, as it appears we are below the main structure of the building. We walk out of a side door, which leads upstairs to the main floor. We walk past the main lobby to an area of stores you would typically find in an outlet mall, and there are several gift shops. The stores opened at ten A.M., yet there aren't many people roaming around. I guess 11:30 is too early to be shopping when you're at a beautiful place like this.

I also see a huge bakery, which is open, and three different restaurants—one specializing in steaks, the other in seafood, and the third restaurant is the resort's main eatery and it is open 24/7 serving breakfast, lunch, and dinner.

"The hotel has four pools scattered throughout the resort. The pools in the back are more private and for adults only. I'll let you guys explore that on your own. We have scuba diving and an aquarium on site if you're interested. We have the brochures up front."

Cindy informs us there will be a party tonight at the adults-only pool at sundown. There will be live music, cocktails, and prizes. "It's somewhat formal for a pool party and only adults are invited. If you need something to wear, go to Ling's boutique in the mall area. She has some nice things in there. Well, that concludes the tour. Here's my card if you need anything or have any questions. I'll be around."

We thank her and watch as she walks back into the main lobby.

"Formal pool party?" I question.

Kelvin smiles at me and pulls me close to him. "Are you hungry?"

"Famished," I reply.

"Steak, or seafood?" he asks.

"Steak."

He grabs my hand as we walk back toward the mall area where the three restaurants are located. Cindy gave a very detailed tour, and this place and it is truly awesome. I wonder if it was really a part of her job description to show us around the resort.

Kelvin and I order steak dinners, which come with loaded baked potatoes and salads. The restaurant has a very royal look, yet everyone is dressed casually. The steak is tasty. With full bellies, we take a stroll through the mall area and visit Lang's Boutique.

Cindy was right. The boutique has many nice things from jewelry to swimsuits to fancy swim cover-ups, and a huge selection of flat rhinestone and high heeled sandals. She even has menswear. I grab a couple of the swimsuit cover-ups and a tan-and-black two-piece swimsuit then enter the dressing room in the back of the store.

The first cover-up I try on is a black sleeveless tassel design. The tassels fall just below my hips, and it hangs in a way that it contours to my body, very sexy, I think. The second is more like a tank top—it's is white, and it scoops down deep at the neck area, revealing a lot of cleavage. It's a crochet lace cover-up tunic, according to the tag. I like both of them, and they are priced reasonably.

Kelvin walks up to the dressing room door. "Did you find anything that you like?" he asks.

I walk out in the tan-and-black bathing suit and the white cover-up. Kelvin's eyes practically bulge out of his head. "Baby, take it off and hand it to me. I'm buying it for you to wear tonight."

I smile and do as he advised. Once I come back out of the dressing room, he grabs the black cover-up from my arm also. "Do you see anything else you like?" he asks.

I walk over to the shoes and pick out a high-heeled metallic silver-and-black sandal. Then I move on to the jewelry section and grab some nice hooped earrings and a few long dangling silver necklaces. As I walk toward Kelvin, he hands me a little basket to place the jewelry into.

"Thanks, Kelvin. I'm going to buy this jewelry," I say to him.

He stares at me for a few seconds before asking, "Why?"

"I don't want you spending too much money on me. You paid for this nice resort..." I rattle off.

He stops me midway, "Baby—" he takes the basket—"listen, I'm going to pay for all of this, and anything else you want for the remainder of the trip." He gazes at me with a slight smile. "This isn't a burden for me. This is something I want to do for you—for us, for our relationship." He walks up to the counter, and the girl behind the register rings everything up for us.

"Will that be all?" she asks, looking at us.

Kelvin looks my way. "I'm good," I reply.

"Your total comes to $215."

Kelvin pulls out his debit card and pays for all of the merchandise.

Once we're back in our room, he hands me the bags. I set them on the storage bench just inside the door, then look up at Kelvin, and we lock eyes. "You are too good to me," I say to him. "Thanks for all of this...this vacation and the things you bought for me downstairs."

Kelvin pulls me into him and kisses me softly on the lips, then he says, "It's not a problem, baby. I want to show you how much you mean to me. If I could, I would give you the world. I'll let you put your things up. I'm going to take a shower then watch a little television."

"Okay," I say to him. He grabs my hand briefly, then walks away.

I head upstairs to the closet and put everything away. While putting things up, I noticed that he purchased himself some black-and-gray swim shorts with a black top and matching flip-flops. I neatly fold his things and place them in the drawer.

CHAPTER 21—THE POOL PARTY

I awake to find Kelvin lying beside me in the bed. When did he get here? Last I remember, I decided to relax a little after putting things away. Kelvin was downstairs watching television. I look at the clock, and it reads seven thirty P.M. I get up and walk down stairs, brush my teeth, and turn on the shower. After pinning my hair up, I rub my facial cream in a circular motion on my cheeks and forehead. I notice I feel so alive standing in the mirror looking back at my reflection. I am in this beautiful resort with a man I absolutely adore and who I feels adores me the same, and I just can't think of anything that could ruin this moment or feeling for me.

I rinse my face off and sit on the bench to rub some Nair hair removal on my legs. Once I have both legs thoroughly covered in the pink cream, I get up to wash my hands. I wet my feet, lather some soap on the bottom of my heel, and I grab my pumice scrub and begin exfoliating while sitting on the edge of the sink. After I'm done with my feet, I organize and clean the sink area, open the shower door, and step in. The water is pouring out so powerfully. It feels like a massage to all of the muscles in my body. I take my towel, lather it up with the hotel's body wash, which smells like roses, and proceed to clean every inch of my skin.

Just as I'm about to turn around to shut the water off, Kelvin opens the shower door and walks in. He doesn't say a word, he places a condom over his already erect penis, and moves in closer to me, kisses my lips gently, then pauses holding his mouth to mine, waiting. I wrap my arms around his neck pulling him down toward me and continue the slow, seductive caresses. Before long, my legs

147

are wrapped around his slender body, and he is leaning me against the shower wall and slowly penetrating me. He begins to grind in and out of me. It is like a slow dance where both of our rhythms are perfectly in sync.

I can feel myself reaching my peak. My moans are getting louder, and he is keeping his pace slow, stroking in and out of me, kissing my neck, squeezing my breasts. This drives me wild. I love it when he plays with my breasts while penetrating me. I can feel my body pulsating all around him. He thrusts harder and more deliberate, hitting my G-spot, prolonging my orgasm.

Shortly after I have cum, I hear his moans, and I can feel his penis jerking, releasing inside of me, he thrusts a few more times, then holds me up against the wall, my legs still wrapped around him. He kisses my shoulder and positions me back toward the water, slowly. I put my legs down one at a time and let the warm water cascade over my satisfied body. As I take the hand towel to lather it up- preparing to wash his body- he disposes of the condom. Kelvin smiles at me, then closes his eyes as I shampoo skin gently. When I look down to wash his private area, I can see his erection has returned. I smile at him, then open the shower door to exit, handing the towel over to him.

He grabs the towel and raises that arm in the air, "Baby, you're just going to leave me like this?" he asks very seductively holding his penis in his other hand, rubbing it.

"You are just being greedy, and we have a party to attend." I rush out the shower before he tries to pull me back into his sexual web.

I rub lotion over my body, take my partially wet hair down, and braid a French braid across the top. Then I put some Jam on the edges of my hair, taking a brush to pull down some baby hairs. I pull the rest of it up into a high ponytail. It looks very retro. I put some pink blush on my cheeks and mascara on my eyelashes, spray some body fragrance on and go upstairs to put on my black-and-tan bathing suit with the black tassel cover-up. I grab my black stiletto heeled sandals and sit on the bed to put them on. When I look into the mirror, I am so happy for the look I accomplished, a sexy, sassy, glowing woman. My breasts look good in the bathing suit; the cover-up accents my curves, and it looks like a party dress. The heels bring out the calf muscles in my legs and brings attention to my thighs. I walk back into the closet and grab the silver-hooped earrings and long dangling necklaces as a final addition.

"Perfect," I say to myself, then grab Kelvin's clothing and shoes and walk downstairs.

I walk into the bathroom, and Kelvin eyes me from the mirror as he is brushing his teeth. He turns around, "Baby, you look hot."

I spin around for him a couple of times, and he just leans back on the sink admiring my new look. "So you like the outfit?"

"I like you in the outfit," he says slowly as he rinses his mouth and walks over to me with a towel wrapped around his waist, puts his arms around me, and pulls me close to him. "You left me wanting more, and now looking at you, I don't know if I can wait." He presses himself against me, and I can feel his erection.

I kiss his lips softly. "I will take care of you tonight, Kelvin. Get dressed." I pull away from him and hand him is clothes and walk out of the bathroom. I can feel him staring at me as I walk off.

As Kelvin and I step off the elevator, we walk the opposite way of the lobby then outside toward the pool. It looks completely different from the main pool area near the front. Two adjoining pools are lit up, which gives it a seductive and mysterious glow. Women dressed in bikinis are walking around with champagne on trays offering it to the guests. Men dressed in Speedos are walking around with appetizers, which consist of crab cakes, cheese, olives, and grapes. *This is not a formal party,* I think reflecting on what Cindy said.

Kelvin grabs two glasses of champagne off the tray. The woman holding the tray stops and looks at Kelvin a little longer than she should, according to my standards. He smiles at her and turns to hand me my drink. I can sense he's wondering if I noticed her flirting with him. I choose to ignore what just happened and the ping of jealousy I feel for the first time in regards to him, which I must say is a new emotion for me because I use to believe I wasn't the jealous type.

As we scope the scene, we notice people are dressed a little less conservative than we are. Women have bathing suit tops on that seem to only be covering their nipples, and there's a lot of butt cheeks showing on both the men and women. Most of the men are topless, and even the staff is loosely dressed. Behind the bar, the waiter has on an apron and nothing else. The reason I know this is because when he turns around, all of his back, including his butt is exposed. Then I see a familiar face.

"Hi. You guys made it," Cindy says, smiling at us, wearing a see-through cover-up with a skimpy bathing suit underneath.

"Hi, Cindy. What type of party is this?" I ask her.

"It's the kind where anything goes." She stares at Kelvin as she says this, then says, "Have fun." And just like that, she is off mingling. Kelvin looks very interested in the scene, but for some reason, I'm not in the party mood.

"Sweetie, let's go to the bar and order some food and some real drinks," he says.

"Can you order me another strawberry daiquiri? I'm going to have a seat over here." I point to a table in the corner that seems secluded enough.

"Are you okay?" he asks.

"Yes," I reply as I walk over to the small round table with two chairs and sit. This area reminds me of being in Italy. It is quaint, romantic, and it has a single rose in the center of the table in a small glass vase. I feel like I need to gather my thoughts. I am picking up on so much right now psychically that it makes me feel as if I am flickering in and out of reality, which is making me kind of dizzy.

I can see Kelvin in view chatting with the friendly blond-haired bartender and glancing back at me once in a while. In this moment, I just feel like I want to run off somewhere to escape my escape. Kelvin walks back over with our drinks.

"Do you want to sit closer, baby, so we're with the crowd?"

"No. I'm good here." I look at him, and I can see he's in a very social mood and is totally feeling the vibe of this party. "You can mingle. I'll be around after I get a little liquor into my system, then we can eat."

"You sure?" he asks.

"Positive. I'll catch up with you," I respond.

Just like that, he's off mingling, smiling, and toasting drink glasses with strangers. I sit there for a while trying to sort through what I feel, as I take a sip of my daiquiri. It seems as if, the more I drink and the more I think, the more unnerved I feel. I don't know what is wrong with me. Why am I feeling stressed on my vacation?

I look down at my phone, and I get a text message from William: *Hi Love. Casey is out on bond. I don't know who bailed her out.*

I call William. "What?"

"Yes. I found out today she was out. I had my locks changed on my doors, and I changed the alarm code," William says.

"Wow. So how's everything else with you?" I say, trying to change the subject from a deeply disturbing one to something a little lighter.

"Okay, I guess. Where are you? I hear music."

"I'm in Key West. Just needed to get away for a few days," I reply, sounding gloomy.

"Okay, well, is it helping? You sound sad," William says.

"We just got here earlier today. We're at a pool party, and all of the people are half naked. I don't know how I feel about it. Everything is so exposed."

"Sounds like my kind of party," William says.

"Actually, it's exactly your kind of party." I add with a chuckle.

"Well, what's the problem, love? Is Kelvin there with you?"

"Yes. He's mingling. He looks to be having a good time. I don't know what's wrong with me. All of a sudden, I just felt sad, and like I want to withdraw."

"Can you video phone me and show me the party scene?" William asks sincerely.

I hang up and call him on the video phone. He is sitting at a desk with a t-shirt on.

"You look beautiful, love. Stand up so I can see your whole outfit." I stand and move the phone so he can see me from head to toe.

"Breathtaking. Why did Kelvin leave you there alone?"

"I told him to go. I was feeling anti-social, I told you." I flip the camera around so he can see the people and the party scene. I get up because I realize I don't see Kelvin anywhere. I'm not panicked, but I do feel the need to find him. As I walk through the crowd, I feel more estranged and the need to disconnect comes back strongly.

I can hear William talking to me over the video phone. "Thanks for inviting me, Sabine. I feel like I'm there," he says. I have the phone pointed in the direction of the crowd as I'm walking through searching for Kelvin.

"Thanks for being my cyber date," I respond to William, finding it strange that I feel comforted when I talk to him. As I walk through the crowd, I see people dancing so close they may as well be having sex—they are half-naked anyway. Then I stop in total shock as I see Kelvin dancing with Cindy very seductively. He has her leg up around his waist, and he is grinding her like he did with me in the shower minutes ago. I almost drop the phone. I quickly switch the phone around.

William asks, "Was that Kelvin?"

"I've gotta go, William. I'll call you back." Instead of confronting Kelvin like I normally would have done, I run away. Chills are shooting through my body, and tears are running down my cheeks. I'm not quite sure how I feel, but I know that was totally inappropriate. I walk off toward the beach to gather my thoughts. I am wondering if Kelvin and I moved too quickly. Why would he do this? Now, I feel hurt, betrayal, disrespected, and wonder why he rushed to start this relationship with me if he just wants to play. I contemplate going upstairs, packing my bag, and leaving.

I walk back toward the resort but around through the front entrance because I can't bear to see Kelvin right now. I come to the front entrance and walk through the lobby and downstairs to the heated pool area. I take off my cover-up and heels and step into the pool. The water is so warm that it feels as if I'm in the arms of my beloved, which at this point, I'm not sure who that is.

Then like flashes or visions, I see them together— Kelvin and Cindy. They are somewhere outside taking off their clothes, kissing passionately. Each vision makes me sick to the stomach, but for some reason, the visions keep streaming, and I see him squeezing her breasts, I see her reaching into his pants. I scream, trying to shake the vision from my head. Just as I'm stepping out of the pool, I bump into a man.

"I'm sorry to intrude. Are you okay?" he asks.

"I'm fine." I walk past him and into the restroom to splash some cold water on my face. "What is this?" I ask myself in the mirror. My heart is in my stomach. My mind goes back to the vision. I see Kelvin pulling away from the kiss. It's as if he is looking at me in my mind's eye. He says my name. I send the message out, "Fuck you, Kelvin. Better yet, go fuck Cindy." I walk out of the bathroom and grab a towel off the shelf near the pool.

The man I bumped into earlier asks, "Do you need to talk? You seem upset."

"I'm fine," I say with animosity directed toward Kelvin as I turn away from him gathering my things.

"We can talk. If you're upset, I can just listen." I turn to face him, and he looks at me. "It's best not to be alone when you're distressed like this. We can go to the lobby to talk," he says peacefully. I pause for a few minutes as I put my cover-up on, pat my legs dry and pick up my heels.

"Okay," I finally respond. He guides me very gently upstairs to the main lobby, which is practically empty as everyone is outside partying.

"Are you cold?" he asks me.

"A little." He takes off his suit jacket and places it over my shoulders, then walks over to the area that has coffee and teas. He comes back with two cups of hot water and an assortment of flavored teas. I smile at him and grab the orange-cherry blossom tea bag, open it, and dip it into my cup of hot water.

"So, do you work here?" I ask.

"Yes. I'm the manager on duty tonight. I was doing my nightly checks when I saw you down at the pool by yourself, and you looked distraught. Are you alone?"

I swirl my tea bag around in my cup, looking down the whole

time, then I look up at him. He's a gorgeous older man—could be in his mid-fifties—very distinguished, and it feels like he has a pure heart. "I came here with someone. I will most likely be leaving alone. How far is the airport from here?"

"The Key West International Airport is about fifteen minutes away. You don't want to try and work things out with your friend?" he asks.

"We have only been dating for a little while now, but we moved things along fast. Now, I'm not so sure about how things have played out. I just don't understand. I'm not even sure if what I feel or saw was true."

"Well, before you make any rash decisions, talk to him first. If you want me to book you a flight tomorrow, I can do that." He slides his card to me. It reads, Michael Snapps, Manager. He stands and brings back a plate of chocolate croissants. "Eat. I'll be around. If you need someone to talk to, my cell phone number is on the back of the card." He touches my shoulder and walks away.

I flip the card over to see he has written his cell number down. I eat a few of the croissants and drink all of my tea. After I have cleaned my mess, I walk out of the front door of the resort, looking around in admiration at the beautiful landscaping, admiring the variety of different colored flowers and different shaped bushes. This is a great distraction, a technique I learned when I use to have panic attacks: Focus your attention on something outside of yourself.

The walkway is lit up, and that bridge up ahead looks enchanting, like it's calling me to it. My cell phone rings. It's Kelvin. I silence it and walk over toward the bridge, feeling nice and cozy in the jacket Michael let me borrow. Maybe I need this time alone to process everything that has occurred in the past few days, weeks, and months. I've been running myself ragged trying to balance everything. Perhaps it's time to take care of Sabine. I look down at my phone, and I have two text messages. One from Kelvin and one from William.

I click on William's first. It reads, *Lady, are you okay? Call me if you need to talk.* Then Kelvin's, *Sabine, where are you? Did you go back to the room?*

In my mind, I think, *Wouldn't you like to know? Keep sucking face with Cindy!* I write back, *I am not feeling well; I just need some time alone.*

Then I text William back, *I'm fine. Just processing.* I walk along the path literally thinking on nothing, just focusing on objects outside of myself, the sky, the stars, a rock. Eventually, I circled to the front of the resort. My mind is blank.

When I look at my phone, I realize it's late; I have been walking for an hour and a half. I have ten missed calls from Kelvin and text messages to follow. Where did the time go, and where did I go?

I walk into the resort. Kelvin walks up to me looking extremely concerned and baffled at the same time. "Where have you been, Sabine? I called you a trillion times. I was worried."

I walk past him, take the jacket off and walk up to Michael who is now at the front desk and hand it to him. "Thank you, sir," I say and smile. He nods. Kelvin follows me as I continue to walk toward the elevator. I push the button and turn around. "I was taking a walk. I told you in my text I wasn't feeling well, I just needed some air."

"For over an hour?" His voice gets higher, yet his tone is controlled and even, his hands motioning in the air as he asks the question.

"Yes," I say, monotone as I walk into the elevator.

He turns me toward him and looks me in the eyes. He is searching to see what I know. He tries to pull me in close to him, but I step away. The elevator door opens and I exit, and he runs to catch up with me. When we get to the door, he asks calmly, "Baby, what's the matter? Did I do something wrong?"

I look at him and respond, "I don't know, did you?" I open the door, go straight to the bathroom, and lock the door. I sit on the bench thinking about my walk. It's as if I zoned out for an hour and a half. Where did I go? How did I lose time? Kelvin knocks on the door after trying to open it.

"Sweetie, can you unlock the door, please? I just want to talk.

I won't try to invade your thoughts." I open the door and sit back on the bench. Kelvin walks over, sits right beside me, and doesn't say a word.

"I'm sorry. I really lost track of time," I say to him. "I didn't mean to make you worry." He places his hand on top of mine, and I snatch away without even thinking about what I'm doing. He looks me in the eyes, searching again, trying to get a read on me. I can feel he can't because I've officially disconnected from him and from everything else in the past hour or so. I stand and turn the shower water on, pin my ponytail up, and jump in the shower. Kelvin sits on the bench for a few minutes, then exits the bathroom.

Once I'm upstairs, I contemplate getting in bed next to Kelvin, he isn't asleep, but laying on his back staring at the ceiling. Gently, I slide into bed and lay my head on his chest. Even though I am highly peeved off, I still want to be next to him. He slowly wraps his arms around me and begin to speak. "I only stepped away because you told me it was okay," Kelvin says slowly. "Cindy started dancing with me." He drifts off in thought, "Maybe we took things a little too far."

"How far did you take things?" I ask.

Kelvin sits up. "Look, Sabine, I'm not going to lie to you. I don't know what I was thinking or why I even engaged that woman, but it meant nothing."

"What meant nothing, Kelvin? What did you do?" Kelvin's breathing has changed to deep suctions of breath, and he has a look of anguish on his face.

"Listen, maybe we're moving too fast. I barely know you," I say to him.

"No. Sabine, I love you, and this is moving at a perfect pace."

"Then why, Kelvin? I don't understand. I saw you dancing with Cindy, her leg propped up around you. Then..." I trail off, remembering the visions, not sure if I should talk about them. "How do I know it's real between us?" I ask with a strain in my heart as I hear myself say the words.

"It's real, baby." He takes my hand and places it on his chest.

"My heart beats only for you. One love, one heart, one mind, remember?"

"Kelvin, did you sleep with her?"

He looks at me with pleading eyes. "No, but we came pretty close."

I feel myself choking back tears, and my heart feels like it is in my stomach. Kelvin pulls me to his chest. "I'm so sorry, baby. Please forgive me."

CHAPTER 22—THE AFTERMATH

I wake up the next morning and walk down stairs into the bathroom. My face is so puffy from crying. I start my normal morning routine: brush my teeth, do my facial, and jump in the shower. I plug my flat irons up, blow my hair dry, and use the flat irons to make loose curls throughout. I lather my body with lotion and lightly blush my cheeks, then walk back upstairs and put on one of the sundresses I brought with me. Kelvin is not in our hotel room.

With my purse in my hand, I grab the key card and go to the resort's main restaurant to order breakfast. I am numb and feel empty from the night before. All I want to do is eat and fill myself up with something of substance. I load my plate up at the breakfast bar with bacon, pancakes, sausage, eggs, and grapes. I head back to the table to drop my plate off, then back in the direction of the coffee. As I pour my coffee, I realize how hollow the inside of my chest feels. It's almost hard to breathe. After walking back to the table, I see Kelvin at the entranceway searching the room. When he spots me, he walks over to me. "Hi, baby."

"Good morning," I reply and continue eating breakfast.

"I went for a walk this morning on the beach to think about things."

"About your sexpedition last night with Cindy?" I stare at him blankly, then go on to say, "What I don't understand is why you brought me here. If you want to be with other people, why commit to me?"

"Sabine, I don't want to be with other people. I want you, and we did not have sex. Please, find it in your heart to forgive me."

"I knew something was off the moment I stepped into that party. We should have just left, but then I wouldn't have been given the insight about you I needed."

"What do you mean?" Kelvin asks, looking apprehensive and hurt.

"I mean, I wouldn't have noticed you weren't the faithful type. I could see you on the beach with her. At first, I couldn't tell if it was my imagination running away with me. Now I know it was insight into what you were doing in that moment. You're bold to do that when we were at the same party," I say in disgust.

Kelvin rubs his fingers through his hair. "Baby, I know this isn't an excuse, but I was a little impaired. I wasn't fully aware of what I was doing, and I wasn't thinking clearly. I got caught up." I look at him and shake my head. "I'm sorry I made you cry. I'm sorry I gave you the impression I wanted Cindy and not you. I'm sorry you saw what you saw," he says. I continue eating. "We're going to get past this. You're the only woman I truly desire on every level, Seme." Kelvin says the last few words very slowly and measured. "I'll make it up to you. I promise."

"What made you stop?" I ask him, feeling my heart soften a little because of his admission and apology. He looks baffled, and I proceed, "I mean, why didn't you go all the way with Cindy? I saw you and her kissing and you grabbing her breasts. I saw her reach into your swim trunks and grip your penis. Then everything went blank. How do I know you guys didn't go all the way?"

"I stopped because it wasn't what I wanted. I realized what I was doing and even questioned myself as to why it was happening." Kelvin goes into deep thought as if he's trying to put himself back in the situation. "I had no intentions of going to this party and having sex with anybody but you. I could feel that I was hurting you, and I could feel you tuning into me. Then, all I felt was disgust for the situation and myself. It was uncalled for, and it isn't what I wanted. I can show you what happened." I think about what he is asking me to allow, then realize how I feel can't get any worse.

"Okay," I reply. He moves over next to me and breathes a sigh of relief that he's finally close to me again. He reaches for me to come close. I lean into him, our foreheads touching. It's like a movie playing but only showing the highlights, more like a preview.

I see Kelvin getting our drinks from the bar, him bringing mine back to me. He is walking away as he continues to look back at me. He mingles in the crowd and dances a little, downing his drink then another. Cindy is eyeing him. She walks over to him with another drink and hands it to him. They are dancing a little and talking a lot, but I can't make out what they're saying to each other.

They both put their empty glasses on the tray and begin a seductive dance. Before long, her leg is up around his hip, and they are both caught in a sexual web of desire and passion. I can feel the sexual energy coming from both of them. I almost want to pull away because I just can't stomach the fact that Kelvin is having these feelings for someone else when he is so dear to my heart.

Just as I'm about to pull away, Kelvin says, "Watch, Sabine." He holds me close to him, rubbing my lower back.

Cindy leads him off to the beach, and he looks somewhat torn between his arousal and his loyalty, as if the reality of what he is doing is starting to sink into his mind. They begin kissing slowly, then more passionately. They both fall to the sand, he is squeezing and rubbing her breasts, and she's going into his pants, mimicking what I saw when I was at the heated pool tuning into him.

Kelvin stands. His lips are moving. It looks as though he is mouthing, "I can't do this, I've gotta go." She looks like she's yelling at him. He walks away and goes back to the spot where I was, notices I'm not there, then walks through the crowd looking for me. He walks through the lobby then goes upstairs to the room. When he comes back down to the lobby, he bumps into Michael, the manager on duty that night. They talk for a while. Michael motions toward the front door. Kelvin walks out and doesn't see me. Michael offers him some water to help sober him up.

I pull away from Kelvin.

"Everything you saw is all that happened," he says.

"Well, it was a lot." I pause. "Thank you for not sleeping with her." Tears fill my eyes.

Kelvin wipes them away with his thumb and forefinger before they fall. "We are going to get past this, I promise. You'll see."

I feel betrayal in the sense that when you're dating someone, you hope during that timeframe you're the only one they desire to the fullest. It's upsetting I could feel the sexual pull between the two of them. I felt he wanted to have sex with Cindy. Besides that, I question if Cindy had the intention on sleeping with Kelvin the whole time. She seemed so professional when we first met her.

"What did Cindy say to you on the beach?" I ask.

He hesitates before responding, "She said you wouldn't have to know—that this could be a one-time thing, that I was passing up a wonderful opportunity. She questioned how many men get to play with a woman while they're in a relationship with no strings attached."

I look at him. "How did you respond to that?"

Kelvin looks as if he is carefully choosing his words. "I told her she was very bold—that I was not in the business of cheating on my girlfriend."

I eat the sausage and bacon off my plate and cut into the pancakes. "Aren't you going to get something to eat?" I ask Kelvin.

"Can I have a bite from your plate?" he asks, staring into my eyes. I take another bite, then cut into my pancakes slowly, then I lift the fork up to his mouth. He places his lips around the food and slides it off the fork slowly. As he chews, he stares at me the whole time accessing my mood and me in general. "I like your hair, baby." He rubs my hair and smiles.

"I think I'm going to have pancakes and an omelet," he says, still looking at me. "Maybe after breakfast we can go to a movie?"

"Maybe," I reply, not able to stifle the smile forming across my face. I smile because in this moment, I realize forgiveness is crucial to my healing. No matter how angry I am at Kelvin, I am humbled by this experience. His honesty and self-expression takes me through what I feel is a purification process. I surrender myself to the reality that he's presented to me. My ego is put to the back burner due to him acknowledging my feelings and me facing my fears. I return to the completeness in which I am, by shedding the false perceptions of the situation.

"I'll take a maybe," he says as he stands and walks over to the omelet station, looking back at me in between telling the guy what he wants in his eggs. In that moment, I make up my mind to let it go, and it is done. I realize that this experience is somehow helping me in my healing process. Not just from the situation from last night, but from the hurt I endured with Richard. I realize that it wasn't the fact that my ex was absent during the time that I needed him, it had more to do with us not laying everything out in front of each other, and surrendering to the situation. The act of surrendering is a sign of forgiveness. Kelvin laid out his wrong doings, and I have the opportunity to decide, and I choose him. I choose love. I rise up above the drama, face my fears, which has to do with the insecurity or lack that comes from a lower place and past experiences. That lacks says, "You are not enough for him". In essence, by letting go of my traditional beliefs, I take a leap of faith on the proverbial edge and just believe in a possible new life with Kelvin. Who said this would be easy?

After breakfast, we drive to an outlet mall that has a theater within the plaza. Kelvin purchases tickets for a show that starts at one o'clock, so we have about an hour to spare. To pass some time away, he suggests we walk across the way to the mall. Once we're in one of the stores, Kelvin strides over to the women's section and picks out two pairs of high-rise skinny jeans for me to try on.

"It's my turn to be your personal shopping assistant," he says as he hands me the jeans.

The first pair I try on have a stonewash look to them with rips up and down the thigh. They fit very snug, and the material is very comfortable. I look at the tag. They call these Alisha High Rise Skinny Jeans, priced at thirty-eight dollars. Not bad, I think as I whirl around in the mirror picturing the type of shoes or top I could wear with them.

The second pair are called Tahiana High Rise Skinny Jeans, and they're a wash blue color, and the texture is stretchy, they stop right at my ankles. I could probably wear flat shoes with these and heels with the other.

When I exit the dressing room, Kelvin is holding up a purse. It's hot pink with a long strap and two short straps and the logo hanging on a silver chain. I grab it from him as he takes the jeans from me. I open the purse and notice there's a matching wallet inside. I love this purse; I go to the mirror and model holding it as a handbag with the two straps and then putting it on my shoulder and turning around to look at myself with it.

Kelvin walks over. "You like?"

"I love it," I say as I hand the purse over to him.

"Go try on a few tops," he says as he walks the jeans and the purse over to the register.

After browsing around the store, I don't find anything else appealing. Kelvin walks up to me with a bag in his hand.

"Are you ready, sweetie? The movie starts in fifteen minutes." I grab his arm, and we walk out of the store and to his jeep to put the bag in the backseat, and then to the theater.

Once we're in our seats, I excuse myself to the ladies' room. I come back into the theater with a ton of junk food from the concession stand; a pretzel, nachos, Milk Duds, and frozen blueberry drinks. Kevin smiles at me as I hand off the tray to him that houses the drinks and the nachos. I bite into the pretzel as I sit down then place it near his lips for him to take a bite.

"Thank you for the jeans and the purse. I really appreciate it," I say as I lean my head on his chest and kiss his neck softly.

He inhales deeply then replies by kissing me on the top of my head.

CHAPTER 23—THE RIDE BACK HOME

The next morning, I wait on Kelvin at the mini bar as he checks us out of the room. I drink my last strawberry daiquiri, savoring every sip. Before walking our bags out to the car, Kelvin tells me to wait on him in the lobby—that he will pull the car up to the front. He bends to kiss me on the lips and instead steals a sip of my drink. As he walks off, I swat at his butt and miss. He turns around and flashes those pearly whites at me, melting my heart.

I get up to use the restroom. I walk back out into the main lobby, I take one last look around at this gorgeous place and think, *I am going to miss this.* To my surprise or maybe it was the Universe rewarding me, I see Cindy for the first time since that night. She's holding a tray of drinks for the newly arriving guests. She is standing at the front entrance of the resort, and just past her outside, Kelvin has pulled up. I walk over to the tray and reach for a glass. Cindy turns to face me.

Her expression changes from a smile to a look of concern when she recognizes me, then she says, "I really hope you enjoyed your stay here at the resort" in her fake professional tone.

"It was great. Thank you. Kelvin sends his regards." I smile then flip the whole tray of drinks on her as I walk past casually.

When I open my car door, I turn to look back at her, and she's still standing there in shock, as if she can't believe I just did that. I smile with the deepest feelings of satisfaction. Just as I'm about to get in the car, Michael, the manager of the resort, walks over to me and reaches out to shake my hand.

"I take it that the rest of your stay went well," he says.

"It did. Thank you for everything," I reply.

"My pleasure," he responds and hands me an envelope. "A little gift on behalf of the hotel for any inconvenience you may have undergone. It's a coupon for a free couples massage on your next visit."

I reach out to give him a hug. He whispers a certain employee will be dismissed today. He glances over at Cindy.

"How did you know?" I ask.

"This isn't the first time an incident like this has happened with her, just never under my watch. I was the manager on duty that night; I see mostly everything that goes on, and I don't turn a blind eye on things involving matters of the heart. What one person views as a sick game can cause a great deal of harm to an unsuspecting couple."

After I sit in the car, Michael closes the door behind me and waves his good-byes. As he walks away, I can see him through the side mirror on Kelvin's jeep. He walks straight past Cindy without helping her pick up the broken glass. I watch Cindy on her hands and knees looking for shards of glass and placing them on the tray.

Kelvin asks, "Did you knock that tray out of her hand?"

I shrug.

Kelvin smiles, shakes his head and looks to the road.

We arrive home at seven P.M. on Friday. I go inside to unpack our bags. Kelvin informs me he's going to the office to check in on things and will be back shortly. I kiss him good-bye and tell him to be careful as he did all of the driving coming back, so I know he's exhausted.

After putting everything away, I go into the kitchen to prepare some dinner. I decide on eggplant parmesan. I check the refrigerator to make sure I have some key ingredients—eggplant, ground turkey, Prego sauce, eggs, breadcrumbs, and ricotta and mozzarella cheese. I text Kelvin to let him know I'm cooking dinner and it will be ready in one hour. After I place the eggplant parmesan in the oven, I go off to the bathroom to shower and prepare for the night.

As I look in the mirror, I think on where Kelvin's sexual frustration level must be at this point, and it makes me laugh a little. Maybe I did overreact to Cindy's attempt to come on to him. Sometimes having a gift can be a curse. Me feeling the sexual energy between the two and seeing the visions of what they almost did made me look at the act at a higher frequency than another person would have viewed it. To anybody else, this would have probably been an argument about how close and inappropriate he was dancing with her. For me, as and empath, picking up on the energy of other people makes me want to retreat or escape sometimes, which is what I did at the party, and it made things worse between Kelvin and me. Sometimes having insight into a situation isn't always the solution. I have to learn how to tune some things out when it comes to Kelvin and express my concerns right away, out loud, when it comes to him.

I'm glad to know Cindy was the culprit in this particular situation, and in the end Kelvin resisted. Nevertheless, I had to punish him. We haven't had sex since before that incident, and I know he's feeling it. I noticed at the movies when I gave him a thank-you kiss on the neck; I felt the surge of sexual energy, which I chose to ignore. I also noticed when we went to the aquarium after the movies and he cornered me in a secluded area. He stood so close I could feel his erection. Yeah, I engaged in his soft kisses, but I ignored his needs. It's a shame because he has been so good to me...well, minus Cindy.

I walk into the kitchen to take the eggplant parmesan out of the oven to cool. I pour two glasses of white wine and set out two plates. I quickly run back into the room to change into a sexy nightgown, put some heels on, and fluff my hair around my face, then walk back into the kitchen, I cut the eggplant parmesan into squares and place a slice on each of our plates.

I light two candles at the table and dim the kitchen lights just as I hear Kelvin walk in. I can hear him take his shoes off and hang his keys on the hook that reads "His." He walks down the short hallway and makes his way into the kitchen to find me sitting on the table holding his wineglass out to him.

He smiles, walks over to me, and grabs the wineglass. "What is this, baby?"

"Dinner." I get off the table, walk to his side, and pull the chair out for him. He sits and takes a few gulps of wine.

"I made eggplant parmesan."

"I can't wait to try it," he says, looking at me.

I say a small prayer. "God, thank you for this food in which we are about to receive. I pray it nourishes our bodies. In Jesus' name. Amen."

Kelvin takes a bite, closes his eyes and groans, then says, "This is excellent."

"Thanks," I reply with a smile, really pleased he's enjoying the food. He gets a second plate with two pieces, gobbles that down, and finishes two glasses of wine. Because I'm a much slower eater, I'm still on my first and most likely, only plate.

"Sabine, dinner was excellent." He gets up and takes his plate to the sink. "I'm going to take a quick shower."

I stand, walk over to him at the sink, and hug him from behind. "Don't take too long . . . I want you," I whisper to him. He turns around and kisses me on the lips, lifts me up onto the counter, and pulls me in close to him. I wrap my legs around his body.

"I could skip the shower," he says as he walks to the bedroom with me wrapped around him. He lays me down gently and commences to take off his clothes. Once he is fully undressed, he crawls over to me on the bed and straddles over me naked. I grab at his hard penis as he bends down and kisses me, and I position his rock-hard penis near my sex. He presses slowly with each kiss until he is fully inside of me.

"Should I get a condom?" he asks.

"You can, but just so you know, I'm on the Pill."

He starts slow, opening me up and stretching my body until the fit feels perfect, then he lifts up a bit on his knees, spread his legs, pushes my legs up to my chest, and starts to pound me a little harder than usual. It feels divine, for lack of a better word.

He is in and out of me making my moist vagina wetter, grinding into me deeper and harder with each thrust. I try to wrap my legs around him, but he holds my upper thighs in the upright position.

He slows down his motion, but doesn't hold back on how deeply he's entering me. I can feel him about to cum. He lets my legs down, and I wrap them around him and thrust my hips upward toward his motions. Our bodies are rolling together in harmony, and I can feel myself building up to an orgasm. We both cry out at the same time. He falls asleep instantly.

CHAPTER 24—PREPARATION FOR THE PARTY

The next morning Kelvin is up and showered before I even think about getting out of bed. He walks over to me, kneels, and tells me he has to go in to work; I guess the vacation has set him back a few days. I remind him we have a Halloween party to attend tonight. I ask if he is okay with me picking out his costume. He smiles at me, pulls out $120 from his pocket and places it in my hand. "Do you think this will cover our costumes?"

"Yes, that's more than enough. Don't worry. I'll have you looking dapper."

"I'm a little worried, baby." He smiles and kisses my forehead. "Thanks for last night. You were great, and..." Kelvin pauses and looks into my eyes as he rubs my hair, then he says, "I'm truly sorry for hurting you, Sabine. I promise it won't happen again. Honestly, I don't know what got into me."

"I'm sorry if I overreacted. It's just that our connection is getting stronger, and the fact that we can tune into each other can be a gift and a curse." I say, not really knowing how to address the situation. He kisses my forehead, then he walks away. I can hear him open the front door and lock it behind him.

I call Sammie to check in on her, but she doesn't answer her phone. She texts me a few minutes later saying she's with a client but will call me in a few.

Next, I reach out to William. He answers right away. "Good morning, Seme. How are you?"

"Great! I'm getting ready to go shopping for costumes for your party tonight."

"You know they have a Halloween store out near my office with some pretty good costumes. I could meet you there if you are interested."

"That would be great. Do you know who you're dressing up as?" I ask William.

"I do. But, it's a surprise. Are you trying to make me ruin the suspense? That's partly why the party is so fun, trying to figure out who people are dressed as," Williams says lightheartedly. "Do you think you could go with me to pick up a few things for the party?"

"Sounds like a plan. Let me get dressed, and I'll call you when I get to that side of town."

"Well, why don't you come pick me up from my house? I'll text you my address," William says.

"Okay."

I'm wearing Alisha stone-washed jeans with the rips up the thighs, heeled black-and-silver sandals, and a white tank top with a white cover up, all purchased courtesy of Kelvin. In addition, I put on the silver-hoop earrings and dangling silver necklaces, and I am sporting my new pink purse.

I snap a picture with my camera phone and send a text to Kelvin. *Thank you, baby, for the spontaneous mini vacation. Do you like my outfit, courtesy of you?*

He calls me on the video phone. "Hi, Sabine. I love it. I love you in it." I hold the phone so he can view the entire outfit. "You're so beautiful, baby. Have fun shopping, and don't go too crazy with the costumes."

"I won't. Trust me."

"I love you, Sabine."

"I love you too, Kelvin."

I realize this is my first time visiting William at his home. I pull up into his driveway and admire his enormous two-story home for a little while before exiting the car. Minutes later, I walk up to the door and ring the bell. He answers on the first buzz.

"Wow. Sabine, you look beautiful."

"Thank you." I blush. "Your house is gorgeous."

"Do you want a tour?" William asks.

"Of course I do," I reply.

"Well, come in," he says as he holds the door open. I walk past him to what just seems like open space. I see a stairwell in front of me. The house has vaulted ceilings and skylights.

"This house is very spacious. I like the energy in it," I say as I walk around admiring the atmosphere. When I turn to face William, I realize he's closer than I initially thought, and I almost bump into him.

"I'm sorry. I didn't see you there," I say to him.

He smiles. "Do you want a tour of upstairs or downstairs first?"

"Upstairs, seeing as to how we're right at the stairwell."

"Ladies first." He motions for me to walk ahead of him. I begin walking up the winding staircase. When I get to the top, we're in a loft area, which has a minibar, a sofa, and a flat-screen sixty-inch television mounted on the wall.

"Nice. Are you in this area a lot?"

"Yes. This is one of my favorite spots." To the right is a full bathroom with a Jacuzzi tub. The bathroom is almost as big as the loft area. I look around and see a stand-up shower, one sink with a counter that stretches across the whole length of the bathroom.

"You definitely have enough counter space," I comment, running my hand across the countertop as I walk the length of the bathroom.

"It's for my guests. The master suite is downstairs," William comments, not looking at my face but more in the general direction of my hips.

There is a washroom with a full-size washer and dryer upstairs and two guest bedrooms across from each other. I open the door to look into one of the rooms. It is fully decked out with neutral colors and cherry oak wood furniture. When I open the door to the second room, it is just as beautiful as the first and decorated similarly, but the energy is different from the rest of the house. It feels stifling. I walk farther into the room, and it feels as if there is a weight on my chest.

"Is this the room that Casey stayed in?" I ask William.

"Yes. So, you can feel it too?" he asks.

"It's a suppressive energy. My heart feels heavy," I say as I move through the room. "Is it okay if I open this window?" I ask.

"Sure. Whatever you think will help... I had the cleaning staff detail the room, making it spotless, but it just doesn't feel the same."

"Beautiful room, horrible energy. Do you have a white candle?" I ask.

"Ummmm, yes. I'll get it." William walks out of the room and down the stairs.

As I walk through the room, feeling smothered every step I take, I set the intent on sending lower energies to the light for healing. When I walk up to the closet, I feel dread and fear. I know these aren't my emotions, so I push past them and open the door. Everything seems in place—empty hangers in the closet and a nicely vacuumed floor. I turn my focus to love. I think of every event in my life where I've felt unconditional love, and like flashes, they appear before my mind's eye. I expand that energy outward toward this room, this closet, this house, and William. *Dear God, please release any negative supernatural holds that are currently suppressing this space.* I breathe in the intent of it being done. William comes back with a white candle and some matches.

I take the candle from him, place it on the dresser, and light it. "Let this burn for a little while," I say to William. "Using the white candle brings healing to this space. It symbolizes lighting up the darkness. I use this as a tool, a visual representation, to clear out negative energies. Can I see the rest of the house?"

William nods and takes me on an extensive tour of his beautiful home, which looks like it's made for a family of five. After the tour is complete I comment, "William, your house is huge and beautiful. Where are the wife and kids?"

"Thanks, love. In time... Are you ready to go?"

"You don't have any pets, do you?" I ask.

"No. Why?" he questions.

"The candle we lit upstairs, can we let that burn while we're out?"

"Sure. Let me go close the window."

"I will meet you outside," I yell as William walks back upstairs.

William meets me at my car a few minutes later. "I could drive if you like," he offers.

"I'm good. Get in," I say as I walk over to the driver's side and open my door.

Our first stop is the liquor store. William buys cases of beer and wine. They fill my trunk and backseat. Then he has me stop by this fancy hotel where the party will be held so we can drop off the drinks. When I get out of the car, I grab a case of the beer and walk into the conference room, which is being decorated for tonight. William has two guys help him bring in the remaining cases of liquor inside.

We decide to eat before shopping. He suggests this nice intimate spot, which serves brunch with mimosas. "This place is romantic. Is this where you bring your dates?" I ask as I sit down in the booth.

He smiles. "Maybe."

The server brings the menus to us. I order a bacon-and-spinach quiche, and William orders a loaded meat lovers omelet.

"Listen, William, I want to apologize for missing our appointment on Thursday. That was unprofessional of me. I meant to tell you we had to reschedule, but so much happened on my vacation that it slipped my mind."

"It's okay, love. I knew you wouldn't be here for our appointment when you called me to tell me you were in Key West."

"That's the other thing: I feel like we are getting too close—I mean as friends—for me to be an effective counselor for you..." I trail off, looking for the words to describe what I'm trying to convey. "Well, I'll become biased the closer we get. A lot of counseling is having someone objective and somewhat detached," I finally manage to communicate to him.

"Sabine, are you trying to break up with me?" William asks just as the waiter comes back to our table with two glasses of mimosas and parfaits.

"Sort of." I laugh, then take several sips of my drink.

"I'm sorry, love. I don't accept. I'd like us to continue our counseling relationship and our friendship. I'm okay with you being biased toward me. These are my sessions, and this is what I want—you as my friend and counselor."

"Okay." I pause. "It's your choice." I smile.

"It is, and I choose you, in both capacities." He smiles and stares at me for a while, making me feel a little uncomfortable. Yet, I can't ignore the warm shivers that move throughout my body just from the look he casts on to me. I change the subject as we eat our parfaits and wait on the main course.

"How's your father?" I ask, concerned.

William sighs. "Not good. He's still on life support. We're just trying to establish a date to take him off."

I touch his hand. "I'm sorry." The waiter places my quiche and William's omelet in front of us. We eat quietly.

"I'm going to use the restroom and then go pay the bill. We need to get you and Kelvin a costume," William says as he stands and makes his way to the restroom, but I can feel his sadness in regards to his father.

We end up in the Costumes and More store right around the corner from his house. I swear this place feels like a haunted house, with all the props they have set up to jump out at you upon entering the store, you walk pass and your motion sets them off. I almost jumped into Williams arms when this huge spider seemed to launch at me.

After sorting through all of the adult superhero costumes, I decide on the adult enchantress witch costume. It is a very seductive short black dress with an emerald green sweeping overskirt. It comes with a corset, hat, lacy bolero, and a broom. I pick the adult very cool vampire costume for Kelvin. It comes with a silvery ruffle long-sleeve shirt, black vest, and a red lined cape with a stand-up collar. He can wear his jeans with it.

William and I discuss the schematics of the party, then I spend the next thirty minutes trying to convince him to get some food catered.

"You have way too much alcohol and no food! People are going to get sick from all that drinking and no eating."

He shakes his head listening to my argument.

"You can get something catered and have it buffet style, like chicken, sandwiches, fruit, cheese, crackers." I look at him. "Most people eat dinner around seven in the evening. By ten o'clock at night, that food has digested and is out of their system. Your party starts at eleven, and once they start drinking, they won't stop. It's not safe, William. This is your party, so it's your responsibility to make sure they have something on their stomach."

"Damn, Seme, you should have been an attorney," he finally says, after my long ramble.

"So, what's it going to be? Food or not?" I ask impatiently.

"Food. I'll call a place right now," he says as he pulls his cell phone out and we walk back to the car.

After he finishes the order he asks, "Are you happy, Seme?"

"Very." I smile, and put my hand on his thigh gripping it.

For a second, we both pause, looking at each other longer than we probably should. I turn away and start the car. "It is going to be a great party William. I can feel it," I say to him as I continue to look forward, ignoring the fact that he is staring at me in my peripheral.

When we get back to his house, I keep my key in the ignition. "I will pick you up some sage to clear your house out some time next week when I get back out to the flea market to pick some more up."

"Okay, love." He smiles at me. "Can I have a hug?"

I reach over to hug him. When he pulls away, he gives me a soft kiss on the lips. "See you tonight at the party," he says, then exits the car.

CHAPTER 25—-THE DISAGREEMENT

I get home around four P.M., I lay our costumes out on the bed, then I search the closet and find some fitted jeans for Kelvin to wear with his outfit with a nice pair of black dress shoes. As for me, I pull out my fishnet stockings and some tall black heeled boots. I place our his and her masquerade masks on the bed next to the costumes. Minutes later, I hear Sammie knocking. I walk out and unlock the front door.

"Why didn't you use your key?" I ask.

"I can't find it. You know how junky my purse is. You got my message right? That I was coming over to visit you after work?" Sammie says as she walks in.

"Yes," I respond.

I fill her in on the short getaway Kelvin and I escaped to earlier in the week, minus Kelvin's almost infidelity. I also catch her up to speed on someone bailing Casey out of jail. When Sammie walks into my room, she notices the costumes laid out on the bed.

"Where are y'all going tonight, girl?"

"A Halloween party. William is throwing it at this fancy hotel tonight at eleven."

"Umm, thanks for the invite!" Sammie says with sarcasm.

"You can still go. You and Malik just need a costume. I didn't invite you because at the time I thought that Casey would be there. Now that Casey and William aren't on good terms, it doesn't matter. I'll send you the invitation." I pull my phone out and email it to her.

"Well, I'll think about it," she says, and we both laugh at the fact that she's pretending she has to consider the option, when she was offended a few seconds ago about not being invited.

"Sammie, I was hanging out with William today, and before I left his house, he gave me a kiss...on the lips."

"What?" she questions, smiling ear to ear.

"I mean, it wasn't a passionate kiss. It was just a peck after I hugged him. Is that strange?"

"Uh, no. It is obvious that he likes you." She states nonchalantly.

"What do you mean?"

"I mean, if you and Kelvin weren't together, he would bark right up your tree."

"Interesting, I reply.

"You better tell Kelvin to watch out," Sammie jokes.

"Shut up, girl." I throw a pillow at Sammie, and she catches it.

"Just saying..."

"So, are you going to the party or not?" I ask, waiting on her response before I can text William to add two more guests.

"Yup. Malik just texted me back, and he's game."

"What are y'all going to wear?" I ask.

"Good question...the mall?"

Sammie and I shop at Spooks at the mall, a store that only opens for two months during the Halloween season. She picks out a Cat Woman costume for her and The Joker costume for Malik. We eat at The Bread House, a place that sells sandwiches and soups, and after, we head out to the flea market. I buy an extra bundle of sage to clear out William's house and more essential oils for my office. Time is ticking away. It's already nine o'clock in the evening.

Sammie drops me off at my house and drives off so she can go home and prepare for the party. As I walk up to my door, I notice Kelvin's jeep isn't in the driveway. Once I'm in the house, I place my bag on the table and walk into the bedroom. Our costumes are still laid out on the bed untouched. That's when I realize I haven't spoken with Kelvin since this morning. I immediately call him on his cell phone.

He answers. "Hi, sweetie."

"Hi, baby. Busy day?" I ask.

"So busy. I'm a little exhausted," he replies.

"Oh. Are you still working?"

"Yes, but I'm going to wrap up because my brain can't take it anymore."

"Okay. Do you still feel up to going to the party tonight?"

"Shit, Seme. The party slipped my mind," he replies.

"Well, come home. Did you eat?"

I can hear Kelvin shuffling papers around. "I had lunch earlier."

"I picked you up a chicken sandwich when I was out with Sammie."

"Okay. I'm on my way. See you soon."

Kelvin is home thirty minutes later. He seems frustrated and exhausted. I walk up to him and embrace him. He relaxes with his arms around me, creating our own little fortress of solitude.

"Come on. I drew a bath for you." He smirks and tries to keep up with me as I pull him through the house to the bathroom. He stands in front of me looking deflated and lifeless, as if all of his energy is draining by the minute. I unbutton his shirt, then I pull it off with one tug. I am standing so close to his chest I can practically smell his cologne and feel the heat from his body. I have him sit on the edge of the tub, and he removes one pant leg at a time then his underwear. Once he's completely naked, I step back and admire him for a while. Then I move to my knees and kiss his stomach. Placing both of my hands around his waist, I look up at him. I see desire in his eyes, yet he is not budging. He is not making a move to kiss me nor is he touching me. I can feel his strong desire to have sex with me.

I untie my robe, and it falls to the floor around my knees. I begin kissing below his navel and gripping his thighs. I look up to him once again to see if he's okay with me continuing lower. I place his penis in my mouth— just the tip—sucking slowly, and I massage the shaft. He grips the edge of the tub to brace himself, and I hear his moans softly echoing in the background. I relax my throat and take him deeper into my mouth, opening my throat up to his thrust and clamping my lips around his manhood as he pulls away. His hands are in my hair, pulling me toward him with force. This goes on for several strokes.

He places both his hands around my face and pulls me up, "Stand up, baby." He demands, turn me towards the tub, bends me over and takes me, over and over again. The force of his thrust surprises me; he has never been this rough before. What is even more surprising is that I like it.

He pulls out of me, turns me around, lifts me to his face, and says, "I don't really want to go to this party tonight, Sabine." Then grabs my waist as I wrap my legs around his body. Kelvin has one arm around my waist, the other arm between our bodies using his hand to position his penis into my sex. He inserts himself inside of me slowly. His face is so close to mine, I move in to kiss him; he moves his face away, lifting it upward and begins thrusting with force and pulling my waist down into him hard. My head is tilting back, and I can feel myself about to explode with pleasure.

"Look at me," he demands as he stops thrusting, which interrupts my almost orgasm. I'm squirming around him trying to get that feeling back. He grabs my waist and makes me still.

"The only reason I'm going to this party is to keep William's ass away from you," he states, looking me in the eyes. "You're my woman. Do you understand?" he asks me, demanding an answer.

I open my mouth to try to respond with an explanation. "But..."

"No, I don't want an explanation. I want a simple yes or no." I stare at him for a while and realize he's serious and he's angry.

"Yes. I understand," I say and try to kiss him for the second time. He moves his face away, loosens his grip on me, and my body slides down his and I am on my own two feet again. Just like that, the sexual act is over.

"Don't you want to finish?" I ask, bewildered. "And why won't you let me kiss you?"

"I need to wash up if we're going to this party," he says coldly. "I'll kiss you when I feel like he is out of your system." Then he steps into the tub.

"Who?" I ask.

"William, Sabine," he says as he rolls his eyes, lowering his full body into the tub to soak.

Shit! I think he knows about William kissing me. The nerve of him, getting upset with me over a small insignificant kiss when he was groping Cindy like there was no tomorrow. We're going to have to establish some ground rules about being in each other's head. It's as if we're invading each other's personal thoughts.

I walk over to him. "What do you mean, when he's out of my system?"

He sits up in the tub. "Sabine, you don't think I notice how he looks at you? What he feels toward you? I can feel it when you two are in my presence; I can only imagine what his thoughts are when I'm not around."

I look at him, confused. "What?"

"I mean he really, really likes you, and every time you're around him; you are enticing him and exciting his feelings."

I stare at Kelvin, confused on where all of this is coming from.

"Don't look at me like you don't understand. You know he likes you. You like the attention he gives you—the care he shows. It's interesting he's always around when I'm not there, waiting on his opportunity."

"Opportunity to do what, Kelvin?" I demand, frustrated by his accusations. Kelvin stands in the tub, washing his whole body quickly, rinses, unstops the drain, then steps out, grabs a towel, and pats himself dry.

"The opportunity to be with you in any way that he can," he yells then moves over to the sink to trim his goatee and brush his teeth.

"He just needs a friend. That's all that I am to him, a friend. I have no desire to be with anyone but you, Kelvin," I plead, feeling somewhat guilty about hanging out with William today.

After oiling his body, Kelvin walks into the bedroom, puts on his jeans, then the silver shirt, the red cape and flips his collar up, never taking his eyes off me. Kelvin is kind of sexy when he is this upset. I've never seen him this agitated before. It plays into the character of his costume, but he is defiantly not a cool vampire. Is he an angry or jealous vampire?

"Both," he says interrupting my thoughts.

"What?" I ask, perplexed, knowing I didn't ask him a question.

"I'm angry and jealous." He pauses as if he realizes he answered a question I didn't voice aloud, then he slowly says, "William is waiting on his opportunity to get close to you, waiting on your guard to be down, waiting on me to mess up so he can slide in, Sabine."

He walks into the bathroom and I follow him, ready to argue his points and to bring up some of my own about what happened in Key West, but he beats me to the punch.

"And just so you know, this is completely different from what happened at the resort," he says.

"How so?" I ask.

"William has been lusting after you since the day you two met." He turns and looks at me. "He has wanted in your pants from day one. You two have developed an emotional connection through your 'counseling sessions.'" When he says *counseling sessions,* he puts up two finger quotes. "Can you honestly tell me if I were not in the picture you wouldn't date William?" He looks at me with searching eyes, as I stare in disbelief at his rant. "Sabine, I feel his energy all over you. Emotional cheating is the worst kind of cheating."

"Kelvin, I'm not cheating on you. You can ramble all night about what you think is going on, but it isn't true. I don't know what has gotten in to you lately. First, it's Cindy who you went to first, second, and almost third base with on our weekend retreat, just after we had sex minutes before we arrived at the party." I stare at him, and he looks down, then he focuses on my eyes again, but his jaw is twitching. "Here you are telling me I'm cheating on you for having a male client?"

"This goes way further than that, and you know it. Do you typically have your male clients come over to your house or invite you to parties? Or have discussions outside of the office about people you know?"

"No, but this situation is different," I state calmly, feeling regret for getting so close to William.

"What makes him different from any other client you've had

in the past?" he asks. I don't know how to respond to that, so I remain quiet.

"Case closed," he states matter-of-factly.

"The case is not closed," I yell. "Tell me what got into you at Key West. I don't understand how you could be so comfortable with a woman you knew for five minutes and forget you were with me. Explain how you could ever think that it's okay to almost fuck someone and I'm at the same damn party."

Kelvin shakes his head. "I didn't almost fuck her," he says calmly.

"What do you call it then?" He looks at me, his mouth clinched tightly, his jaw twitching even more, but he doesn't respond.

"Case closed," I say, then turn and walk away.

"We're not done with this conversation." He grabs me, turns me around, and stares at me as if he's searching for an answer.

"Honestly, I don't know what got into me that night. I felt like you didn't want to be there once we got to the party. I was trying to provide an escape for you. There was so much going through my mind about what you told me about Casey the previous day and what I saw. I was worried about losing you. I don't know; call it self-sabotage, I guess."

"Why do you think you'll lose me Kelvin?" He doesn't respond. I walk over to him. "I'm yours. I love you. I'm not going anywhere. I just need to understand what's going on in your head lately. I can feel you pulling away from me."

"Don't you need to get dressed?" he asks coldly, effectively changing the subject.

"I do," I respond.

Kelvin walks away.

We leave out of the house at midnight on our way to the party. We don't say much on the thirty-minute car ride. Kelvin reaches over to hold my hand; our eyes meet for a second. As we pull up to the hotel, I hand him his mask, and we both put them on before exiting the car. We walk together holding hands, then he stops me in my tracks, lowers his face, and softly and gently kiss my lips.

CHAPTER 26—THE HALLOWEEN PARTY

We walk into a room filled with goblins, vampires, witches, fairies, ghosts, and a variety of haunted and enchanted people dressed as creatures. The atmosphere feels almost surreal. There are several fog machines scattered throughout the room creating mystery and suspense, as if it discharges the message that "secrets are supposed to be hidden, feelings should remain unknown, and the only thing that matters is what happens in the moment." Actually, these are the exact words that are posted on the walls as you enter the party.

It's extraordinary how a space can be decorated to create an environment to fit an idea or theme that seems to take on a life form of its own. This room is every bit of scary and mysterious. I wonder if this was the vision William was hoping to accomplish. Just as I think his name, William appears dressed as a magician with a top hat, cane, and a half-white masquerade mask.

"Hello, good people," he says with a smile. "Glad you two could make it." William reaches over to hug me, but Kelvin intercepts the hug, reaching between William and me to shake his hand.

"We wouldn't miss it for the world," Kelvin says with a mischievous grin.

I can feel Kelvin's aura change from sullen and moody to energetic and feisty. Wow, I don't think I noticed it before, but Kelvin's personality changes when he's at a party. His demeanor reminds me of how he was at the pool party in Key West. Well, I'm not going to complain; at least he's in good spirits and not brooding over the situation about William.

A server dressed like Betty Boop in a tight fitted dress with lots of cleavage exposed walks over to us and offers us a drink. "Bloody Mary?"

Kelvin and I both grab a glass. William looks at me, and he seems acutely aware that I am purposely trying not to make eye contact with him. "Well, I'll let you two mingle," William says. "Have fun. Oh, I had some food catered for this party. Eat, drink, and be merry," he exclaims as he walks away.

When I turn to look at Kelvin, he's finished his drink and sets his empty glass on a tray, "Let's get some food," he says as he escorts me over to a table to set my drink down. Kelvin grabs my hand and walks with me over to the buffet where we fill our plates with fried chicken, salad, subs, and chips. He then grabs two bottles of water. "William really knows how to throw a party," Kelvin says as he bites into his sub then put a few chips into his mouth, looking around at the scene.

I eat my food slowly, looking around at everyone dressed up. There are easily about a hundred people in this space. The disc jockey is playing "Remember You" by Wiz Khalifa and the Weeknd. There are two floors to this conference room. The second floor is more of a balcony that encloses the whole room. It reminds me of the nosebleed seats you would see at a concert. There are people mingling upstairs looking down to the center of the dance floor. I look down to my plate and finish my sub sandwich and all of the chips. As I am biting into the chicken, another server brings us more alcohol. This time we are served Smith and Wessons, which consists of Baileys, vodka, and club soda, topped with whipped cream.

I take a sip. "This is delicious." It's exactly my type of drink. It tastes like a creamy, icy drink from The Coffee House, but with infused with alcohol. I drink half of it and finish my chicken.

When I look up, Kelvin is gazing at me. His plate is empty, and he's finishing his second drink. "Do you want to dance, Sabine?"

"Sure." I get up slowly, and we walk out to the dance floor. Rihanna and Future's "Love Song" has just started playing. We slow dance to the hypnotic sound of the music as the rhythm takes us to another level transcending this place and time, taking us up, up, up.

The lyrics echoes and I am rolling my hips as my body takes in the sound of the drums. Kelvin is thrusting his pelvis and undulating his body as he pulls me in close to him, closing the gap between us physically. Rihanna and Future's voices are resonating the words that feel to be bridging this emotional gap between Kelvin and me. As the song ends, the beat picks up with another Rihanna song, "Selfish." "Each song feels as if it is handpicked for us.

I turn around, my back to Kelvin's front, my head leaning on his upper chest, his body supporting some of my weight, our bodies seemingly becoming one as we sway to the beat. My eyes are closed as we trap ourselves here in the moment, taking in the essence of the words in this song, closing out the rest of the world. It is only us in this room, on this floor— at least it feels this way. The next six songs that comes on have us hypnotized by each other in our methodical dance, as if we planned it out like a routine. This feels more relaxing than a meditation session or a long walk on the beach. Music tends to have a healing effect, almost like going to church and hearing the preacher preach, and it feels as if the preacher is ministering to you and your specific situation.

Tonight, each song selected by the deejay feels as if it's talking directly to Kelvin and my situation and healing any transgressions and hostilities we have toward each other. When the last song goes off, and the deejay starts rattling off about the food and drinks, Kelvin and I walk back to our table to see Malik and Samantha sitting there.

"Wow. It looked like you guys were making love on that dance floor," Sammie says smiling, then reaches out with her cat claws making a scratch in the air.

Kelvin and I both smile, somewhat embarrassed. Kelvin reaches to hug Sammie, and I reach to hug Malik. They are both stuffing their faces with food.

Kelvin walks back over to me. "Sweetie, I have to use the restroom. Be right back," he says in my ear. I nod, and he walks off. I sit next to Sammie.

"When did you two get here?" I ask Sammie.

"Long enough to see you two on the dance floor," Sammie says.

I look at her sideways. I can tell she's had a few drinks. She's very playful, and she seems relaxed.

"So I guess Malik is the designated driver," I say and look over to Malik who nods as he people watches and eats chicken and drinks a Coke.

William walks over to our table. "You all enjoying yourselves?" he asks, but he is looking directly at me.

"The party is great, William. The food is great, the deejay is jamming, and the atmosphere...well, it fits," I comment, looking him in the eyes for the first time all evening.

"Thanks, Sabine, and thanks for your help earlier," William says, just as Kelvin walks back up to the table.

Kelvin grabs a chair and sits near me, pulling me at the waist to sit closer to him. "You helped William with the party, baby?" Kelvin asks.

Samantha and Malik look at each other then back at me, wondering how I'm going to respond to that question.

"Yes, I went with William to pick up some of the drinks for tonight." I reply.

Kelvin nods, then lifts his glass and says, "Cheers to great alcohol and a kick-ass party."

Everyone lifts their glass and drink to that. Sammie looks over at me with questioning eyes. She gets up and walks over to me. "Come on, girl. Let's dance." She grabs my arm, and we're off to the dance floor. I look back at Kelvin, and he lifts his glass and smiles at us. Malik looks as if he is a deer caught in the headlights, and William is very cool and collected.

"Seme, what was that?" Sammie questions referring to the awkwardness we just experienced in regards to Kelvin questioning me hanging out with William.

I shrug. "Beats me."

"Oh, no. Is there a love triangle going on with you, Kelvin, and William? Did something more happen today when you hung out with William, besides the kiss? You didn't tell Kelvin you were with William today?"

"No, I didn't tell Kelvin and nothing more happened."

Sammie shakes her head as we continue to dance.

"William is throwing some serious salt in the game. I don't know how long Kelvin will maintain his cool," Sammie says.

Sammie is right. Williams seems bold tonight, not because he thanked me but because he voice his appreciation for my help not just around my sister and her husband, but it seems to be timed just right for Kelvin to hear it too. Maybe because I didn't address the kiss, that made William feel that I was okay with it. I admit I am wrong to feel this way, but I was okay with it. A part of me wanted to indulge with William in that way.

As Sammie and I are dancing on the floor, a woman bumps us from behind. First, into me, bumping my shoulder then into Sammie, bumping into her arm. We look at each other and keep dancing, moving away from her. As we continues to dance, she makes her way back over to us and is randomly letting a hand slip here and there, landing on Sammie's upper thigh and the back of my head. We turn to look at the woman. She literally has on all black. Her gown flows down to the floor, and she has on a black wide span hat with a scarf covering her face, only revealing her eyes, which we can barely see as she has her head tilted.

After a long pause, Sammie finally says, "Listen, Ms. Lady in Black, if you want to dance with me, just ask."

I instantly start laughing, totally understanding Sammie's frustration. She does seem like she is moving in closer to us on purpose, as if she's trying to hear our conversation or get our attention. The woman shrugs apologetically and moves away from us backward, doing some little twirl with her fingers. When she turns around, Samantha puts up her middle finger, which has me laughing even harder. I grab Sammie's hand and force it down to her side.

"Stop it, Sammie," I say as I laugh a little. Sammie smiles, even though, she is still visibly annoyed by our encounter with The Lady in Black. We're interrupted from our little incident by the loud yelling we hear over by our table. When we look over, Kelvin is out of his seat with his arms extending upward, whipping around, and he is walking toward William. Malik grabs Kelvin by the waist and pulls him away from William, who is calmly looking at Kelvin, waiting on him to make a move.

"Oh my God," I scream and run over to Kelvin, jumping between him and William.

"Kelvin, calm down," I say to him. Kelvin effectively ignores me and continues to speak.

"Will, if you've got something you want to say, I'm right here," Kelvin states, lowering his tone trying to appease my request of him. "Or we can handle this some other type of way. There's nothing but space and opportunity here." Kelvin pats his chest. Twice. Very hard.

"Kelvin, what's happening?" I ask calmly.

"What's happening, baby, is that your boy Will here thinks he has the upper hand. He keeps making these smart-ass remarks, speaking on things he knows nothing about," Kelvin says, not taking his eyes off William.

"Okay, well, can you just take it down a few notches?" I ask calmly, sort of embarrassed.

Sammie walks over to William, who looks as cool as a cucumber. It wouldn't surprise me if this was exactly the response he was trying to elicit from Kelvin. William's expression looks pleased that Kelvin is in an uproar.

"Listen, Kelv. I wasn't referring to you in the scenario I was speaking on earlier, but if the shoe fits..." William trails off.

I can feel Kelvin wanting to lunge at William. But, he calms himself down as he feels my grip tightening on him. Kelvin finally puts his arms down, wrapping them around me. Continuing to stare at Williams as he tightens his grip on me.

Then Kelvin says, "This right here is mine. I'm going to need you to back the fuck off, and we won't have any problems."

William opens his mouth as if he's about to say something to retaliate, but decides against it. He walks away mumbling, "Enjoy the rest of the party."

Kelvin stands there for a while with me in his arms, looking as William walks away, obviously pissed. I look up at Kelvin and he plants the most adoring kiss on my lips.

Malik walks up to us. "Listen, we're going to need a little less drama tonight," he says as serious as he can, then laughs., "What was that, man?"

Kelvin turns me loose. "Mannnn!" Kelvin seems to sing the word. His mood has gone from confrontational to very animated and hyperactive. Kelvin explains to Malik the conversation was necessary and that he had been waiting on the opportunity to speak his mind to William. After communicating this to Malik, Kelvin smiles as if he's accomplished what he hoped to tonight. I'm still stunned at how Kelvin's emotions have gone from annoyed before the party, to party animal during the party, to aggressive, to an emotional contentment over the span of a few hours.

Sammie asks Malik, "What happened?" Malik looks at Kelvin who is just as calm now, smiling and drinking a beer.

I turn to look in Kelvin's direction. "How many drinks have you had?" I ask.

He hesitates and stumbles before answering, "Four, maybe five."

"So, would this be the fourth or the fifth drink?" I ask.

"More like the sixth," he adds, and he and Malik start laughing.

I let him take one last sip of the beer, then I switch out his drink for a bottled water, "Drink two of these," I say to him firmly.

Sammie jumps in, "Okay, I want to know how their conversation escalated to where it was," she demands.

Malik responds, "William was telling these stories about guys he knew from his past and how they treated their women. He was talking about infidelity and not making enough time to cater to your lady." Malik drinks more of his soda and bites into his chicken. "But, when he was telling the story, he was looking out on the dance floor at you, Sabine." Malik chuckles and chews his chicken thinking about it. "It was more of the way he was looking at you—his eyes were fixed on you."

Kelvin adds to the conversation after finishing one bottle of

189

water, "Yeah, he told this story about this party this couple went to, and at the party her dude was dancing with this other woman in a way that was inappropriate and totally disrespectful to his woman." Kelvin looks at me.

Malik jumps back in. "Yeah, he did say something like that... and something to the effect of, 'if I had a beautiful woman, I would only have eyes for her.' Sabine, he was looking right at you," Malik finishes.

I wonder if the only reason Kelvin had even come to this party was to give William a piece of his mind about his position on our friendship.

And as if right on cue, Kelvin says, "You know, I considered not coming to this party, but I knew Seme wanted to attend." He puts his arm around my shoulder. "I'm so happy I did. I'd be damned if I was going to let her come by herself." He smiles at me. "And to be honest, this really is a kick-ass party." I can tell the liquor is getting to Kelvin. His eyes are bloodshot red; he is talking more than usual and out of character. I open another bottle of water and hand it to him. "I've gotta use the restroom," Kelvin says as he gets up from his seat.

As soon as Kelvin is out of sight, Malik asks, "Sabine, are you cheating with William?"

Samantha hits Malik on the shoulder. "Of course she isn't." They trail off into their own side conversation about cheating and the likes.

I look over a couple of tables and see the Lady in Black looking our way. "What is up with her?" I say aloud. Sammie looks in the direction I'm looking toward, and the woman gets up and walks away. Kelvin comes out of the restroom, and I walk over to him. "Are you okay, baby?" I ask him.

"I feel like I should lay down," he says.

"Do you feel sick?" I ask.

"The room is spinning a little." I use my weight to support him, pulling one of his arms around my shoulder. We walk over to the bar, and I order a ginger ale. I sit with him on a sofa near the front entrance, open the ginger ale, and have him take a sip.

He lays back and falls asleep instantly. I look at my watch and it is already two thirty A.M. I contemplate getting us a room for the night at this hotel.

"Sweetie, I'll be right back," I say to Kelvin. He mumbles something incoherent. I walk out of the conference room and up to the front desk. They are asking for $189 for one night. Thinking about the long car ride home and getting Kelvin in and out of the car is what helps me decide to book the room. Malik assist with getting Kelvin in the elevator and upstairs to our room. Once Kelvin is in the bed, I remove his costume and place a trashcan near the bed in case he gets sick.

Samantha, Malik, and I take the elevator downstairs to the main lobby to just chill out for a while. We watch as the party dies down. People are leaving, some exiting the hotel and others checking in for the night. I see no sign of William. I do see the Lady in Black. She is checking in to Room 345. At least that is what I think that I overheard. Lady in Black slips off to the elevator.

Sammie and Malik decide to head home. We say our good-byes, and I go upstairs to check on Kelvin. He is sound asleep. I take off my costume, shower, then put on the hotel robe. After looking at my cell phone and reviewing a text from Samantha saying they made it back home safely, I send a message to William: *Are you home, or did you get a room?* I am curious to hear Williams standpoint on what happened tonight.

He texts me right back to my surprise: *I'm checked in.*

I write back: *Is this where you come when you want to get a break from your house?*

He responds: *Yes, it is.*

My reply: *I'm sorry about what happened at the party.* Trying to lead the conversation to that direction.

His reply: *No worries, love. Maybe I overstepped my boundaries just a little. I blame it on the alcohol.*

My response: *I don't know. I wasn't there until after it escalated.*

His reply: *Probably best you weren't. Is Kelvin sleep?*

My response: *Yes, more like passed out. You both were abusing the alcohol a little too much tonight it seems.*

His reply: *Are you home?*

My reply: *No. I checked into a room.*

His response: *Nice. Do you want to meet me in the lobby? We can talk in person and give our fingers a break.*

I hesitate for a minute, walk over to Kelvin, and kiss him on the forehead, then text back: *See you in 10 minutes.*

CHAPTER 27—THE CONFESSION

I slip on my skirt and top from the witch costume, put on some hotel room shoes, grab my key card, and take the elevator down to the main lobby. I walk past the front desk and out toward an area that looks like a cathedral. William is sitting in a chair on the sidewall of that room. I walk up to him and have a seat in the empty chair beside him. It looks as though he is deep in thought.

"Penny for your thoughts," I say.

He smiles at me and grabs my hand. "Kelvin was right to blow up like he did. I have feelings for you, Sabine. I've never met anyone like you before."

William looks me in the eyes then continues, "You know that I saw Kelvin dancing with that woman when you were at Key West right before you hung up on me. I didn't like what I saw, and I may have brought that up in conversation with him at the party. I know that was none of my business. I'm sorry for causing conflict in your relationship. Kelvin was right. I don't know anything about that. Wait. . . . this isn't what I wanted to talk to you about, I'm stalling," William confesses.

"What is it?" I ask with concern.

"The first day that we met? I was at lunch with Casey at the Chinese restaurant in your plaza. She told me about you and your sister. She wanted me to come to your place of business and find out what you were all about," William declares.

I pull my hand away from his. "What?" I ask angrily.

"She was trying to get more information on you and your sister." He stares at me as I process what he's saying. "You were so warm and welcoming, and I really did need those counseling sessions with you." He sits up in his chair, "You helped me so much. From the moment I met you, I knew I didn't want to know you under those circumstances. I really wanted to get to know you on a personal level—for my own knowledge. Just as a man gets to know a woman he's interested in. I got to know you on a professional level, and you are a wonderful counselor." After he completes his statement, I stand, not really knowing how to take what he is saying to me.

"Please, Sabine, sit down. Let me explain," William pleads.

The curious part to my personality takes over, and I sit back down, at the edge of my chair physically and metaphorically speaking, wanting to know where his story is going.

"That day I came to your house, I really was afraid. I had seen something that disturbed the core of my being." He pauses for a second, as if this is extremely hard for him to talk about, then he continues. "I became suspicious when I found the photos that had been taken of you and Kelvin and your sister and her husband. Casey's obsession with you two took me by surprise." As William speaks, he looks straight ahead. "I also realize now that she was messing with the dark arts to try to manipulate situations. I know I never finished the story that day—about when Casey was in the closet on the floor." William pauses for a few seconds then continues, "She turned to look at me, I didn't recognize her. I mean, she looked like herself, but different at the same time. Does that make sense?" William looks me in the eyes.

"Yes, kind of like what I experienced in the police station," I respond.

"Exactly. Her eyes were dilated, her breathing was heavy. When she moved to get up, it was like gravity was working in reverse, helping to lift her to her feet with no effort on her part. She walked up to me and stared into my eyes for seconds, but it felt like an eternity. I was so afraid." William shivers, staring off into the distance again. "It makes me feel icky just thinking about it now. I wish I could permanently erase that vision and experience from my mind." He looks back over at me, coming out of that memory. "I felt the difference being around you— someone with a pure heart—in comparison to her, a person with a dark soul. I knew which side of the field I wanted to be on. I am so sorry for not being honest from the beginning." William seems very sincere in what he's communicating to me.

I take a deep breath, trying to sort through and process what he's telling me.

"Life has been hard for me without my father being around. I feel lost most of the time." William stands. "Do you want to go for a walk outside to watch the sunrise?" he asks.

"Okay," I reply with hesitation, and then stand up with William.

As we walk out to the balcony to watch the sun rise, William continues, "There's so much pressure on me with the business in regards to what direction we should go in—pressure on when to take my father off life support. The truth is I've never felt as complete as I do when I'm around you. When I'm around you or talking to you, I feel like I'm not alone and that I don't have to make decisions on my own. I feel like you're my partner and go-to person so to speak. I also feel I'm that for you, too." He looks in my eyes, questioning. "I know God provides everything a person needs, and I think you were sent to me as an earth angel to guide me through this time. I really appreciate our friendship, Sabine. I know you're with Kelvin, and I won't try to come in between you two again...I want you to know the truth about me. Because, when a person truly loves someone, they're honest about who they are." William swipes a piece of my hair out of my face then kisses my cheek. "I really love you, Sabine, and because I love you, I want the best for you, and if that's Kelvin right now, so be it."

I'm shocked by his confession in regards to Casey, mostly. It forces me to reflect back to different points of time like; him coming to my home to show me the pictures and the journal, the counseling sessions- more specifically- the vision quest. I think back to what his father told me in regards to Casey. And now, William finally completes the story about what happened when Casey was on the floor in the closet at his home. All the empty holes are filled in, and even though I am angry at William for being deceitful in the recent past, I can appreciate his honesty currently. I feel gratitude for this experience. The duality of this situation has come to an end, and in it I see Divine Perfection, a plan working out beyond what could have ever been done at a human level. When William started his counseling sessions with me, it was to help him process his feelings in regards to Casey, and that is what happened. William has grown from the experience and developed a new found integrity. With the help of the counseling, it seems as if he has found comfort and peace with the situation. He was able to gracefully unlock the secret to me and all of the pieces are falling where they should be.

"I will apologize to Kelvin," he says, then turns to look at the sun. "Beautiful, isn't it?" he asks me.

"Yes, it is," I reply in a daze.

"Well, I'll let you get some rest and check on Kelvin." He hugs me, pulls away, shakes his head, and walks away.

My thoughts are running all over the place. I take the elevator back upstairs, use my key card to open our room door, lay in the bed next to Kelvin, and drift off to sleep around six A.M.

I awake around eleven in the morning to the sound of shower water running in the bathroom. I lay in bed thinking about this morning and what William confessed to me. As I walk toward the bathroom, Kelvin is stepping out of the shower.

"How are you feeling?" I ask.

"Okay. Slight headache," he says. "You got the room because of me?"

"Yes. You passed out. Malik helped me walk you up here," I respond.

"I'm sorry," he says with guilt in his eyes. "I guess I was exhausted from the work day, and maybe I did have a little too much to drink." He looks at me as if he's trying to gauge my mood.

"It's cool. Maybe we should've stayed home. Maybe this whole thing was a bad idea. I'm sorry for dragging you out so late, when you worked so hard yesterday," I say to him.

"Seme, it's fine. You have nothing to be sorry about. I called to the front to see if we could have an extra hour. I wanted you to sleep more. They were okay with it, which is why I didn't wake you. I was calling to pay the bill, but they said William Witford had paid it for us."

I look at Kelvin, waiting on his disapproval and the argument to follow. Surprisingly, he doesn't argue. He leaves it at that. I walk back into the room and lay down, thinking to myself, I'll take my shower once I get home.

Kelvin walks out of the bathroom, slips on his jeans, and lays down beside me. He wraps his arms around me and hugs me tightly, then he begins to speak. "I apologize for my mood yesterday. When I came home from work, I was upset about a deal that fell through. Instead of telling you what was going on, I took my frustration out on you. I have no right to tell you who to counsel or who to be friends with. You're your own person, and you make those decisions."

He pauses for a minute. "What I'm really sorry about, Sabine," he says as he takes a deep breath, "is for what I did in Key West with Cindy. It was uncalled for, and I know it hurt you because it hurts me knowing another man has your time, energy, and efforts." He swallows hard and shifts. "I am afraid of losing you."

He hugs me tighter. "When you love someone, there are two extremes: One, your love for them, which feels awesome and two, your fear due to the fact that you love them so much you wonder what it would feel like if you lost that, and that feeling is unbearable. I realize now my thinking was self-sabotaging. I was upset before we went on our trip to Key West, about you inviting William into our home. I was nervous about seeing Casey on that video in what looked like a real-life demonic possession and the threat that was made to our relationship as a result of that experience with Casey, combined with me wanting everything to be perfect between us. I pondered how we could be dating going on two-and-a-half months and have all of these issues come up already. Was it a sign this union wasn't meant to be?" he asks rhetorically.

"Then, I realized that it was a test—the trials and tribulations of a relationship. If you want something bad enough, God will test your resolve in the matter... Am I putting you to sleep, baby?" he asks most likely because he cannot see my face as he talks to me because I am in his arms and not looking into his eyes, and I am so quiet.

"No. I'm listening," I respond as I take everything he says into my mind and heart.

"What I'm trying to say is that I kept thinking something outside of our relationship could threaten what we have. I was wrong." He pauses for a second. "Something from the outside could cause great damage if we allow it. I made a decision to let Cindy flirt with me—going all above and beyond with her dance moves. I took a walk with her on the beach and engaged in whatever else followed. I made a choice. You made a choice not to kick my ass out of the house after something like that." He chuckles a little. "William has every reason to love you. You are beautiful, soulful, and skilled at many things. You have that nurturing touch, and it feels like I've known you my whole life. Maybe William feels the same. Regardless, who am I not to trust you? Who am I not to be able to let the future come naturally and whatever comes up, deal with it at that time?"

I turn around to face Kelvin, and I say, "That was beautiful," then I smile.

Maybe my smile was a little too wide, which warrants his next statement. "Okay, make fun of me," Kelvin says.

"I'm sorry, but it really was beautiful. Is this what you do when you come down from your high? You're very philosophical right now," I state.

"It needed to be said." Kelvin simpers. There is a knock on our door. Kelvin gets out of bed and opens the door. He steps out further into the hallway looking as if he is narrowing his eyes on something or someone. He stares down the hall for a few minutes, then slowly walks back into the room. "Strange," he says.

I put on my boots and put our capes to our costumes and my stockings into one of the hotel's dry cleaner's bag. "Who was it?" I ask.

"No one," Kelvin replies, "Although I could have sworn I saw someone ..."

"Maybe it was maid service. Let's go. We asked for an extra hour, and we got it. Now our time is up," I say, as I double-check the bathroom to make sure we haven't left anything. Once we're downstairs in the main lobby, we cross paths with William. He is directing the crew that is picking up the fog machine, the remaining liquor, and props in the conference room where the party took place last night.

Kelvin walks over to William and reaches out to shake his hand. "Nice party last night."

"Thanks. The company has an annual Christmas party also," William replies. "Listen, man, my apologies about stepping out of line last night. You were right. I had no idea what I was talking about."

Kelvin looks at him. "It's all good. Maybe I was being a little too protective. Sabine is her own woman, and she makes her own decisions." Kelvin shrugs. "Thanks for paying for the room."

"It's the least that I could do," William replies as they shake hands once more and give a half hug to each other.

Kelvin informs me he's going to pull the car around to the front, and with that said he turns, kisses me on the forehead, and walks out of the front door, leaving William and me alone.

William walks up to me. "I saw Casey this morning. She was right down the hall from me in Room 345."

"What?" I question, shocked.

"Yes," he replies.

"She was the Lady in Black. She kept bumping into me and Samantha on the dance floor, and I saw her check into Room 345 early this morning."

"Her court date has gotten pushed back by a month. Detective Mack called me this morning asking about our visit to the club a few weeks ago. He was questioning if Casey was with me the entire time. I think they're trying to get evidence she poisoned your sister's husband."

"Was she with you the entire time?" I ask.

"I think we both know the answer to that question," William

replies, then looks at me with eyes that speak volumes of impure resolve.

In that moment, I'm taken back to that night at the club when I looked up to find William watching Kelvin and me perform in that semi-private room. My thoughts are brought back to this current moment, as Kelvin pulls up outside just as William and I are walking toward the front door. Kelvin gets out of the jeep and walks over to my side to open the door, then he asks William if he would like to join us for dinner tonight.

"I'll take a rain check. I have to be at the hospital today. The family made a decision to take my father off of life support," Williams says sullen.

"I'm sorry to hear that." I walk over to William and touch his shoulder. "Let me know if you need anything."

"I will. Thank you, Sabine. I'll talk to you two later," William says as he walks away.

CHAPTER 28—THE AFTEREFFECTS

The weeks go by slowly. I spend full days in my office across town taking on six clients per day. I'm able to focus more on counseling now that I've stopped the catering business until the opening of the café and lounge. I haven't spoken to William in more three weeks, ever since they pulled the plug on the life support for his dad. I sent flowers to the funeral, and I texted William to let him know I'm here for him if he needs to talk. No response. My guess is he's going through the process of grief.

Kelvin has been out of town the whole week in Michigan on business. We talk often on the phone about our day. Although we're talking every day and night, I can feel the slight disconnect that seems to loom in our relationship lately. Part of it has to do with respecting each other's boundaries, and the other part has to do with accepting our current reality and the choices we've made in the past few months. If I had to label it as anything, I would say we're in a time-out emotionally. Respectively, we're in our corners, licking our wounds and thinking about how our actions affected each other. I guess this comes with being in a committed relationship, when you realize your actions don't affect you alone—any choice that needs to be made, any actions to be sought come with the concern of the other person in mind, and if not, the consequences hurt.

Neither one of us care to elaborate on the subject of us. I'm staying busy with my clients, which exhausts me emotionally. When I come home, I don't have the energy to discuss any subject that requires empathy, patience, or understanding, which means I've barely acknowledged how my relationship with William could have affected Kelvin. I often wonder how much of what transpired between William and I could have been avoided had I kept things professional. But I also choose not to go down that road of guilt and would've, should've or could've. What's done is done; I just choose not to look at it right now. However, I have to admit, in William's absence, I miss the friendship.

Of course, I miss Kelvin more. He's busy building up his empire in both Michigan and Florida. Our conversations focus on the details of our day, rather than the emotional components of our hearts, which most likely need to be explored at this time. Based off his confession at the hotel, Kelvin is nervous also. This is new for both of us, and things are happening extremely fast, so we just need to adjust, that's all. What's that saying about time and healing? Oh yeah, time heals all things.

"So, I hired a driver for the cafe," I say to Kelvin over the phone.

"That's great, baby," he responds casually.

"He'll work Monday through Saturday from ten-thirty to five-thirty."

"So, everything will be in place by the end of the month for the big reveal of the café?" Kelvin asks.

"It looks that way. When are you coming home?" I question.

"I'll be home tonight, sweetie. I have to go. Love you."

"Love you too." Just as I hang the phone up, it rings again. "Yes?" I answer, expecting to hear Kelvin's voice on the other end of the phone.

There's a long silence and then, "Hello, love."

"William?"

"It's been a long time. Did you miss me?" William asks.

"Actually, I do miss you," I answer honestly. "How are you holding up?"

"I'm fine. It's been an emotional week for me, but I got through it all okay, I guess," he replies.

"I'm happy to hear that, William."

"The flowers were lovely. Thank you." He pauses. "And for the record, I wasn't ignoring you, I was just..." It seems as if he doesn't have the words to describe what he wants to express.

"It's okay. You don't need to explain anything to me. I understand. I just wanted to make sure you're okay, and hearing your voice is confirmation that you are."

"Thank you, Sabine. Your concern means a lot to me." There's a long silence again. "Well, I'll let you go. I just wanted to check in. Tell Kelvin I said hello and that I'll take him up on his dinner offer soon," William says.

"Thanks for calling and checking in. It feels good to hear your voice. Call me whenever you need to talk. I'm here as a friend or counselor, however you want to use me."

I hear a chuckle on the other end. "However I want to use you?" William questions.

I giggle. "You know what I mean." We both laugh, holding the phone a little longer.

"We should meet for lunch on Monday," I state.

"Lunch sounds good," William replies.

"The Chinese restaurant near my office?" I ask.

"Yes. I'll see you at noon on Monday. Good night, love."

"Good night, William."

After a nice long bubble bath, I feel relaxed, a little more at ease now that I've spoken to William and convinced him to meet with me after the weekend, even if it is just for lunch. I feel I'll be able to gauge him more in person and get more insight into his mental state. I slide into bed, look briefly over at the clock, which reads ten P.M. Where is Kelvin? It has been hours since we last spoke.

To take my mind off him, I grab a book and begin to read. My mind becomes engaged in the fantasy of the fictional life of Nathanial and Abbigail. After getting halfway through the book, I set it down on the nightstand and switch the lamp off beside the bed. It's midnight, and I'm a little worried about Kelvin. He said he was only a few hours away the last time we spoke. I call his cell phone, and it goes directly to voicemail. I say a prayer for protection to keep him safe wherever he is. As I fall off to sleep, I wonder why he hasn't taken me to Michigan to meet his father and brother. If my mom and dad were still alive, I would be excited about introducing him to them.

CHAPTER 29—SURPRISE, I'M HOME

I awaken to lips touching mine ever so gently. "Kelvin!" I reach up and grab him, making him fall on top of me.

"Hi, babe," he says smiling in between kisses.

"What time is it?" I ask, trying to look at the clock.

"It is a little after two A.M. I'm sorry; I took a little longer than expected. There was a really bad accident on the expressway; I had to take an alternate route."

"I was worried. I called your phone. It went straight to voicemail."

"Yeah. I lost my charger. I'm here now. No worries, sweetie. I missed you," he says, then looks at me like he's looking through my soul. "You are so beautiful." He kisses me once more. "I'm going to shower. Go back to sleep," he whispers.

My eyes are already closing as I ask, "Did you eat? Are you hungry?"

"I'm fine, baby. Just rest. I just wanted you to know I'm here." He rubs my hair until I drift back off to sleep, then he lifts up off the bed. I fall back into a more restful sleep.

When I awake the next day, I'm delighted to find Kelvin wrapped around me. I turn to face him, and he appears to be in a deep sleep. I kiss his lips, rub his arms, and trace the outline of his lips. After laying with him for a while, appreciating this time with him, even though he is asleep, I slowly take his limbs off my body; starting with his arms then his legs, as quietly as I can, and get out of the bed. I want to make him a spectacular breakfast to show him how much I missed him and appreciate him. As I'm walking from the bathroom, through the bedroom, toward the kitchen, I see a long-stemmed rose laid out on the floor. As I continue to walk, I see another long-stemmed red rose, then another. A trail of red roses leads to the kitchen, highlighting my path and directing my steps. I walk into the kitchen to see dozens and dozens of roses, all red, displayed on every countertop.

"Wow," I manage to get out as I walk over to the counter to smell them.

"Do you like them, baby?" I hear Kelvin's voice from behind me.

I turn around shocked to hear his voice, knowing I just left him in the room sound asleep. He's wearing pajama pants and no shirt.

I reply, "They're beautiful." I turn back to look at the display again. It really is a sight to see.

"I thought you'd like them," he says.

When I turn back around, Kelvin is on one knee holding a little black box. My heart drops, and tears are rolling freely down my cheeks as I walk over to him.

"Don't cry, baby. I want to ask you something," he says sincerely. "We've been through a lot in these past few months. I know everything seems to be moving at lightning speed between us—from how we met outside of your café to our first date at The Sweet Spot on that same night, to a few weeks later when I moved in. It has been a huge adjustment for me, and I'm sure for you too, but I wouldn't have it any other way." He pauses, swallowing hard. "I know I don't want to spend another second without making this official between us." He pauses for a few seconds more. "I knew it would come to this moment of me asking you for your hand in marriage. I just hope you feel the same for me as I feel for you. I love you. Sabine, would you spend the rest of your life with me as your husband?" He opens the box and gazes into my eyes.

I nod.

"Was that a yes?" he asks uneasily.

"Yes," I respond. He stands, takes the ring out of the box, and slides it on my finger, then he embraces me in a hug followed by a passionate kiss.

We decided to eat breakfast away from home because I can't bring myself to move all of the roses from the kitchen just yet. It is such a beautiful sight.

"Call Sammie and Malik and have them meet us at the restaurant for breakfast. Let them know I'm treating," Kelvin yells from the bathroom as I busy myself with snapping pictures of the roses and my ring. I wonder if Sammie knew that Kelvin would propose.

I call Sammie on her cell phone. "Hey, girl."

"Good morning," she replies.

"So, Kelvin wants you and Malik to meet us at Keke's Breakfast Café, his treat."

"Oh, what's the occasion?" she asks suspiciously.

"Will you be ready in an hour?" I ask, ignoring her question.

"Yes. See you there," she says then hangs up the phone.

Kelvin comes out of the room fully dressed in jeans and a t-shirt. "Just think, sweetie, in ten days, we'll be eating breakfast in you and Sammie's cafe." He walks over to me and holds me in his arms.

"Does Sammie know about all of this?" I motion around the room.

"She may have an inkling." He smiles. "Let's go." He grabs my hand and walks me to the car. "How are you feeling?"

"Surprised. Happy. This doesn't feel real." I look at the ring again. "I had no idea..." I trail off in a daze.

He studies me for a while then says, "I have to make a quick stop by my office to check in on things."

"Sure," I reply.

During the drive, I contemplate my current reality. Is this my life or am I in an alternate universe? It seems as if every major piece of the puzzle is starting to fall into place. Almost two months ago, I was a single woman with no prospect of a boyfriend. Plus, I was jaded about how my relationship ended with my longtime friend and lover, Richard. I was still mourning the death of my parents and months away from opening a business that Sammie and I had been planning for a year. Now, it's days left until the opening of the café and lounge, I'm engaged, and I'm accepting everyday new blessings into my life. Kelvin has become a great part of my life—I can't imagine being without him.

Kelvin interrupts my thoughts as we pull up to Frey Transportation., "Baby, can you come inside with me for a second?" He walks around to open the jeep door for me. I walk in behind Kelvin and watch as a man who looks very similar to him—tall, slender with angular features, yet, much older, walks up to us.

"Sabine, this is my father, Matthew Frey," Kelvin says.

I smile and step toward him to shake his hand, and Kelvin says, "It's okay to hug my father." I reach for a hug, and Mr. Frey embraces me.

"Nice to meet you, Mr. Frey," I say as we pull away from the hug.

His father stares at me, looks me up and down and then finally says, "Nice to meet you, young lady. I heard an awful lot about you over the past two months. You're all Kelvin seems to talk about lately." He smiles, "Now, I see why."

"Dad," Kelvin interrupts, "are you ready to go to breakfast or not?"

"I'm ready, son. I'm just admiring your fiancé." He grabs my left hand and looks at the ring. "Kelvin made a good choice," he says as he turns my hand loose.

"It's beautiful, isn't it?" I ask, admiring the ring.

"You are beautiful. The ring is nice," Mr. Frey says, grinning at me.

When I turn to look at Kelvin, he shakes his head. "Let's go."

CHAPTER 30—THE ANNOUNCEMENT

Upon entering the restaurant, Sammie runs over to me. "Hey, girl. Do you have anything to tell me?" she asks excitedly.

I look at her for a few seconds then lift my hand up to show her the ring. She screams happily, jumping around, then looks at the ring again. Malik shushes Sammie, and she lowers her tone. Kelvin introduces his father to them, and shortly after the hostess shows us to our seats. Breakfast is filled with questions about how he proposed, when are we setting a date, what will be the venue of the wedding... These questions came mostly from Sammie.

"Girl, this is going to be so fun. Now I get to help you plan your wedding."

The men are quiet and smiling at the excitement Sammie and I are displaying. We decide to make a day out of hanging out with the family. After breakfast, we head up the road to Golf Stop, a restaurant and resort-style golfing experience. We all have a few drinks and try our luck at hitting a few balls. When the men become competitive and start keeping score, Sammie and I opt out and just watch them play. Hours escape in what feels like nanoseconds.

"Doesn't this remind you of when we use to spend Sundays with Mom and Dad?" Samantha asks, looking out toward the gulf course.

"It does. This whole day reminds me of them, and of how it feels to be a family again."

"Yeah. We have to do this more often." Sammie turns to look at me. "So, any thoughts as to where you want to have the wedding?"

"I was thinking of a remote wedding, maybe in Costa Rica or

Hawaii a week before Christmas of next year. This way, we'll be settled into our business and be comfortable with us both leaving the country at the same time. Plus, it would give us all enough time to prepare financially." As I say this, I realize I've actually given this wedding more thought than I gave myself credit for. "I'll contact a travel agent and get the cost of an all-inclusive resort after I run it by Kelvin of course." I smile at the idea of making decisions together with Kelvin.

"That would be perfect, girl," Sammie says. "I'm so happy for you. I think you and Kelvin are great for each other."

Mr. Frey has been in town for eleven days staying in the spare bedroom. Kelvin purchased an airline ticket to fly his father back to Michigan later this evening. I say my good-byes early as they head back to the office to work. I decide to go to the mall to kill time and to get my mind in the right place before the walk-through of the café tomorrow morning.

I browse around in different department stores at the mall, finally strolling in the intimate wear section of one of the stores. I get an idea of how I want to spend tonight with Kelvin. It definitely involves sex to celebrate our engagement. I thought it was too awkward to have sex with Kelvin's father in the other room this past week. Besides, our weekdays were spent working and afternoons watching movies together and playing board games. We were also busy with several recreational activities throughout the weekend—the beach, tubing, and outdoor barbecues. I have to admit, this has been a delightful week, and I'm about to put the icing and cherry on top of the cake tonight. I pick out what I feel is the sexiest gown, which is also the most expensive. Next stop: The Chocolate Shop.

As I'm leaving the mall, I get a text from William: *Sabine, I cannot believe you're engaged. I guess I was a day late and a dollar short. Just kidding. I am so happy for you, love. Remember, I expect an invitation to the wedding.*

I chuckle at the text remembering our lunch date this past Monday. William is in a good space right now, considering his circumstances. I have to admit, I do care for him a lot. One of the reasons I wanted to meet with him was to make sure he was okay emotionally in recent wake of his father passing away. I also wanted to open up the line of communication with us again, I have come to view him as family, and I missed him.

When William saw the ring, this past Monday, he asked, "Sabine, do you have something to tell me?" motioning his head toward the ring.

I smiled and responded, "Kelvin proposed to me yesterday."

"Wow. Congratulations," he said as he grabbed my hand to look at the ring. "Well, he was smart to lock you in., I can respect that." I could sense the hint of disappointment in his voice.

"So, how are you dealing?" I asked as he held my hand looking at the ring.

"I'm not going to lie, Sabine. It's hard. I miss my dad, but things are running smoothly at work. My brother just finished his law degree, so he'll be joining me at the firm taking on some of the responsibility. That helps a lot."

"William, I'm so proud of you. You are so graceful in this whole process. I know when my parents died..." I pause, trying to hold back tears. "It took a part of me with them. So, if you ever need to talk, day or night, I'm here."

"Awwww, love. I'm sorry. I didn't know." He looks me in the eyes, and it seems as if the roles have changed and he is supporting me now. "We can heal together," he said.

As I pull into the driveway, I'm transported back to this current moment. Kelvin's jeep is gone. He is probably driving his dad to the airport. Upon entering the house, I put the nightgown I just purchased in the closet on a hanger so it won't wrinkle, and the chocolate covered strawberries in the refrigerator to chill. I pull the Keurig, which I purchased on sale, out of the box. It was one of the many items I bought today on my little shopping spree. All of this in an effort to clear my mind about any issues that may come up on the final walkthrough of the cafe tomorrow.

Sammie and I would be very disappointed if we are not able to open on the day that we've advertised over the past few months.

Everything is already in place: the decorator is coming out the morning of the opening, the caterer will have the food delivered by five in the afternoon, and I plan to bake some things from the menu. *No worries,* I say to myself to clear my mind, then I quickly glance over the directions for my new coffee maker for a third time. I set the timer to six thirty five A.M. on the Keurig and place a K cup pod into the machine.

I pan sear two steaks then place them in the oven to bake, along with two potatoes. I then quickly steam some broccoli. After cleaning up the house and washing the bedding from the guest room, I take the food out of the oven to cool, head to the bathroom, and draw a bubble bath. I soak for a good half hour washing the day off me, framing my mind for a romantic night with my fiancé. It feels good saying that word, *fiancé.*

As with every major event or milestone in my life, I go into meditation and I thank God for bringing me to this point, for bringing Kelvin to me, for giving my life purpose again, and sparking the excitement in my heart. I then call on my romance angels to surround me, to make this night a magical one for both Kelvin and me.

CHAPTER 31—THE PRIVATE CELEBRATION

Dinner is prepared and laid out on the table. Our plates are perfectly proportioned with T-bone steak, steamed broccoli, and a baked potato loaded with cheese, bacon, chives, butter, and sour cream. Two glasses of sangria filled with fruit: oranges, peaches, limes, lemons, and red apples. The decanter in the center of the table contains the remaining liter of sangria. I've also place a few of the chocolate-dipped strawberries on a saucer in the middle of the table.

I just washed my hair, and it smells like flowers and candy. Because I let it air dry, it has a wavy loose curl look to it. I bathed in Amber Romance bubble bath, so the smell is infused into my skin. As I light the last of the two tall unscented candles, I hear Kelvin walk into the front door. I walk over to the foyer as he is taking off his shoes. He looks up at me and beams the most beautiful smile, showing all of his teeth.

"Hi, sweetie," he says as he walks up to me, kisses my lips, then pulls away staring lovingly into my eyes as he holds me in his arms.

"Hi," I say softly. "I made you dinner." I pull back from his embrace and grab his hand. He follows me to the kitchen.

"Wow," he says, then turns to look at me. "You never cease to amaze me."

"Just thought we should celebrate our engagement," I say.

"This looks wonderful, you look beautiful, and I'm starving." He pauses then pulls me close. "I'm ready to eat, and I'm not just talking about the food on the table," he whispers. I smile and allow him to trail kisses down my neck.

"Let me go wash my face and hands, sweetie. I'll be right

212

back," he says as he eases away from me. Kelvin comes back out dressed in blue pajama pants and a white t-shirt, and it appears he's done more than washed his hands and face. He took a quick shower to freshen up for dinner. He sits down at the table, grabs his glass of sangria, and takes several gulps, leaving the glass only half-full. He then takes his knife and cuts into his steak, which is now piping hot because I just took his plate out of the microwave, and pops a piece into his mouth. He shakes his head. "Oh my, Sabine, this steak is just..." He keeps chewing and closes his eyes, "heaven," he says when he opens them.

I laugh a little, pleased my cooking is giving him so much pleasure. He takes several more bites, then some bites of broccoli and the potato. "Baby, you just don't know how famished I was. This is exactly what I needed. If I hadn't asked you to marry me, I would right now," he says with all sincerity, which causes me to blush as he continues to devour the food. "My father likes you a lot, Sabine."

"Awwww, that's sweet. I'm so happy I got to meet him. This past week has been perfect, hanging out with you and your dad," I say.

"It was perfect, minus the fact that you withheld sex from me," he says, staring directly into my eyes. "We've only had sex once within a two-week period. Is this how marriage is going to be with you?" he asks with a slight grin.

I giggle. "If you continue to take all of these long road trips, and if your dad is in the house with us, maybe." I pause for a long time as I notice he has stopped chewing, and a serious look covers his face. Then I continue, "This is my apology. What do you think so far?" I ask.

"I think you should grab those strawberries, meet me in the bedroom, and I'll let you be the judge of what I think so far," he says seductively.

"Seriously?" I ask in shock.

"Yes, sweetie," he says calmly.

Once I'm in the room, I set the strawberries on the nightstand and go use the bathroom, then brush my teeth and floss. When

Kelvin enters the room fifteen minutes later, he has brought the liquor decanter with the remaining sangria and two wineglasses, which he carefully places near the chocolate-dipped strawberries.

"Sabine," he whispers tenderly to me. I sit up with my legs curled underneath me and my back against the headboard. "When I come out of this bathroom, I want that sexy-ass gown on the floor and you naked laying on top of these covers with your legs spread and ready for me. Do you understand?"

"Yes," I reply halfway shocked and halfway turned on by the authority in his tone.

When Kelvin exits the bathroom, he is naked, and at his request—or more like command—I am lying across the bed undressed with my knees bent and my feet flat on the mattress. He slowly crawls between my legs, inching up to my face. Once he has reached my face, he whispers, "Good girl," then he kisses my lips briefly, moves down my body circling his tongue around my areola then bites down softly on my nipple. He then moves over to the other breasts and does the same thing. I moan aloud in pleasure. "Don't you miss this?" he asks as he trails kisses down my body, gripping my butt with one hand as he spreads my legs wider with his other hand. He nibbles on my inner thighs, sending tingles straight to my sex.

"Kelvin, I want you," I say to him.

He places his fingers near the opening of my vagina and slowly slides two fingers inside of me. "Sweetie, you'll have me, but I'm going to take my time and ravish every part of your body tonight."

And with those words, he bends over, positioning his face between my legs and begins to flick his tongue all over my throbbing clit. My body is hypersensitive to each flick. I naturally want to close my legs in around his ears. As I do this, he uses both hands to open my legs and hold them in position as he wraps his lips lightly around my clit and sucks slowly, moving his head back and forth, pulling gently with his lips when he pulls backward and lapping his tongue out when he comes towards me. He pushes his finger inside my sex, then lifts his face briefly to tell me, "We're going to try something a little different tonight. I don't want you to cum until I tell you that it's okay. Agreed?"

I nod.

"Baby," he demands, "try really hard, okay?"

I nod in between my heavy breathing. He places his mouth back around my clit. He is flicking his tongue one minute and gently sucking the next, all the while sliding his finger in and out of my vagina.

I moan out in agonizing pleasure. "Kelvin," I scream as I sit up, feeling like if I didn't stop him right then that I would be dishonoring his request of not cumming until he gives me the okay. Kelvin comes up to my face and kisses me, forcing me back down to the bed, then he places his penis at my vaginal opening. I move my pelvis up toward his hard pulsing penis, trying to get it inside of me in a hurry. He holds my waist down.

"Slow down, baby." He continues to kiss me passionately, all the while keeping his man part at my opening, only sliding the head in and out. I use both my hands, grab his butt, and slam his body into me, pushing him deep inside of me. He moans out in pleasure and slides in and out of me forcefully.

"I am so close, I don't know if I can wait," I whisper to him. He slows his motions down, pulling all the way out, then forcing himself back in. "Cum for me, baby," he says finally as he presses himself deeper inside of me. He draws back slowly again and powerfully pounds back into me. In that moment, he sends me over the edge. I am spasming all over him, yelling out in pleasure. He pulls out of me, and I can feel warm, thick liquids squirting all over my vagina, then I feel him slide back inside of me slowly. He is fully hard, continuing in and out of me.

"See what you do to me, Sabine?"

I don't say a word, but just let the pleasure take over my body. "I can't get enough," he says with passion in his voice. The night is long and filled with one pleasurable act after another. After round three, I drift off into a deep sleep.

215

CHAPTER 32—POST CELEBRATION

One day before the opening (November 28)

The smell of freshly brewed coffee wakes me up this morning. I turn to look at the clock and it reads six thirty five A.M. The exact time I had set the Keurig to brew. I had half expected it wouldn't work, even though I had followed all the directions to a T. My mind was scattered last night thinking about today and everything it entailed.

I roll over to Kelvin's side of the bed, hoping to feel his warm body. Yet, there is no body on his side. He must have gone into work early today. I get up, brush my teeth, and turn the shower water on. As I look in the mirror, the thought that has been on my mind since Kelvin proposed to me comes to my attention yet again: How did this become my life? Being engaged to this handsome, loving man who I have only known for a little over eight weeks, and the grand opening of the café in less than thirty-two hours. My life has gone from zero to one hundred in a matter of months.

I step into the shower, and the memories from last night flood my mind. The warm water hits my skin, jolting the sensations along with visions of our sexual escapades. I think about the progression of our sexual acts from the time we met until now. The sex has always been out of this world, so much in fact that it doesn't feel real when I think on it, but when I feel his hand rubbing over my body, I am instantly put in a state of pure pleasure. I feel so much love for this man. This kind of love is like the kind I've never felt before. It's like the kind you see in the movies or read about in a romance novel. It feels so intense, as if our experiences have surpassed this lifetime and several others.

My mind takes me back to the last round in our escapade, my top lip perfectly interlaced between his top and bottom lip, gentle sucking, tongues dancing, and the occasional crashing of our teeth as our mouths stayed slightly parted, allowing each other access to the sweetness of each kiss. My lips crave more as our kisses lingered on. Our bodies perfectly align. He flips me around gently, bends over me, and as I am lying on my back looking into his beautiful brown eyes, he tells me how much he loves me and how he vows right now to always give this to me. His pelvis to my pelvis, we are joined together in an act of pure pleasure and enjoyment. We seem to fit each other just like a glove.

"Seme, where are you, girl?"

Shit. My pleasurable thoughts interrupted by my sister's loud, fretful voice.

"Sammie, I'm in the bathroom," I yell, as I turn the shower off and grab my towel.

"Oh, I called your phone and you didn't answer, so I let myself in."

"I didn't hear it, girl," I respond.

"Why? Were you in here fantasizing about your fiancé?" she asks sarcastically.

"Ha. No," I say, caught in my lie.

"Come on. You said we would start the day early, go for breakfast before the walk-through," Sammie whines.

"Okay. You're extra perky today. Can you pick me out an outfit while I lotion up and do something to my hair?" I shout out from the bathroom as I pop a B12 vitamin and a Motrin into my mouth. My energy level is definitely lower than Sammie's, and my limbs are sore from last night. I come out of the bathroom and notice that Sammie has made my bed and laid out a nice pair of fitted jeans, a pink-and-tan off-the-shoulder paisley cut top, and tan sandal heels.

"Perfect," I say. I look at her, and she has on the same thing except her top is light purple and turquoise.

"I bought this outfit for you so that we can start our birthday off right, girl." She walks out the room and into the kitchen.

We'll be turning thirty-nine tomorrow. Since we can remember, every year we celebrate together. We go for breakfast at some nice fancy location out where the rich people stay and have mimosas, a farmer's omelet, and strawberry crepes, then we hit the malls for some shopping. We decide to kill two birds with one stone today: celebrate our birthday with each other, then meet with the building inspector, Gloria, at eleven. I walk out into the kitchen to find Samantha sipping on some coffee and nibbling on a few chocolate-covered strawberries she found in the refrigerator.

"So, Sabine, chocolate-covered strawberries? What happened last night?"

I smile. "Here, girl. I bought you these earrings. Put them on," I say as we walk out of the door.

CHAPTER 33—THE WALK-THROUGH

Samantha and I drive by the storefront before making our way to the other side of town for breakfast. We exit the car to admire the sign in white cursive letters posted above the door, S & S Café and Lounge. It looks beautiful. The backdrop to the sign is burgundy, which matches very well with the two awnings on either side of the door, shading the top portion of the windows. The brick storefront protrudes out a few inches more than the connecting shops. The red brick stands out as the two shops beside S & S Café and Lounge are a cream color. Just looking at the building itself, it is very inviting. It looks like it's saying, "Come dine here."

I think we picked a great location. We're between a bookstore and a hair salon. I can just imagine the customers we'll get by just sight and location alone: Salon workers stopping by to get breakfast, lunch, and dinner. Salon clients stopping by to pick up food before they leave the area. Avid readers from the bookstore stopping by to pick up a muffin and read a book they just purchased from next door. Sammie and I could not have coordinated this any better. We should have friendly and noncompetitive neighbors.

As we look through the windows, we see several dining tables made of glass and chairs posted around the table in a metallic and silver color, but because the lights are off, it's hard for us to make out much more. When we come back at eleven for the walk-through, I'm sure we'll be surprised and excited to see the finished product. All of the smaller but very important details were added within the last week.

Sammie and I jump back into the car smiling ear to ear. We are so excited. Today is the day we officially get the keys in our hand. Breakfast is filled with talk about the details for the party tomorrow night. Sammie contacts Lamar, Julissa, Wendy, and Lydia to remind them that their official start day is tomorrow afternoon at five P.M. They're all just as excited as we are. Sammie shows me the picture of the T-shirts the staff and we are to wear. It has the logo on the top right, and it's burgundy with white letters just like the sign on the outside of our building. We have black aprons with pockets in the front. We decide the staff can wear jeans and black gym shoes for comfort. As we are leaving the tip for the waiter, my phone rings.

"Hello," I answer.

"Hi, may I speak with Sabine Stallworth or Samantha Marcs?"

"This is Sabine."

"Hi Sabine. This is Gloria Wilson, the building inspector. I'm just confirming our appointment for today at eleven."

"Yes, we'll be there," I respond.

"Okay. See you two in a little while," Gloria says very chipper.

As soon as I hang up the phone, Sammie and I are jumping up and down as we walk outside to her car.

"This is it, girl, the final walk-through," I say, a little nervous.

"Everything is going to be just fine, I know it," Sammie replies.

We get back to the storefront at exactly ten forty-five A.M. As we pull up, we see a woman standing outside of the café, we can only assume it's Mrs. Wilson, the building inspector. We also see Gus, the property owner, outside with Gloria. Sammie and I put some lip gloss on, check ourselves in the rearview mirror, then say a quick prayer that everything will be in order for this walk-through, then we exit the car.

As we walk up to the storefront, Gloria greets us. "Wow, I didn't know you two were twins," she says, looking shocked.

We shake her hand and smile. "Are you two ready for this?" Gus asks as he unlocks the door.

"Yes," we both answer excitedly.

"Well, let's get started," Gloria says.

When Gus flicks on the lights, the sight is amazing. The vintage-style furniture we picked out online looks even better than we envisioned inside of the lounge. The café side has seven round glass tables that seats four with vanities and mirrors posted all around, matching the silver-and-gold vintage color scheme. The lounge side has six sofas that extend around the walls of the building with coffee tables in front of each sofa. A long dining room table that seats eight is placed in two separate locations—one near the window that is in the front of the building and another more private toward the back of the building.

In between the lounge and the café is a bar area that has a glass encasing to hold desserts and other foods of our choosing, which we can advertise. To the right of the encasing is two cash registers then a long counter space that curves around making a half circle with bar stools around the counter. Behind this bar is an archway that leads to an open style kitchen that can be viewed from where we stand, which is right in front of the bar. Inside the kitchen are three convectional stoves, an industrial size dishwasher, two refrigerators, tons of cabinet space and three sinks. The middle of the kitchen has an island counter space.

The artwork on the wall pulls together all the colors in the space—the grays, the blues, burgundy, silver, gold, and the cherry oak. The lamps, with their subtle glow, accents the calm feel the space is conveying. To the right of the kitchen is a stairwell made of cherry oak wood, with a black handrail. When you get to the top of the stairs, if you look to the left and the right, there is a women's restroom to the left and a men's restroom to the right. Straight ahead are French doors that open out into Sammie's and my personal space. The French doors have glass on them so you can see inside of the room. There are two desks right across from each other and two doors toward the back. One room will be my counseling area; the other will be Sammie's Reiki and massage room.

Everything looks perfect. Now, let's just hope everything checks out with this inspection. We wait patiently as Gloria Wilson completes her assessment, ensuring everything meets OSHA standards and that there are no safety hazards. Gloria is very thorough in her examination. She has a clipboard and is checking off things as she inspects them. Gus is doing his own walk-through to make sure everything is up to par with what he had the contractors complete. He shows us the refrigerators and stoves and explains the warranty on them. Gus shows us the back door from the kitchen entrance, and where the Dumpsters are located out back. He also gives us the alarm code to the building and shows us how to operate the key pad.

I'm admiring the six Keurigs in the bar area, along with blenders, a mini refrigerator, small sink, and an icemaker, all courtesy of the vendors Kelvin connected us with. Sammie and I check our email to ensure the supplies and food will be delivered tomorrow morning around seven A.M., as we plan to be up early in the morning at the café, organizing. We confirm with the caterer she will be here around eleven A.M. and the decorator here at noon. Julissa, Wendy, Lamar and Lydia will be here at five P.M. They will assist in making sure everything is running smoothly. Lamar will be in charge of the photo area, Julissa and Wendy will walk around to serve food on trays to the guests, and Lydia will manage the employees. I set it up for the cleaning staff to come in at five P.M. tomorrow, to ensure that the space is sparkling before the party—I mean, the opening—then again at eleven P.M. to clean up after.

Sammie is upstairs checking out her massage studio and organizing our offices, plugging up our computers, scanners, and copy machines to ensure everything is working properly. She calls the cable company to get the internet connection started while I start an email on my smart phone to send out to all of my contacts in regards to the opening tomorrow at seven P.M. I wait to send it out until Mrs. Wilson gives us the okay.

Gus comes to retrieve both Samantha and me so the inspector can give her report.

"Okay, ladies. It looks like everything is in compliance. You're ready to open," she says with a smile.

"Thank you so much, Ms. Gloria Wilson. We really appreciate this," I say. Sammie and I both shake her hand.

"No problem. Now all of the real work begins." She smiles. "Good luck with everything." She exits the building and walks toward her car. As soon as she leaves, Sammie and I hug each other and jump up and down with excitement for the third or fourth time today. I push send on my email. I then call Kelvin to relay the good news as Sammie goes off to call Malik. Gus is smiling at us and waits on us to finish our phone conversations.

After we finish up on the phone, Gus hands us both three sets of keys and have us sign off on the lease agreement, which locks us in the contract with him for five years. "Okay, girls. You have my number if you need anything. Good luck tomorrow," he says as he exits the building.

Sammie and I sit down on one of the sofas. "I can't believe we did it," I say.

"I know, right?" Sammie responds.

"If only Mom and Dad could see this," I state, looking around at the café and lounge in amazement.

"I think that they can." Sammie smiles and touches my hand. We have a moment of silence and bask in our creation.

Sammie breaks the silence by saying, "The cable company will be here between nine A.M. and eleven A.M. tomorrow."

"Let's go get our hair done next door to celebrate," I say. We turn out all of the lights, put the alarm on, then exit the building.

As we walk next door to Mz. Ingram's Hair Salon, the receptionist up front greets us. We inform her we both want a wash and curl. She takes our names and has us sit in the waiting area as the stylists finish up on their current customers. Sammie and I sit quietly on our smart phones, finishing loose ends in regards to the café. We switch the utilities over; Sammie calls the electric company, and I call the water and gas company.

As I am sitting in the chair after getting my hair blown out, Michael, my stylist, starts to converse with Michelle, Sammie's stylist, about the owner of the salon being out on bail and how he is worried about not having this job if she goes back to jail.

"What did she do?" Michelle asks as she puts a perfect curl in Sammy's hair with the hot curlers.

"She got a battery charge for attacking her boyfriend in his home. They said the police witnessed it," Michael states as he turns my chair around to look at what he has done so far to my hair. "Plus, I heard through the grapevine she poisoned a man at a club," Michael adds as he puts some hair product on the edges of my hair.

The minute Michael says this, Sammie gets choked on the Pepsi she's drinking, then she speaks up, "I'm sorry to be eavesdropping, but who is the owner of this salon?" Sammie asks looking at Michael.

"Her name is Casey—Casey Ingram," Michael says.

The End
Book Two is coming soon.

Printed in the United States
By Bookmasters